AMBIVALENCE

Noel Davern

This novel is entirely a work of fiction. The names, characters, and incidents portrayed in it were created in the imagination of the author. Any resemblance to actual persons, living or deceased, is purely coincidental.

National Library of Australia Cataloguing-in-Publication entry
Creator: Davern, Noel
Title: Ambivalence / Noel Davern

Paperback ISBN: 978-1-7635773-0-5
Ebook ISBN 978-1-7635773-1-2

Publisher Noel Davern
Website noeldavern.com
Email noel@noeldavern.com

This book is dedicated to all the people who have shared
and helped shape my life.
Thank you.

ambivalence /am-**biv**-uh-luhns/
n. coexistence in one person of opposing feelings
towards a person or thing.

The Australian Pocket Oxford Dictionary

1

The Surveillance Operator lurched bolt upright. If not for the embrace of his harness, the shock would have catapulted him from his seat. He stared disbelievingly at his display.

"We have a bird coming out of Gauzhou!"

His shout evaporated the boredom of everyone on board. The other analysts frantically reset the pages on their monitors, beginning the urgent analysis of the data steaming into the sensors festooning their aircraft.

The pilots' idle chatter dissolved. They had been paying superficial attention to their instruments while looking forward to the thrill of their next refuelling rendezvous. Now, they snuck a furtive eye to the west, wondering if they would see the missile's plume as it arched skywards.

Amidst all this turmoil, the autopilot remained unwavering, not having the sense to appreciate the unfolding drama. The autothrottle couldn't hear the whine of the engines either, but was monitoring their performance as both systems steadfastly guided their RC-135S Cobra Ball along its path, just off the coast of China, through what most countries defined as international airspace.

Of course, it wasn't actually their aircraft. It belonged to the people of the United States of America. And they hadn't chosen to be here. Those same people, through their government, had done it for them. And they had placed them here to witness the beginning of the end. Not just for them; for everyone. For everything.

The operator continued to stare at his display, but he allowed himself a moment of self-reflection. How had it come to this? Those same people had precipitated it—his people—with their relentless prodding; their arrogance; their self-importance; and their ego. Pushing, pushing, pushing. Poking the bear. And the bear had had enough.

But the time for contemplation was long gone, stolen by the events unfolding around them. His training kicked in, and, with almost instinctual behaviour, he became laser-focused. Now objectivity became the order of business. Where was the missile heading, and to what purpose? It was tracking 175 degrees. Out towards the south-west Pacific and not towards mainland USA. OK, good. Maybe it was just a test firing or a warning shot.

The computers then, in their deadpan way, reported the probable target. Central Australia. What was in central Australia that could warrant an ICBM attack?

Pine Gap!

"This isn't happening, this can't be happening," he mumbled, almost under his breath.

The frantic messages being exchanged with command informed him multiple systems were reporting detection of the missile launch. The goddamn Chinese had rolled the dice. Fortunately, they were still tumbling, and it remained to be seen how they fell. And they were no longer playing penny ante.

~

Incidents between the two superpowers had been becoming more serious with each passing day. The latest of them had been the use of a laser device on a fast-mover coming out of North Korean airspace on an intercept course with the RC-135V/W Rivet Joint, the other electronic surveillance aircraft deployed to the theatre of operations.

When the hostile aircraft had established missile lock on their charge, one of the escorting Raptor pilots thought, "Enough of that buddy," and used his targeting laser to illuminate the offender.

The targeted aircraft, later identified to be a Chinese J-11, had abruptly pulled away and headed for the safety of the mainland. The guidance provided by ground control allowed the pilot to get his aircraft back to base, but the laser had caused such severe damage to his eyesight, it made it impossible for him to land. He had ejected and was currently being treated in hospital.

The aircraft had been lost, along with what the Chinese commanders considered a considerable loss of face. They had been busy running scenarios for a suitable response.

~

Petty Officer Bethany Marks sat with her customary military ramrod posture. The constant background of the air conditioning system was the only sound, but it wasn't a distraction; her mind blanked it out as irrelevant. She focused on her tracking and targeting displays as they constantly updated with the data streaming into the Arleigh Burke-class destroyer *USS Henry Teak's* Aegis Combat System.

She had the responsibility of tracking, intercepting, and destroying the ICBM. It was an enormous workload, but she was now confident she could orchestrate a successful intercept. All she needed was the launch authorisation.

"Please come, please come." She could hardly breathe; such was her anxiety.

Within a few seconds, the confidence level of an intercept would decrease exponentially. A few seconds more and it would be out of range. The Exec Officer was hovering over her shoulder, mimicking her thoughts.

When she determined she could wait no longer, she threw a quick glance at the Exec. "I'm all in." Her finger jabbed the button as she let her pent-up breath release.

The ship's deck immediately erupted with the sound and fury of a RIM 161 Standard Missile being spat from its tube and darting skyward, leaving a dense smoky trail in its wake as it sped hell-bent towards its prey.

She glued her attention to her monitors. Tracking data was within acceptable limits, and time seemed to dawdle as the distance between hunter and prey diminished. Finally, the tracks intersected, but then both continued on their individual paths. She had missed.

No, no, no.

Exactly two seconds later, the ICBM vanished from her screens.

Thank you, Lord, thank you. They had got it!

Her software confirmed the kill, uploading the status to

Command. She leapt from her chair and hugged the Exec, her expression a mixture of pride, excitement, and dread. She had done her job. Pity those up the chain of command hadn't seen fit to do likewise.

The Exec gave her a hurried pat on the back. "Well done, Beth." He didn't have time for anything more elaborate, as he dashed off to the bridge to confer with the Captain.

Beth's professionalism quickly reasserted itself and she returned to her station. Then the nagging doubts started. She was sure she had seen the two tracks briefly continue past each other. She re-ran the logged data. Sure enough, there was that two second period between supposed impact and the target vanishing from her screens. And her missile showed no signs of impacting anything. This wasn't what a kinetic energy intercept should look like. Something strange was going on, but she couldn't put her finger on it. She re-ran it over and over, hoping for some insight, but everything else seemed normal. Maybe there was a system malfunction. No; diagnostics on her systems revealed no anomalies.

She was convinced that her interceptor had missed. But what had happened to the Chinese missile? Maybe they had hit the kill switch. Triggered its self-destruct mechanism. If so, she expected to see signs of the resulting debris on her screens, but, except for her interceptor, they were blank.

Then a creeping dread seeped into her mind; there could be a second scenario. What if the target didn't exist at all? What if the Chinese could hack their systems and spoof the whole thing? That had far more devastating consequences than if the ICBM had done its terrible work and obliterated Pine Gap in a nuclear inferno. The entire US war-fighting strategies were based on its sophisticated electronic capabilities. If these were compromised, all bets were off. She keyed her mic and reported her conclusions.

2

Fashion designers and boutique owners mingled with the models from the show. Perhaps a quarter of the guests were on the dance floor, the rest milling around and talking in small groups. Drinks flowed freely, and the various conversations were loud, vying as they were for ascendancy over the music throbbing from near the dance floor. Expensive clothing and jewellery were on display everywhere, with the entire scene oozing power and opulence. The rich and famous had gathered to party.

Viktoria was enjoying herself, still on a high from the parade, and a little tipsy from the cocktails she had consumed. She was on her own at the moment and approached a small group of designers and, more importantly for her, a popular casting director from a major film studio. Her mission was to get an introduction to him, and, with luck, expand this into getting some roles with his studio. But she was hesitant to interrupt them, so she hovered around, waiting for an invitation to join their group. Even amongst all this glitz and glamour, she was the kind of girl who would soon be noticed.

She caught the eye of a pretty blonde woman looking directly at her, showing some interest. She recognised her, of course. It was Elena Fricker, the fashion house heiress. She matched her gaze for a few seconds, then blinked as she snapped her attention back to her target group.

About a minute later, still having no luck breaking into their conversation, she felt a soft touch on her arm. It was Elena.

Seductively squeezing her biceps, Elena leaned in to her ear. "I loved the apricot Louis Vitton, the most elegant frock of the entire parade, adorning by far the most beautiful model."

Viktoria swivelled her head. "Thank you. It was my favourite as well."

OK, she's coming on a bit strong. How do I get out of this one? With her connections, she would be handy to have as a friend. The trouble is, that's all I want. She seems to want a lot more.

Viktoria gently removed her arm from Elena's grasp. "Your father's line was the star of the show. I felt so pleased when they selected me to model some of them."

While remaining focused on her task, she saw a way to use this distraction to her advantage. "I love this part of the event. There are so many influential people here, and not just from the fashion industry. I wonder why Pierre Voisard has come. Do you know him, by any chance?"

"I do. Quite well, actually. He's such a socialite. He comes to all these events. I bet he's hit on you once or twice."

"Well, I've never met him, but I'd like to. Not to get hit on, mind you. I've just broken into acting, and contacts in the film industry are always handy," Viktoria said with a wry smile.

"Well, I can solve that for you straight away. Let's go over and say hi."

Taking her hand, Elena led her to the group, causing their conversation to die as they turned their attention to the two newcomers.

Elena said, "Hi, Pierre, enjoying the evening? I hope our gowns have inspired you to purchase some of our line for the ladies in your life."

Pierre laughed good-naturedly and leaned forward to kiss her on each cheek. "Hello, Elena, you look lovely as usual." He turned his attention towards her companion.

Giving him no time to continue, Elena said, "This is my friend Viktoria. Do you two know each other?"

Pierre responded, "In fact, no, but naturally, I'm aware of her." He extended a hand towards Viktoria. "I loved your portrayal of Émilie in

The Witches."

With a warm smile, Viktoria gracefully accepted his hand, and said, "Thank you. So pleased to meet you, Mr Voisard."

Viktoria steered the conversation towards the film industry and focused most of her attention on Pierre, although she was careful to shoot smiling glances at Elena from time to time.

Elena soon tired of their conversation, excused herself, and went off to talk to some of her other friends.

Mission accomplished.

After being brought several more cocktails during a lot of general chit-chat, Viktoria excused herself, short-circuiting any chance of the conversation getting more personal, and retired to the room she had reserved in the hotel.

~

She was quite tipsy and fell asleep easily.

When she awoke, she stretched and glanced at the clock. It was 8:30 a.m. Early, but she needed the bathroom. She slid out of bed and headed in that direction. While there, she took a shower. It refreshed her somewhat, but she returned to bed, not being a morning person by any stretch of the imagination. She curled up on the bed, hugging a pillow, and drifted back to sleep.

Viktoria's body shimmered with an iridescent blue light and abruptly disappeared. A short time later, the shimmer returned and Viktoria reappeared back in her bed, in the exact position she had been lying moments earlier, still fast asleep.

3

A blue light flashed across the room as Viktoria appeared. A short time later, the event recurred, causing a second Viktoria to appear. Both versions wore identical bedclothes.

The two women woke, blinked and looked at one another in utter confusion. Suddenly, the first one grabbed at her forehead and grimaced, unable to understand the booming voice seemingly coming from inside her head.

"Stop it, stop it—" She startled upright and swung her legs off the bed. Everything went quiet as the voice abruptly ceased.

"Who are you, and where are we?" a voice enquired.

The first Viktoria looked at her companion and asked, "Did you just say something?"

"Yes. Who are you? What's going on?"

"I'm Viktoria. I don't know what's happening."

They were talking to each other in Ukrainian.

The other girl stumbled out of bed, but felt a little giddy, so she went over to a chair and sat down. "My name is also Viktoria. I see you look like me, but how is that possible? What's happening?"

The first Viktoria joined her at the table. They again scanned their surroundings, but nothing looked familiar. The room resembled a studio apartment, if somewhat spartan. As well as the table and chairs, there was a small kitchenette, and the king-sized bed that they had just vacated. A doorway, with the door ajar, allowed access to an en suite. The only other feature to break the starkness of the walls was a set of sliding doors, which were also open, revealing several sets of clothes hanging inside what was obviously a cupboard. There were no windows, and the walls were devoid of any pictures or other adornments. The ceiling seemed to emit a stark white glow. They could not see a door to leave by and all they could hear was their own heavy breathing. Both women felt a little claustrophobic.

The expression on the first one changed back to alarm. The voice had returned. Then she seemed to relax somewhat, but her eyes remained wide in amazement.

Her companion again asked, "How did we get here and why do you look like me?"

She raised her hand. "Wait a minute, I'm just collecting my thoughts."

The voice inside her head said, *"Please listen to me. I have something to tell you. And I would also like to speak to your companion. Please ask her to listen to me as well."*

My God, I've gone mad. Go away.

The voice left her, but she felt so distressed she became nauseous. Her companion moved closer to comfort her. They sat together cuddling each other, and after a little while, the nausea passed.

"Can you hear anything in your head?"

"No, what do you mean? What's going on? How did I get here?"

"Try to see if you can hear anything."

The second one just looked back at her, wondering what she meant, then she stiffened in alarm.

"Please listen to me. I realise you are confused, but if you listen, I will explain. I will not hurt you; in fact, I will protect you from any harm. You just need to understand."

She heard the words clearly, but she didn't understand where the voice was coming from. Her pupils dilated and her skin tingled with her body's fight-or-flight response.

"Did you just hear that?" she whispered.

"You are hearing things, too?"

"Yes, but who is speaking?"

"I am your mother. Please ask A to listen to me as well."

What do you mean, you're my mother? She's dead. What's going on?

"Please ask A to listen to me as well. I have to explain some things."

"Can you hear her? She wants to speak to you now."

Her companion hesitated, breathed deeply, and closed her eyes. As if it was in a dream, the voice returned.

~

One girl woke and rolled over to gaze at her companion sleeping peacefully beside her. She still couldn't get over how alike they were. Not only in looks, but in their mannerisms, likes and dislikes, and habits.

She stretched lazily, then headed towards the en suite. When she returned, she found her companion standing beside the bed.

"Good morning. How did you sleep?"

Her companion smiled back, seemingly happy with herself. They were growing more accustomed to each other, but their situation still left them utterly confused. "At last I had a restful night. You?"

"Mmmm. Me too." She also looked to be in a good mood. "I'll make us some breakfast while you have your shower."

As she revelled in the embrace of the warm water streaming over her, the second one pondered her predicament. It was baffling. What in the hell was going on? At least she had a companion to help her through it all. And she felt a deep emotional attachment to her double. They were so alike. But none of this made any sense. She dragged herself back into focus, left the shower, dressed, and made her way to the kitchenette.

The smell of toast hung in the air as they sat together at the small servery bar, enjoying breakfast. The first Viktoria held her coffee cup up to her nose, savouring that aroma as well. She loved coffee.

Her companion cast a scanning glance around the room in frustration. "We have to find the way out."

The first one put her cup down and looked around the room, just in case things had changed. "But there are no doors. We've looked everywhere."

"How do you think we got in here? Is it a prison?"

"This doesn't feel right. Perhaps it's just a dream. Will you shake me to see if you can wake me up?" She could see and feel her companion shaking her, but nothing changed. She put her hand to her head and said, "Do you want to try to speak to our mother again?

Perhaps she'll let us out now."

Her companion nodded. They stood face to face and clasped hands, then locked eyes and concentrated.

"Good morning. I hope your rest was successful."

Yes, I slept well. We would like to leave now. Will you let us?

"It is important that you do not return to your civilisation until you are ready. As I explained, I have much work for you to do. It appears you will take a little time to adjust. Until then, you are safe here and I will give you anything you ask for. But you must remain isolated for now."

But we have to go outside, it's driving us crazy in here.

There was a sudden blue flash, and another doorway appeared. Actually, it more resembled the entrance to a lift. Both girls rushed to it and pressed the adjacent button. The doors slid open, revealing what was indeed a lift. They almost jumped inside, such was their excitement, and pressed the button marked 'Surface'. Almost instantly, the doors reopened, and they looked out to see a beautiful vista of rocky outcrops interspersed with pristine vegetation. A little way off, they could see, hear, and smell the ocean. The air was chilly, and both girls hugged themselves, trying to combat the cold. But only for a moment. Looking at each other, then down at themselves, they were amazed to find themselves now clad in tracksuits and parkas.

They embraced their surroundings. It was such a relief to be rid of the confines of the room. They flittered around, sometimes coming together and hugging, revelling in their new found freedom.

With her face flushed and panting slightly from her exertions, but all smiles, one girl said, "Isn't this beautiful? But we appear to be alone here. I can't see any signs of anyone else."

She received a nod of agreement. *Thank you, Mother, but where is everyone else?*

"There is no one else on this island. You can enjoy it all by yourselves."

But it'll be so lonely here with just the two of us. Please let us go back to Paris.

"Your work for me is not in Paris. And as I explained, you are not really who you think you are."

Who are we then?

"You are A and B."

4

The Sydney Opera House was filling fast. A small group of friends excitedly walked down the aisle towards their allotted seats. Along with the rest of the audience, they were smartly dressed and exuded an air of excitement. They were about to be treated to the premiere performance of the touring Symphony Orchestra of the National Philharmonic of Ukraine.

They all had a love for music, and at a recent social gathering in a jazz bar, Heidi had teasingly suggested they should get a little culture and listen to some real music. She was, of course, referring to her great love—classical music. When she informed them the Ukrainian Philharmonic was about to tour Australia, they had taken her up on the challenge, and had been lucky enough to get some of the few remaining seats.

Besides going to the concert, it was a perfect opportunity for a weekend away together. They all had many activities planned during their visit to the *Big Smoke*, as Sydney is colloquially known to Australians. Friends to catch up with, places to visit, and fine dining to be enjoyed. And, of course, a trip to Bondi Beach.

They settled into their seats, Heidi being on the left of the group and Bernie to her immediate right. This suited Heidi just fine, thank you very much; she was becoming quite keen on Bernie. And he had been showing some interest in return. He was based in Sydney, so obviously it was a chance for him to catch up with mates, but it was her secret hope she was the main reason he had come. Flirting with him, she occasionally leant towards him to brush his arm in order to reinforce some remark she was making as their idle chatter filled in the time before the concert began.

A latecomer briefly interrupted their conversation as she excused herself and shuffled elegantly past them to take her seat further down their row. Heidi was turned towards Bernie and didn't notice her approach. He noticed her, though, in his peripheral vision. Noticed her all right; she was gorgeous! The woman offered a fleeting smile of thanks as they shifted their legs to allow her passage. It was all over in a moment, and Heidi would have barely registered the event if not for the lingering fragrance of the woman's perfume. And she admired the woman's elegant and expensive looking dress. The other thing of note was that she seemed unaccompanied. That was unusual. Women who looked and dressed like that must have a host of admirers only too willing to spend an evening with them.

The performance began, and they turned their attention to the music. Distracted by the memory of the woman's perfume, Heidi cast her the occasional glance. There was no reciprocal interest. She stared at the stage, paying rapt attention to the performance.

~

The concert ended, and after giving their applause to the orchestra, the group stood to leave. As they approached the exit, Heidi excused herself and made for the ladies' room. Emerging from her cubicle, she found the room unoccupied except for herself and the woman who had shuffled past them before the performance. Heidi recognised her immediately, remembering her dress, and, as she approached, that beautiful perfume. The woman was touching up her lipstick. As she was preparing to wash her hands, Heidi cast a glance at the woman's reflection.

Oh my God, she's so beautiful.

They made eye contact in the mirror. Smiling politely, the woman turned to look at Heidi directly, then reached up to touch her lightly on her earlobe.

"These are beautiful earrings, are Chopard, yes."

Her action surprised Heidi, and she recoiled a little, but then relaxed at her gentle touch. This lady knew her jewellery, strengthening Heidi's appraisal of her as rich and sophisticated. They were indeed Chopard and were her most prized possession.

Heidi now knew the woman was foreign but couldn't quite place her accent. Eastern European possibly? It just added to her exotic mystery.

The woman let her touch linger a little longer than was necessary, then reached down for her handbag.

Heidi belatedly answered, "Yes. A present from my parents. I only wear them on special occasions."

As the woman turned towards the exit, Heidi thought her parting smile conveyed a little loneliness. The clicking of her stilettos on the tiles faded with her departure.

5

They gathered in the conference room at 9:30 a.m. Most of them had no idea what the meeting was about. And many did not know each other at all. Some had never experienced the security procedures they had just undergone, either. Full body scans, metal detectors, iris scans, and ID photographs had all been performed prior to the issuing of a one-time security pass. All electronic devices had been temporarily confiscated, including watches, smart or otherwise. They had also been required to sign an official secrets document before being admitted to the room. And these were just the checks they knew about —frantic work had been going on in the background, collecting all kinds of information on them.

There was, however, one person in the room who everyone but Beth recognised. The Minister for Defence called them to order. He thanked them for their attendance and introduced a middle-aged woman attired in a smart business suit as the Director-General of the Australian Signals Directorate, Judith Morton. She would chair the meeting.

"Thank you, Fred. Ladies and gentlemen, thank you for agreeing to attend at such short notice. I apologise for you not being given any information on what this is all about, except that it concerns an emergency of national importance. I also apologise for the security procedures you had to undergo, but you will soon realise why we needed them, and why we chose this particular location. And I must warn you that, after this meeting, your lives will probably never be the same again."

This statement did nothing to settle their anxiety.

The attendees were exchanging worried glances when Judith resumed. "Let's start by briefly introducing ourselves."

She started, re-informing them of her name and occupation. Unsurprisingly, that was the extent of the information she offered about herself.

Next, although somewhat unnecessarily, the Minister for Defence introduced himself. He never missed a chance to talk about himself. Fredrick Brown. At least he disclosed his age: 52. He explained directly to Bethany, and in some detail, what his role entailed, and offered her a personal thanks for her attendance. He acknowledged she was the only non-Australian in the room.

Since she had just been addressed, it was natural for Beth to follow.

"Petty Officer Bethany Marks, 24, Missile Officer, United States Navy. Currently deployed on the *USS Henry Teak*." Delivered while standing to attention. And with the clear, strong, somewhat staccato voice instilled in the US military. She stood out from the rest of the attendees with her accent and pretty African-American features, and also in her attire. Before she informed them, it was obvious to all where she worked; dressed as she was in the elegant, tailored Dress Uniform of the United States Navy.

Next was another person in uniform. He had been paying rapt attention to the fetching naval officer since they assembled. He was still somewhat traumatised by the events of the preceding days and felt at least some sense of connection with her among the mostly civilian group. Besides, she was cute.

"Pilot Officer Philip Lawson, 26, F-18 Pilot, No 1 Squadron, Royal Australian Air Force." He had a formal way of standing, and his voice and tone showed respect.

The baton was quickly passed around the room in no particular order.

"Jessica Gordon, 27, Emergency Medicine Registrar, Gold Coast University Hospital." Jessica wore light grey slacks and a blue cotton top. She appeared a little overwhelmed by her present company.

"Sergeant Bernard Ambrose, 28, No 2 Commando Regiment,

Royal Australian Army." Bernie was dressed less formally than the others in uniform; he wasn't wearing the dress uniform of his regiment, but the fatigues he wore in his day-to-day duty. He also had a much more relaxed stance than Philip or Bethany and spoke with the drawl common to Australian men.

And finally, the last of the attendees.

"Heidi Almendinger, 26, Cyber Specialist, Australian Signals Directorate—I work for Judith," she added with a tilt of her head.

With the introductions over, the incredible events of the previous few days were sequentially revealed to the meeting.

Judith motioned for Heidi to start, asking her to inform them about the message she had recently received, adding they were all cleared to discuss everything concerning it while here at the meeting, but not a word about any of this was to be discussed beyond these walls.

Heidi started by telling them of a mysterious file that had appeared within the downloads folder on her home computer. She had first noticed it after returning from a concert she had recently attended in Sydney. This had both alarmed and intrigued her; she had no idea where the file had originated. Of course, she knew the dangers of opening such files, but she had powerful anti-virus software running on her computer and had various tools at her disposal that she could use to examine it safely.

The file was encrypted, but the software she had available at home didn't dent the encryption. Now her interest had well and truly been piqued. Apart from her ignorance of its origin, a file with this level of encryption wasn't the sort of thing usually encountered in ordinary day-to-day life. But it was in her professional one. She had considered the possibility of a sophisticated hack, possibly by a foreign power, targeting her as an entry point to government systems. That sort of attack was something she was involved with quite often at work. She had approached her superiors with her concerns, and asked for permission to analyse the file using the official, highly developed tools available to her at work. She had toiled all day before finally cracking it.

Heidi's narrative enthralled Beth. *That's what I'm doing here.* She had been correct about her hack hypothesis. *The Aussies are onto it. And it looks like they've cracked it.*

Heidi's voice interrupted her thoughts as she carried on to inform the meeting the file contained a list of names, two short videos, a date, and a time. The list of names, to her amazement, included her own, and she recognised one other name: Bernie's. Her name was at the top of the list. This had certainly got her attention, but it was what she saw when she ran the videos that blew her mind. She had raced to inform her superiors.

Judith re-took control of the meeting. This included turning on the large computer monitor mounted on the wall and displaying the list of names, time, and date. Today's date; 10:00 a.m. Everyone immediately realised the reason for their invitation. Their names were on the mysterious list. The only ones missing from it were the Minister for Defence and Judith. They, for different reasons, had invited themselves to the gathering.

Judith pointed out that no venue had been mentioned in the message. So she had chosen one. And what better location than a highly secure room in her department's building? She didn't know what to expect. Most probably, it would be another message. She explained she had convened the meeting to start early to allow time for everyone to introduce themselves and be made aware of the contents of the message. She added that, although classified as top secret, she had received permission to show them the videos. Presumably, if further contact were made, the sender of the message would refer to its contents.

She played the first video. There was no soundtrack, but those present stared spellbound at the footage. It showed, in ultra-high definition, a near view of an ICBM in the boost phase of its flight. Displayed on the bottom of the video were the rapidly updating GPS coordinates and the time and date to millisecond resolution. Suddenly, another missile flashed past it in a near miss. Two seconds later, the ICBM pulsed an iridescent blue, then abruptly vanished from the screen. The video ended, leaving its audience to stare in mute fascination at the monitor.

A pregnant silence dragged on until Judith broke it with her understatement: "You can see why this captured our attention."

The room exploded into several conversations at once. Everyone was trying to voice their interpretations simultaneously. All, that is, except Jessica, who had no idea of what she had just been shown. And

Bethany, who had a very good idea, but who couldn't quite believe it. She remained stoically silent; she had been ordered to secrecy about her theory. Attend the Aussies' meeting and report back. But say nothing. Her commanders had no desire to let anyone, including their firm ally Australia, know of China's suspected abilities, and the possible compromising of their command-and-control systems. Not yet anyway.

Judith brought the meeting back to order, inducing silence by playing the second video. To most of them, especially Philip, this one was even more dramatic because they recognised what they were looking at. It showed video, again with no accompanying soundtrack, of an Australian Air Force F/A-18E Super Hornet flying a steady course in the dwindling light of early evening. It was a view taken from the starboard side of the aircraft. As in the previous video, on the bottom were GPS and time readings. Philip's blood ran cold. He recognised the identification markings on the aircraft, and the reference to the time and place that had turned his world on its head. He knew what was coming next. The others just watched, seeing what they thought was stock Australian Air Force promo footage. After a few seconds of play time, the missile on the wingtip pylon shimmered with the same blue iridescence as seen with the ICBM, and vanished.

They looked at each other in disbelief, trying to digest what they had just seen. Philip struggled with his thoughts. Should he tell the meeting of the now highly classified footage he had taken on that day? Probably better not. Although Judith had given permission to discuss everything, she was not his commanding officer. And a civilian, no less. He didn't want to do jail time for disclosing national secrets without express permission from high command.

Judith resolved his dilemma. She said she had one more video to show. Philip recognised it immediately; he had taken it himself, recording it on his phone. It showed a view from the starboard side of the cockpit of his aircraft. In the centre of the video, at what he had estimated to be thirty metres distant, was a jet black diamond-shaped object, holding a rock-solid formation with him. It appeared to have a very smooth surface and was symmetrical in both the horizontal and vertical planes. The front and back angles were quite acute, and the top and bottom ones obtuse to complete the structure. Included in the frame was the starboard wing with its pylon mounted AIM-9

Sidewinder missile. A pinpoint of beautiful blue light suddenly emanated from the object. Simultaneously, the missile shimmered with the now familiar iridescence and disappeared from the pylon. The video became chaotic as the framing changed sporadically, showing a frantic movement of the camera.

The room again erupted into animated conversations. Everyone was talking at once. Everyone, except Philip, who silently stared at the monitor, his mind in a different time and place. And Bethany, who with slightly watery eyes, was trying to swallow the lump in her throat. She knew what she had just seen. There was a third scenario as to what had happened to the ICBM, one that would not have occurred to her in her wildest dreams.

They were here! And it seemed they were friendly. With the Aussies at least.

Heidi reached out and touched Philip's arm. "That was you, wasn't it?"

Almost subconsciously, he replied, "Yes."

His mind was still re-living the events of that day. He hadn't believed what he was looking at, and he was going to get evidence of it, because he knew no one else would believe it either. It already had his head spinning, but he'd nearly shit himself when the missile had vanished. He'd jammed his phone back into the pocket of his flight suit, checked to confirm the object was still there, and quickly scanned his flight displays to see the status of his aircraft. No armaments on board. The entire weapons load had disappeared! Then his heart skipped a few beats. Fuel level was extremely low, perhaps fifteen minutes of flight time left till he ran out at the present rate of consumption. That was nowhere near enough to make it back to his base at Tindal. He had quickly contacted the USAF KC-10 tanker he'd been conducting mid-air refuelling drills with on this training mission. The second of three of them was due in twenty minutes. He informed them he was fuel bingo and requested an immediate tanking. He made the rendezvous with moments of fuel left on-board.

Judith said to Bethany, "You stated you are a missile officer on the *Henry Teak*. We know it was on station in the South China Sea at the time of the ICBM vanishing. It was your interceptor flashing by in the video just prior to the missile disappearing, wasn't it?"

"Yes ma'am. I presume so."

~

The clock on the wall flicked to 10.00 a.m.

Right on cue, the phone in the centre of the table rang. Judith recognised the tone; it was an internal call. Still, she felt a little trepidation as she reached over, pressed the speaker button, then picked up the handset.

"Judith Morton."

"Excuse me, madam. Two young women have just walked into reception and informed us they are here for their scheduled meeting with a woman named Heidi. Ah, they are a little unusual, madam."

Judith cast a glance towards the dumbfounded Heidi. "Thank you. Please expedite your security scans and escort them here as soon as possible. And although I'm certain this request is unnecessary, please be sure to extend them every courtesy. They are extremely important guests."

So; not another message. A personal visit!

But how did they know where the venue she had chosen was? She was now doubly glad for her choice of room. Detailed security scans of their visitors would be available and security personnel would be close by if needed. However, judging by what they had all just seen in the videos, she doubted their protection would be needed or effective. It was a comforting thought, nonetheless.

Judith was beginning to realise that somehow Heidi was central to this whole incident. She had received the initial message, and the women now being escorted towards them had just named her. She took Heidi by the hand, squeezed it reassuringly, and led her to stand beside her near the door. Everyone present seemed frozen in place with apprehension. The eerie silence was broken only by the occasional clearing of a throat or nervous shuffling of a foot. Then came the much-awaited knock on the door.

After a nervous smoothing of her clothing, Judith glanced towards Heidi and opened the door, stepping aside slightly to dodge its inward arc.

A security guard stood in front of her. He extended his hand in a gesture to both introduce his guests and invite them to enter. She greeted him with her eyes and politely thanked him with a slight bow of her head. As he stepped aside, she turned her attention to the young woman standing beside him.

She was simply stunning. Early twenties. Tall, slim figure.

Beautiful face with high cheekbones. Slightly almond-shaped eyes with sparkling hazel irises. Flawless, lightly tanned skin. Long, dark, wavy hair held neatly in place in a ponytail, with just a few strands hanging free to frame her face. No discernible makeup. The only visible jewellery was a pair of sparkling stud earrings. Her outfit composed of comfortable black sneakers, black yoga pants that hugged her lithe body and a tight-fitting black top, high in the neckline and with sleeves down to her delicate wrists. She wasn't carrying a purse or bag, simply standing there with her arms by her side. A security visitor pass hung around her neck displaying the government insignia, the department name, her photograph and the simple inscription—A.

She was looking Judith directly in the eye as if studying her, giving her the uneasy feeling she was being scanned. Assessed. Judith couldn't quite put a finger on her expression. It seemed to be a juxtaposition of friendly interest and slight aloofness.

All of this took mere moments, and the spell broke when the young woman flicked her gaze towards Heidi. Her expression immediately melted into the radiant greeting of a long-lost friend. She said softly, "Hello, Heidi, so pleased to see you again," and stepped forward to kiss her on each cheek in the traditional European greeting.

Judith couldn't place her slight accent.

Heidi, for her part, was in shock. She returned the greeting automatically, knowing enough of the etiquette to reciprocate. This was the woman who had commented on her earrings during that brief encounter in the ladies' room. It must have been her who uploaded the file. But how did she know her name? How did she access her computer? And why did she act as if she knew her?

Bernie also recognised her. She was dressed far more casually and had her hair done differently, but there was no question this was the girl from the Opera House. However, acting on a gut feeling, he remained silent.

As these greetings were exchanged, Judith turned her attention to the other visitor. She had to quickly look back to check that the first one hadn't somehow switched places with her. They were identical—in every detail. Same slim bodies; same faces; same eyes; same hair; same clothes. Same everything! Except, perhaps, for the expression on the second one's face. Maybe it was a little more tense and less friendly? Maybe a little more judgemental? Perhaps it was her imagination. They were identical. Identical! The only way to tell them apart was by the security tags they were wearing. This one displayed the letter B. No wonder security had said they seemed a little odd. Judith forced herself to smile a greeting and extended her hand in an invitation to enter. It was accepted; her grasp soft as B stepped forward.

As she entered the room, Heidi thought, "Oh my God, she has a twin sister and has brought her to the meeting as well."

The visitors let their eyes scan across the room to acknowledge the others present. There was a fleeting, almost subliminal pause as the first one's gaze encountered Bernie's, giving him the feeling she recognised him.

Then, with that almost seductive inflection of hers, she introduced them both.

"Thank you for taking time to meet with us. I am A," and with a delicate twisting of her wrist in an upward direction towards her companion, she added, "B."

Silence greeted her. Interpreting the nonplussed looks on the meeting attendees as these names being unacceptable, she quickly updated them. "Annabelle." Accompanying the last syllable with the same hand gesture.

Giving Judith no time to recover her composure and proceed with her own planned introductions, Anna, followed by Belle, approached the large oblong table in the centre of the room and said, "Please, let us start. We have much to discuss."

They sat in adjacent chairs. The others hurried to comply, the Defence Minister rushing to claim the chair adjacent with Anna. He wanted a position of prominence at the table to show them his importance. The others took whatever chair was close to hand. Heidi was the last to be seated and ended up sitting opposite their two striking visitors.

Anna hit them with a bombshell. No preamble. No small talk. No beating around the bush. Short, if not sweet. Straight to the point. And the point made them reel.

"Nuclear war between your so-called superpowers will destroy habitability of this planet. We will not allow this."

As if everyone's hearts weren't already in their mouths, the mention of nuclear weapons supercharged the emotions flowing around the room.

When Anna's gaze met Heidi's, her expression transformed. She said, "Do not despair, Heidi. We like you. It is just that this planet is more important. It is very precious to us. All we need to agree on is to protect it."

An uneasy silence settled, no one quite knowing how to respond.

Finally, Beth found her voice. "What do you propose to do?"

She saw the implications for her country if their attitudes and actions did not change. Pronto. They were no longer the big kids on the block. That was a pill many would find hard to swallow. She was only a junior officer with no influence over the people who'd have to make the hard calls. But she was the only American here. And there were no Chinese. She assumed responsibility as spokeswoman for her country and was desperate to return with as much information as possible.

Her eyes boring into Beth, Belle replied with the none-too-veiled threat, "Nothing further, we hope, but this is entirely in your hands." It was the first time she had spoken since her arrival. Even their voices were the same.

So, you're the bad arse.

The one with the big stick. And she had a goddamn enormous one.

The Defence Minister puffed himself up in his seat. He was the highest ranker here; the one used to doing the talking, and making the big decisions. "Could you please confirm it was you who intercepted the missile and disarmed our aircraft mid-flight?"

Anna looked at him briefly, then ignoring him, flicked her eyes to Philip. She reached over and placed her hand on top of his. "We are sorry we caused alarm with fuel reduction. It was meant as demonstration." Her action surprised everyone in the room almost as much as her words.

He bobbed his head, his throat too dry to venture to speak. The Defence Minister glared at Anna in annoyance. Didn't the stupid woman realise he was the most important person in the room? The only one actually capable of making a decision.

Anna decided to terminate the meeting. There were people here who were not invited, one of whom she had no desire to spend further time with. Anyway, the main objectives had been achieved. The selected group had now met and also encountered Belle and herself. Their presence here was demonstrated and their purpose unequivocally stated. Just one final thing to do.

She touched Belle on the arm, stood and said to Judith, "Time to change your ways. We will be watching."

Belle stood to join her, triggering the others to do likewise. Anna walked around the table and approached Jessica, then taking her by the hand, she gently turned it palm up and placed a USB memory stick in it, then curled her fingers closed, leaving her grasping it in her fist.

The intense look in her eyes faded into a smile. "For you, Jessica."

Anna moved her hand upwards and rubbed Jessica's arm, then turned towards the door.

Jessica stood motionless, shocked she had been singled out after having seemingly been a bystander for the entire meeting.

Belle followed Anna out of the room.

Judith rushed after them. "Who are you, and how do we contact you?"

Anna turned, and after a moment's delay, said, "We will call you."

The escorting security guard, who had been waiting patiently outside, led them down the hallway.

The room fell silent. Jessica opened her hand and stared at the USB stick.

Having reached the doorway in her pursuit of Anna and Belle, Judith turned to face them and said, "Well, ladies and gentlemen, I don't think we're in Kansas anymore."

This broke the suspense, and the room burst into various overlapping and excited conversations.

Judith snapped back to the present when she noticed Jessica still staring at the USB stick. What did it contain? It was probably encrypted, but she was desperate to see its contents. And she was astute enough to realise it wouldn't be wise to just confiscate it. It had very expressly been given to Jessica. Confiscating it would most likely annoy Anna. Annoy was probably not the correct term, more like infuriate. And a furious Anna wasn't someone Judith wanted to have around.

Judith approached Jessica. "Would you like us to have a look at that? It's probably encrypted, but we should be able to crack it."

As if in a stupor, Jessica handed the USB stick to Judith, who immediately passed it to Heidi. She sat down behind the computer, inserted it and scanned it for viruses. The report came back clear. The monitor was still turned on and everyone could see that the stick contained a single file, *Jessica.pdf*. A large file: 2.4 GB. Heidi offered the mouse to Jessica, indicating she could open it if she wanted to, hoping she'd do so and end everyone's suspense.

Jessica bent over and double clicked on the file. It wasn't encrypted and it opened to reveal what appeared to most of them to be some kind of scientific document about Multiple Sclerosis.

Jessica's face paled as she glanced through the abstract. Then, with a shaking hand, she scrolled through the document, stopping occasionally to read some of its content. When she was about a quarter of the way through, with her face now drained of all colour, she collapsed into the nearest chair.

Heidi pulled her chair beside her and put her arm around her.

Jessica wiped her eyes, and Heidi pulled her in closer.

"I'm so sorry, Jessica."

Jessica produced a brave smile. "I've recently been diagnosed."

The others shifted about uneasily, not sure of what to say.

Beth thought, "And Anna has a goddamn big carrot."

6

When Bernie reported to Major Spencer, he found the Chief of the Defence Force and the Special Operations Commander present as well. When he had received the order, he had presumed it concerned the meeting from the previous day. Their presence convinced him of it; he didn't mix in their circles.

The CDF opened the proceedings. "Good morning, Sergeant, at ease."

Bernie snapped to comply.

The air hung thick with intrigue. The three officers studied Bernie, who looked back, his face an impassive mask.

The Chief of the Defence Force opened the file he had in front of him. After studying it for some time, he said, "We are here to discuss the meeting you attended yesterday. As I'm sure you're aware, the entire event was recorded, and we have studied it carefully. You can imagine our reaction when the two visitors turned up, and with what they had to say. Their indifference to Fred Brown was surprising, and the lack of any politicians on their list perplexing."

Once again, he referred to the document and turned a few pages, then suddenly closed it and looked directly at Bernie.

"Of note is the fact that you had nothing to say. And that nothing was directly said to you." He paused, inviting a response.

"That's correct, sir. I thought it best to remain silent at that stage. But I was all ears."

"Any insights you'd like to share?"

"Still mulling it over, sir. It was quite an experience. But I can tell you, when put in context, those girls are the scariest two people I've ever met." Bernie followed his gut and let the fact he recognised Anna from the concert slip his mind for the moment.

"I wholeheartedly agree. But it seems you and that select group of young people, for reasons unknown to us at this stage, have their attention. The centre of this attention appears to be the young woman, Heidi Almendinger — the two of you are in a relationship I'm told."

"Yes, sir, you could call it that. Early days, but we are seeing one another."

"Congratulations, Sergeant, and this places us in an advantageous position. Given that, as far as we are aware, she is the first person they have contacted, we need to keep a very close eye on her. That is where you come in."

Although the CDF had just offered his congratulations, his intense look conveyed to Bernie that he had no genuine interest in Bernie's love life. The meaningful part of his statement had come at the end.

He pushed back slightly in his chair and exchanging glances with the Special Operations Commander. Bernie assumed they were going to discuss something between themselves, but after a few moments, the CDF looked back at him and resumed.

"We don't know what liaison the visitors have had with the Americans or the Chinese, but it's overwhelmingly likely they have done so given their central role in all this."

Bernie's glance shifted between the two senior officers, his mouth clamped shut. He wasn't going to say anything further until asked to.

"And military issues are not the only thing the visitors seem interested in. What did you think about the fact that they specifically invited a doctor? And provided documentation regarding a disease she is suffering from?"

Bernie shook his head. "Don't have a clue what to make of that, sir. It seemed completely out of context to me."

The group remained silent for some time, then both senior officers cocked their heads towards Major Spencer.

His cue to speak. "Sergeant, your orders are to observe, collect any intel you can, and report back to me. This includes anything Heidi says about the matter. And anything regarding the Chinese. Anything at all, no matter how trivial it might seem to you."

Bernie acknowledged this and stood to attention, anticipating, correctly, that he was about to be dismissed.

After saluting, he turned to leave, but stopped mid-stride when the Chief of Defence added, "Sergeant, if the visitors contact you again, please inform them we are desperate to cooperate with them and want to establish a two-way communication process. And thank them for the destruction of the ICBM. We seem to have overlooked that during the meeting."

~

At the same time that Bernie was receiving his orders, Judith was sitting in her office with reports strewn all over her desk. She had been busy since first finding out about the message. And so had the host of technicians and specialists who had been doing analysis and preparing the reports she had in front of her.

Overnight, she had attended several meetings with high-ranking military figures and government ministers. She had, of course, told them what had transpired at the meeting, but had kept her cards close to her chest on any further information she had gleaned. She wanted to guard against leaks, and with politicians involved, that was almost inevitable. Everything had to be conducted on a need-to-know basis. That was also the reason she was sitting here, pondering the situation alone and not with a panel of experts. If any such experts existed, that is.

The report she had open and was staring at blankly fascinated her. Well, actually, it was the person central to the report that really fascinated her; Heidi Almendinger. What was it about Heidi? What did the aliens see in her? She was convinced that was what Anna and Belle were—aliens. When she saw the video showing what could only be interpreted as a UFO, it immediately came to her mind. As far-fetched as it was, no other explanation seemed possible. And the aliens were definitively interested in Heidi. Their only message, that she knew about at least, was to Heidi. They had greeted her like a friend; had even told her they liked her. What on earth was so special about Heidi?

Judith pored through the report again. Seemingly normal upbringing, if somewhat privileged. The only child of affluent and successful parents. They had emigrated from Germany when she was eight, her mother accepting a position at Monash University, lecturing in mathematics. She was now a professor there. Her father was a neurologist at the Royal Melbourne Hospital.

Heidi had attended a prestigious private school where she had excelled in mathematics and physics. The reports on her character and involvement in school activities were excellent. She had been a member of the school swimming team and was an accomplished distance swimmer. Heidi was also a musician, playing the clarinet in the school orchestra. She had undertaken the International Baccalaureate curriculum, matriculating with a high distinction in every subject. Then gone straight on to higher education and had graduated from The University of Melbourne with a Bachelor of Science and a Master of Software Engineering. And she was multilingual, being fluent in English, German and Finnish.

Heidi had applied for a position with the Signals Directorate immediately after completing her Masters, breezing through the selection process, and had been with them for two years now. Her annual performance appraisals showed nothing noteworthy.

So, Heidi was an intelligent, well-adjusted young woman. But why select her from all the people in the world? There were millions of intelligent, well-adjusted young women out there. And young men, for that matter.

Judith put her head in her hands and sighed, then gathered all the reports and placed them in the filing cabinet beside her desk. It was time to talk things through with Heidi.

~

As soon as she took the call, Heidi logged off her computer and headed straight to Judith's office. It was the first time she had been there, and she was high with a mixture of excitement and apprehension. The DG wanted to talk to her. Wow! It had to be something to do with the meeting. With Anna and Belle. Had Anna made her promised call?

Judith didn't get up when Heidi knocked on the open door, just responding by inviting her to enter. She asked her to close the door behind her, then indicated Heidi should sit in the vacant chair on the opposite side of her desk.

Judith looked at Heidi, sighed and shook her head.

"OK, let's talk things through. How do you know Anna?"

"I don't know her. I have seen her before, though. At the concert we were at prior to the file appearing on my computer. She was sitting in the same row as us, and I had a brief conversation with her in the rest rooms just prior to leaving. I thought nothing of it at the time."

"Heidi, she acted as if she knew you."

"I can't explain that. But it freaks me out. Well, I mean, she does."

Judith frowned, intensifying her gaze. "What was your conversation about?"

"She commented on my earrings, that's all."

"And she was alone? Belle wasn't with her?"

"No. There wasn't anyone with her at all."

Heidi's statement that she and Anna were not acquainted surprised Judith. She puzzled over it for the moment and move on.

"What do you make of them?"

Heidi wrung her hands together, then placed them both palm downwards on the desk in front of her, gripped the edge and leaned forward, almost conspiratorially.

"Please don't think me mad or anything, but my first thoughts were they may be time-travellers from the future or maybe even aliens. That's what occurred to me when I saw the videos in the file. Either that or it was a hoax. But that video and personal confirmation of it by the pilot seems clear enough. He saw a UFO. And it had amazing capabilities."

"My thoughts exactly. And we dodged a bullet with that missile, figuratively speaking. It would've been the end of life as we know it if it had reached its target."

"Judith, I think it's the end of life as we know it because it was prevented from reaching its target. Or perhaps that'd be better phrased because of how it was prevented from reaching it."

Judith pushed her chair back from the desk and swivelled it from side to side. The two women peered at each other, sombre looks etched on both their faces, but Judith hinting at a much greater level of confusion.

"Heidi, I can't get the image of Anna greeting you out of my head. Think back. Maybe you knew one another in Europe, as children, before you came here. It's very important that we find out everything we can about them. Maybe they've been here all that time."

Heidi shook her head in denial. "I was eight years old when I left. And Anna and Belle look a lot younger than me. Their accent is European, though."

Judith eased her chair back closer to her desk.

"OK, let's allow it to rest for the moment. If anything comes to you, anything at all, you tell me straight away."

"Of course."

"What did you make of the people on the list?"

Heidi shrugged and shook her head, wondering why Judith would ask a question like that.

Judith let out an exasperated sigh. "The entire episode is mind blowing. My God, we've been talking to aliens! But the most intriguing thing to me is, why you? It beggars analysis."

"I know. When I first saw those videos, I didn't know what to think. And, after I had slept on it, I became quite scared, well, apprehensive anyway. After talking with them, I'm not so sure. I don't think they want to hurt us. It's all so confusing; you saw what they can do. But they haven't directly attacked us. We've probably got a choice here; with them or against them. I'd like it to be with them."

Judith reached over and patted Heidi on the hand.

"Don't you think it a little odd that the list didn't include any of our leaders? And Minister Brown seemed to be given the cold shoulder."

"My guess is they're probably not ready to talk to them yet. Just sounding us out. I'm sure it won't be long before that happens, though."

"Let's hope so. But I think their agenda might be a little more urgent that just sounding us out. If they make contact again, you must tell them that our government wishes to meet with them. Surely they realise they are the ones to negotiate with."

Heidi bobbed her head emphatically. "Yes Judith, I'll be sure to do that."

Judith stood and held out her hand. Their discussion was over. "OK, Heidi, thanks for your thoughts. And although Sergeant Ambrose has a high security clearance, it's nowhere near the level of yours. No discussing any of the things you discover with him."

"Of course not; my lips are sealed."

Bernie knocked on the door. Almost immediately, Heidi opened it to greet him.

Bernie savoured their kiss and smiled as he handed over the bottle of wine he was holding, his contribution to the dinner she had invited him to.

She examined the label briefly and handed it back. "Thanks, that looks nice. I'll get some glasses."

Bernie poured their drinks while she brought over the cheese platter she had prepared for their entrée. He thought she seemed a little preoccupied as she raised her glass to return his salute.

After taking a sip, he casually reached for some cheese. "Looking good, Heidi. Come to grips with that meeting yet?"

Heidi gave an uneasy laugh, then also reached towards the platter. "Bernie, I'm so scared. I know we've been told not to discuss it, but I've got to talk to someone about it. What did you make of Anna and Belle? And that UFO? Oh my God; that was crazy."

"Yeah, that's probably the best word for it. One of them was at the concert, sitting just down our row. Did you notice her?"

Heidi nodded in affirmation. "And, Bernie, get this—she was in the ladies' room when I went there. She spoke to me briefly."

Bernie recoiled slightly with surprise. "Really, what about?"

"Just some idle chitchat, nothing really ... girl stuff. But she seemed friendly; she wasn't threatening at all. But you know a lot more about this stuff than I do. What are we going to do?"

Bernie shrugged. "Well, I agree with your original comment that they're frightening. Bloody terrifying, actually. Who knows what they're capable of? But I'm none the wiser about how to handle all this than you are. There's no standing operating procedure on how to fight off a UFO."

"But what about those two women?"

He shook his head to emphasise his appraisal. "Don't have a clue what to make of them. Except they're dead set dangerous. Oh, and real dolls. What about you?"

Heidi leant in close. "Bernie, crazy as it sounds, I think they're time-travellers. Or aliens. They had a UFO, for goodness sake! They went to a lot of trouble to set up the meeting, but they didn't hang around long. I don't get it."

"Yeah, but they had a hell of a message."

He regarded her for a moment before continuing. "Heidi, I was wondering why Anna treated you as if she knew you. Do you think it was because of your exchange in the ladies' room, or do you know her from somewhere?"

Heidi shook her head vigorously. "I've got no idea who she is. This is so weird. I don't have a clue why she acted like that. But it must have been her who put the file on my computer."

"It's bloody weird all round. We've got to be on our guard with them, but it seems to me Anna likes you. If you get the chance, cultivate that. It might just save us all."

Heidi looked at him with wide eyes before nervously reaching for another piece of cheese.

"I feel so sorry for poor Jessica, though. She's all alone up there and has that terrible illness. I wonder what's happened with the document Anna gave her."

"It's pretty unlikely to see the light of day. The powers that be won't want anything to do with this coming out if they can help it."

She reached out and squeezed his hand. "That's even sadder for her, knowing there's a treatment but not being able to access it."

Bernie nodded, then after a moment's pause, he became even more serious. "Heidi, why didn't you tell me about the message?"

"You know I'm sworn to secrecy. I was tempted to—don't worry about that. Your name was on it, after all. Anyway, when Judith told me to go to that meeting, I presumed you'd be there as well. You'd find out all about it then."

"Yeah, I understand. But if you ever need a shoulder to lean on, you've got mine. Okay."

Heidi shifted her position and leant against him. "I know, babe, from now on, no secrets about any of this between us. OK?"

Bernie cuddled her gently. "Absolutely."

He tried to take Heidi's attention off the meeting and lighten the mood of the evening. "Let's just wait and see how things pan out for Jessica. Early days and all. And I'm sure it's not the last we'll see of that pair. Let's put some music on and enjoy that meal you've promised me."

7

Heidi picked her parents up from the airport. Her dad had the weekend off and they had surprised her with a visit. Their phone call had excited her. It was always good to catch up with them—not that she got the chance to do it all that often these days.

On the drive home, her parents politely asked how work was going.

"Let's just say it's been a hectic week. You know I can't talk about work, but, oh my God, you would not believe what I'm mixed up with at the moment." To change the subject, she mentioned Bernie.

Both her parents immediately went into full inquisition mode, demanding all sorts of information about him. Most importantly, they wanted to know how serious she was about him … and he about her. Her mother was ecstatic that she was finally getting into another relationship. Her father was his usual self on the subject. He wanted to find out a lot more about Bernie and suggested he could join them for lunch.

"I'll ask him. With luck, he won't have anything on. It is Canberra, after all."

~

Heidi called Bernie once they got back to her house. "Hey, got anything on today?"

"Was thinking of going to the rugby this evening with some mates. The Brumbies are at home to the Chiefs. Didn't ask you because

I know you aren't interested in rugby. I'm up for something during the day though—was actually just thinking of calling you."

"Well, I'm embarrassed to ask you this, but my parents have given me a surprise visit. They're here for the weekend. I let it slip I'm seeing you and they suggested we could all have lunch together. You'll love my mum, but my dad is a handful, especially where guys and I are concerned. I'll completely understand if you don't want to. It'll be easy to come up with an excuse. Something like blaming it on the short notice."

This caught Bernie completely off guard. Things had been going great with Heidi. Meeting the parents, though ...

"Heidi, I've got to tell you, this is new ground for me. No one has ever actually asked me to meet the parents before. Don't get me wrong, I'm glad you like me enough to ask, but are you sure we aren't rushing things a bit here?"

"Yes, of course, shouldn't have asked. I told you I was embarrassed."

Bernie thought he could detect some disappointment in her voice. And although he was not all that interested in her parents per se, he thought it might be an opportunity to find out more about Heidi and her upbringing. Besides, he had been ordered to keep an eye on her and report back on anything he found out. This might turn up something relevant.

"No, listen, I'd love to meet them. Honestly. Sounds like you'd better sit between me and your dad, though."

"Thanks so much, Bernie. I'll pick you up around eleven thirty." She sounded happy with his reply.

~

"Mum, Dad, I'd like you to meet Bernard. Bernie—Ursula, Kurt."

Everyone exchanged handshakes. Kurt was polite if not openly smiling. Ursula looked impressed, beaming at her daughter after the introductions. Bernie was at his charming best and her father was hiding any misgivings that he may have been harbouring. Heidi began to relax.

Things are going OK so far.

It didn't last long, though. Her father would not make it that easy. "So, Bernard, why the army and what's that like exactly?"

"Well, sir, that's a bit of a long story. I've kind of been dabbling in it most of my life. I was in cadets in secondary school, a drummer, actually. After school, I did an apprenticeship as a carpenter. And I enlisted in the Army Reserve. I saw it as a chance to get out into the bush and enjoy the outdoors while keeping fit. And to get some extra money, of course. Apprentice wages are a bit light on."

Kurt was looking back with a neutral expression.

"After boot camp, I was selected to join 1 Commando regiment, which is partly manned by reservists. They're stationed in Sydney, close enough to my home at Arrawatta. Fast forward to me finishing my apprenticeship and a lot of training with the reserve. Mum wasn't too fussed with all this military stuff I was doing. She thought the perfect way for me to spend my life was building homes for people. Then I was posted on a tour to Afghanistan. That was almost the last straw for her, but my sister gave me a lot of support."

Bernie grinned as he thought of his sister.

"Trish's the alpha in our family. Better than me at everything she tries. Could probably even shoot straighter if she gave that a go. Anyway, while on deployment I realised this was the life for me, and when I returned I enlisted in the army full time. I'm now a member of 2 Commando."

Bernie had never mentioned being a carpenter to Heidi before. In fact, he rarely spoke about his work, or family for that matter.

Ursula commented, "Quite the exciting life you live, Bernard. I understand a little about that lifestyle. In my youth, I spent two years in the Finnish reserve. I come from Finland and men have to undertake two years' military training once they turn eighteen. It's voluntary for women, but being very patriotic, I enlisted as well."

"That's great to hear, ma'am, good on you. And I had better remember to be on my best behaviour around you, with all that training you have," he said with a wink.

Kurt wanted to press further. "So, exciting lifestyle, tell me more. And please, it's Kurt, you can drop the sir."

"Never a dull moment, Kurt. All kinds of training. Meeting interesting people. Flying around in helicopters. Jumping out of planes at night. All expenses paid travel to far-flung places. Some days, I wonder why they pay me"—a look of fleeting sadness overtook him as he remembered past events—"but some days, I know."

The conversation died as their main course was served.

Having finished their meals, as Kurt was reaching for his glass of wine, Heidi suddenly asked, "Dad, what's MS?"

Bernie quickly glanced at her, and with an almost imperceptible shake of his head, warned her not to pursue this any further.

Ursula gasped and Kurt froze with his glass halfway to his lips. Both parents looked aghast at Heidi, fearing what was coming next.

"Darling, why do you ask about that? Have you been feeling ill?" Kurt asked, his voice laced with concern.

"Oh my God, Dad, no. I'm fine. I'm just curious because a colleague has been diagnosed with it, that's all."

Both her parents breathed a sigh of relief, relaxing somewhat, but Bernie still had a look of concern.

Kurt said, "Your poor colleague, it's a terrible diagnosis, sweetheart. It's a progressive disease that damages the insulating covers of nerve cells in the brain and spinal cord. We speculate that anomalies in the immune system or certain infections may cause it, although we do not understand the mechanisms involved. There is no cure, but it is an area of vigorous research. If we can understand it, the flow-on effects to numerous auto-immune diseases will be enormous."

Bernie was desperate to change the subject, realising the dangerous ground Heidi was treading. He quickly chimed in with what he thought would be the favourite topic of any Victorian. He asked about football. Not just any footy. The AFL.

"I see the Hawks are top of the ladder at the moment, Kurt. What team do you follow?"

"Actually, I follow the Hawks. Going great at the moment, aren't they? To tell the truth, I'm not that interested in football. But I know enough about fitting in with life in Melbourne that you must have a club to barrack for. I'm an immigrant from Germany and my favourite sports are winter related. Ursula and I have a chalet at Merrijig and visit there whenever we get the chance."

"Do you ski, Bernard?" Ursula enquired.

"I've had a few goes at it since I've been here, but I've got to say I suck at it. I'm not too bad at snow-boarding; picked it up fairly quickly as I used to surf in my youth. But skiing, no, not so good."

Heidi chimed in. "Well, I'll have to give you some lessons, Bernie. If we're ever on the slopes together, Mum and Dad wouldn't be seen dead with some bogan on a snow-board."

Bernie laughed and burst into a verse of Lee Kernaghan's *Boys from the Bush*. This got him a playful push on the chest from Heidi, trying to shut him up. Ursula smiled, noticing the easy way Bernie had about him, and Heidi's obvious attraction to him. Kurt just grunted.

Bernie then skilfully steered the conversation towards discussing Kurt and Ursula's childhoods. Heidi found it surprising how interested he was in their respective countries of origin and what it was like to grow up there. He was full of surprises.

~

Her parents were staying with Heidi at her house. That stood to reason, not only because it had lots of spare room, but because they had bought it for her in the first place.

Later, when they were alone in their bedroom, Ursula said, "He's a nice guy, and Heidi seems so happy with him. She did seem a little on edge today, though—probably anxious about what we'd think of him."

"Yes, you're right. She can do a lot better than some soldier whose fall-back plan is carpentry. I hope this doesn't go anywhere."

"Kurt, please, she has her own life to live, you know."

"She can do a lot better than him, that's all I'm saying."

8

Judith glanced at her phone. She recognised the ring tone; it was reception.

"Excuse me, madam, I have a Jessica Gordon requesting to speak with you."

"Thank you. Please switch her through." If Jessica wanted to talk, she could guess what it would be about.

She keyed the phone. "Judith here, nice to talk with you again, Dr Gordon."

"Hello, Ms Morton. Thanks for taking my call. It's about the document Anna gave me. I'd very much like to discuss it with my treating specialist, but I realise that everything that happened at the meeting is classified as top secret. Do you think that'd be possible?"

"Please, it's Judith. Ms Morton sounds so formal. I understand how much the document means to you, Dr Gordon, and it is yours after all. But we are dealing with a complicated situation here. Perhaps we could meet to discuss this in person. As I'm sure you appreciate, I have quite a full timetable at the moment, but if you could find the time to visit Canberra, I'll be happy to schedule a meeting. My department will cover your expenses, of course. Could you let me know when you can travel here?"

"Thanks, and by the way, call me Jess. I've got Tuesday and Wednesday off in two weeks' time. Is that convenient for you, or is it too soon?"

"No, that'll be fine. I'll get my assistant to make the arrangements for that Tuesday. Looking forward to our meeting. Is there anything else I can help you with, Jess?"

"No, that's it. See you on Tuesday and thanks again for taking my call."

Judith hung up with a resigned sigh. *This was bound to happen, but how am I going to persuade my superiors to let Jessica divulge the info, and what cover story can we concoct to explain the document?*

9

Despite all she'd been exposed to recently, Bethany found herself overwhelmed by her surroundings. She was in the Pentagon and was being ushered into a room which, as far as she could tell, contained the entire group of decision makers within the government, along with the upper echelon of the military.

As she glanced around, she reflected this was going to be even more daunting than the debriefing with Naval Intelligence she'd been through yesterday. She tried to slink into the background, but a greying naval officer immediately approached her.

"Petty Officer Marks, I'm Admiral Blake, commander of the Pacific Fleet. I'm very pleased to meet you."

Bethany didn't quite know how to reply; she had never conversed with an admiral before. She settled on a stammered, "Thank you, sir."

"It's I who should thank you, Petty Officer, for your initiative and conduct in undertaking the ICBM intercept. I'm proud to have sailors of your calibre in my command. Please, let me introduce you to the Secretary of the Navy."

As he led her in that direction, she briefly scanned the placeholders on the large table in the centre of the room. One jumped out at her—POTUS.

"Oh my God," she thought, before turning her attention to the gentleman being introduced to her.

The Secretary of State interrupted them, requesting they all be seated. Bethany found her placeholder next to the Admiral's and took her seat along with the others. Her gaze flitted from person to person, and she was fidgeting, obviously ill at ease.

Admiral Blake reassured her in hushed tones. "Relax, Petty Officer. Just answer any questions you're asked. No one here is out to get you. In fact, they'll hang on your every word. The President is another matter. We'll have to see how that plays out."

Before she could answer, the room fell into silence and everyone stood as the President bustled into the room. He glanced around, barely acknowledging any of those present, until his eyes settled on Beth. He held her gaze for a moment, then took his seat.

The Secretary of Defence addressed the meeting.

"Welcome, Mr President. Thank you for attending." He looked around the table. "We are indeed in uncharted waters and, excuse the paraphrase ... there be dragons here."

Expressionless faces looked back. No one appeared to be in the mood for humour.

He adopted a much more formal tone. "I'm sure you've all read your briefs. We are still struggling to understand what has transpired and its ramifications."

He cast an eye towards the President, trying to gauge his level of attention. Although no confirmation was given, he presumed he had at least read the reports. What he understood about their contents was anybody's guess.

"I must stress the importance of Pine Gap to our global and, more specifically, Asian area military capability. Unless they are intent on precipitating a full-scale war, it's inconceivable the Chinese would consider, let alone undertake, such an attack. It's possible a rogue element was involved. Intel shows they have just replaced the head of their Strategic Missile Forces, but we have received no communication from them since the launch. Nothing."

Distracted by the President fidgeting with his placeholder, the Secretary took a noticeable breath. The moment passed, and he refocused before cocking his head in Bethany's direction and continuing, "Petty Officer Marks conducted the intercept. Please accept our commendations for your actions on that day."

With a mixture of pride and embarrassment, Beth lowered her eyes.

He turned his attention to the Director of the CIA. "We were seriously considering her postulations about what might have occurred. That was until she returned from her meeting in Australia."

Then he pointed towards Bethany. "Petty Officer Marks, everyone here has seen the videos presented at that meeting, along with a video of the actual meeting. We'd appreciate hearing your firsthand account of what transpired."

Bethany rose to her feet and gave a quick precis of what had occurred, finishing with, "Quite extraordinary, I think you'll agree. And the black object in the video can only be described as a UFO. As far-fetched as it seems, perhaps we're dealing with aliens."

No one spoke, although some moved about in their seats.

"Whatever this is, it's something big—very big."

Beth glanced towards the President and found she suddenly had his full attention.

"To me, the most amazing thing was when the two visitors turned up. It was quite an emotional experience. The power they command is terrifying. I have to tell you, actually talking with them, after having seen the videos, had my hair standing on end. Thinking about it still does."

She lightened the moment briefly by touching one of her braids. "No mean feat in itself."

A smile lightened her sombre expression. It was fleeting, though. Realising this sojourn was not being well received, she allowed the moment to pass, then once again looked around the table. The President had pushed his placeholder back into position.

Beth steeled herself and carried on. "But the two women didn't appear to think they needed any personal protection. They walked into that building and submitted to the security scans as if they didn't have a care in the world."

She raised both hands with palms facing upward in a gesture to reinforce her deductions.

"The fact they were unprotected was either an illusion, or their masters considered them expendable. Either way, as far as I am aware, the Australians did not attempt to detain them."

This concluded her report, and Bethany resumed her seat.

The President was clearly becoming bored with all this rhetoric and blurted out, "So, what do you suggest we do about this China problem? We can't back down to them."

"It's a complicated and delicate situation, Mr President. We have to consider this very carefully."

No. The President had well and truly reached the end of his attention span.

He stood and growled, "If they're trying to stop a nuclear war, why talk to the Australians? They don't have any nukes. They should talk to us. Get onto the Australians and find out how to contact them. We need to deal with them directly. If not the so-called aliens, then those people helping them. Let me know when we have the details."

The President turned towards the door, then, almost as if it was an afterthought, said, "I want a list of targets for a retaliatory strike against China. Something that will hurt them. My preference is their manufacturing hub. I'm sick of them flooding our markets."

With his somewhat stiff and self-important gait, he left the room.

~

Continuing as if the departure of the President was of no consequence, the Chairman of the Joint Chiefs of Staff asked, "Have we analysed these videos? Do they appear authentic? Or could this be another ruse from the Chinese?"

The Director of National Intelligence stood and entered the conversation. He directly addressed the Chairman of the Joint Chiefs. "We've analysed them forensically. Given the state of AI-generated deep fake news, and the absurdity of the alternative we're considering, it might be the most believable explanation at the moment. However, the video taken from the F-18 is almost certainly genuine."

He now widened his audience by looking at the others gathered around the table. A brief nod from the Chairman encouraged him.

"The other two videos are peculiar in many respects. There is no metadata attached. They exhibit breathtaking clarity. No artefacts or distortion due to lens imperfections are detectable. The focus is perfect, and no camera shake is evident. If they are genuine, the camera used was exquisite, the likes of which we don't have in our possession at the moment. This points to the inevitable conclusion they are most probably fake, that is, if not considered in light of the other evidence to hand."

He paused, and looked towards his seat, indicating he was

finished commenting.

The Chairman interjected by holding his hand up and saying, "Anything further to add?"

The DNI first looked at the Chairman, then let his gaze sweep around the table, and offered his opinion. "The events in the various videos are consistent and the timelines match. My view, gentlemen, is they are genuine. And if so, we are dealing with extremely advanced technology. I suggest we tread carefully from here on."

There was a moment's silence, then the DNI continued. "If my assumption is correct, the other elephant in the room is China. Have the aliens contacted them? And if so, what was the content of that contact? If they have, we're behind the eight ball on this. We can't afford for the Chinese to get the upper hand here. We've been directing intensive efforts to determine what's occurring in China at the moment, but we aren't making much progress. Things are certainly not progressing as usual, though. Which, of course, you'd expect just after launching a failed nuclear strike. But they are circling their wagons; something has them spooked."

The Secretary of State, in a gruff voice, said, "I'm not convinced this has anything to do with aliens. It's the goddamn Chinese. Aliens, for God's sake! There must be another explanation. It's inconceivable that if aliens have arrived, we wouldn't be their first point of contact. And gentleman; no contact. A meeting in Australia, of all places. A few videos. And a couple of girls. Please. Don't you think their arrival would be a little more overt?"

His outburst had completely disrupted the meeting. His next comment finalised it.

"I'll contact the Australians and confirm they're sharing everything, including any means of contacting those girls. Could the Joint Chiefs remain for a moment, the rest of you are excused."

~

The Joint Chiefs stood huddled together in a small circle. The Chairman swallowed several times, trying to stifle his inner turmoil. The others looked at him, their apprehension also apparent.

He closed his eyes. In the meantime, the rest of them cast glances at each other, wondering why they had been called together.

Finally, the Chairman, in a hushed but deliberate tone, said, "He has to go. He doesn't have the intellect for this. Nothing remotely like it. China flooding our markets is our biggest problem? Goddamn! The man doesn't have the mental capacity of a three-year-old. He's barely past the learning to talk stage. And, since that's the only thing he can do, he doesn't shut up."

The others took a step back, propelled by the vehemence in his voice.

The Chief of the Navy was the first to respond. "Like it or not, he's our Commander in Chief. We've already got enough on our hands, what with China and goddamn aliens thrown in the mix. A dead president would tip the country over the edge."

"I wasn't talking about killing him. Maybe something as innocuous as him suffering a stroke or the like. As long as he's out of the loop until we can resolve this. We'll get absolutely nowhere with him pulling the strings."

The Chairman looked at the others, either trying to gauge their support, or to conjure it up. He received blank stares in reply.

~

As soon as he got back to his office, the Director of the CIA summoned his aides. He gave them an image of Anna extracted from the security video of the Australians' meeting. He requested a top priority search to locate her, telling them she was a person of interest in a classified operation. Once they had located her, he was to be informed immediately.

Within an hour, there was a knock on his door.

"We have her, sir, one Viktoria Miroshnychenko. Currently located in Paris, France." The aide handed him a folder containing the target's details.

"Thank you, good work. Close the door on your way out."

As soon as he was alone, the Director rang the Chief of Staff of the Army.

"Jack, Bruce here. Can we meet regarding the Australian incident? As soon as possible."

"Of course. Your office or mine?"

"Let's make it mine."

Bruce studied the report on Viktoria word by word. It seemed odd that a French model and actress would be involved in all this, but the confidence of a positive match was 99%. She was one of them all right.

Maybe her being an actress offered a clue. He ignored the fact that there had been two of them at the meeting. A bird in the hand ...

When he arrived, Bruce handed Jack the file.

As he flicked through it, Bruce explained, "We've located one of those girls. I don't want to speculate on exactly who we're dealing with here, aliens or whatever. If that's indeed what they are, I'm not sure of how we'd go about having a conversation with them. But people are a different matter. I have staff who are experts at having very forthright and direct conversations with people, whether they're cooperative or not. And you heard the President. He wants direct contact with them. I say we report her whereabouts to him, and request authorisation for a delta mission to bring her in for a little chat. That should put us back on the front foot. And let us know what involvement they've had with China."

This drew a hesitant frown from Jack. "My boys are more than capable of doing the snatch, especially in a friendly nation such as France. But you saw the videos. We could be playing with fire here. I agree; we need authorisation from the President himself on this one."

"Good, I'll get straight onto it."

~

Viktoria was panting slightly, but she felt at ease; she loved to exercise, and this was her favourite form. As she was about to leave the park, with only a few blocks left until reaching home, a fellow jogger approached from the opposite direction. He stumbled as he was about to pass and accidentally brushed against her.

She dismissed the incident as the man apologised profusely for being so clumsy. He spoke in French, but with an American accent. As she resumed her run, Viktoria felt a little dizzy and stumbled, then stopped to take a few breaths, hoping the feeling would pass. It didn't. In fact, she felt quite ill and took a seat on a nearby bench. Her mind then went blank as she fainted.

The jogger returned to offer help, telling a few curious passers-by that the woman had fainted, and that he'd called for emergency services. He laid her down on the bench and knelt beside her, supporting her head until an ambulance arrived. Nobody seemed to notice its response time was less than a minute. He conversed briefly with the paramedics, and then, as she was still unconscious, they placed her on a gurney and rushed her off to hospital.

10

Jessica's wellbeing had been playing on Heidi's mind since the meeting. She wanted to do something to help and suddenly had a brainwave.

She called Bernie. "I've just thought of something. Why don't we go to the chalet for a weekend? We can ask Jessica to come. It'll give her a chance to talk to someone, at least."

"Yeah, can't see any harm in that. In fact, it sounds bloody brilliant. And it'll give you a chance to give me the skiing lessons you promised," he added with a chuckle.

"I'll see if I can arrange it."

~

"Hey, Mum, I was wondering if I could have the chalet for a weekend? A few friends want to do some skiing and it'll be a great place for us to stay."

"How many friends, Heidi, and I assume Bernie is one of them?"

"Of course he is. What did you expect? But don't worry, he's a decent guy, and I know what I'm doing. It's just a few of us … please."

"OK, but don't let your father know if you can help it. You know what he's like."

~

Heidi rang the Gold Coast University Hospital and told them she was trying to contact Dr Jessica Gordon. If possible, could she please leave a message to inform her Heidi Almendinger would like to contact her?

About an hour later, Heidi's phone rang.

"Hello, Heidi, how nice to hear from you. Sorry, I've been busy. How are you?"

"Well thanks, Jessica. I hope you're feeling OK. This is a bit out of the blue, but I'm planning a weekend at my parents' chalet for a skiing trip. So far it's just my partner and me. He was at that meeting. The soldier. Bernie. Don't know if you remember him. Anyway, we were thinking you and your partner might like to come and join us. It'd be a great chance to catch up and get to know each other a little better, and to discuss all this craziness we're mixed up with. What do you think?"

"Please, it's just Jess. I'm still in shock after that meeting, and I'd absolutely love to catch up with the two of you. I'm dying to talk to someone about it. Believe it or not, I've got the coming weekend off. Hope that's not too soon for you. Might even get a colleague to cover for me so I can leave a bit early. I'm owed some favours. Let me know the details, times, places etc. Oh, and I'm single at the moment, so it'll just be me if that's all right."

"Wonderful, Jess, so looking forward to it. Why don't you fly to Canberra Friday after work? We can drive down from here. The chalet is in Merrijig in the Victorian Alps."

~

Heidi and Bernie met Jess at the airport. After exchanging excited greetings, they all piled into Bernie's twin cab 4WD and headed straight for the chalet. Heidi sat in the back seat with Jess.

As soon as they got underway, Heidi asked, "How are you feeling, Jess? Is the MS showing any more symptoms and have you read through Anna's document? Does it describe a treatment?"

"Of course I've read it. From beginning to end. It's exceedingly technical, but I can understand enough of it. There's a *lot* of biochemistry described, and it contains details of what causes the disease and a revolutionary treatment, one that I am more than willing to undergo. It's unbelievable, really. I know we're all sworn to secrecy, but I've arranged a meeting with Judith to discuss permission to show it to my specialist. It's on this coming Tuesday."

"That's great, Jess. After what we've seen Anna capable of, I'm sure it'll work. That's great, isn't it, Bernie? Judith will let her, won't she?"

Bernie glanced back at them in the rear-view mirror. "Yeah, great news. I'd think she'll have to let you show it to him, Jess. But she'll have a doozy of a cover story, that's for sure. Can't wait to hear what it is."

Jessica said, "Oh my God, could you believe that meeting? I'm so glad I can finally talk about it with someone."

That was all they talked about for the rest of the trip.

They arrived at the chalet late that night, got the fireplace going, and had a nightcap or two before retiring to get some rest prior to their big weekend.

11

The sudden blue flash caught the two guards unawares. As it faded, they felt a constriction around their necks. Their hands flew to their throats, panicked fingers desperately tugging at the bands as they tightened unmercifully; choking them. Their legs thrashed about as their desperate struggles continued, their lungs burning, their faces reddening and their eyes bulging as they suffocated. Then they succumbed to the inevitable and fell to the floor, unconscious.

As abruptly as they had appeared, the bands vanished. The room assumed an eerie quietness, the only sound the almost imperceptible hum of the surveillance equipment.

The CCTV screens showed nothing but static, no longer witness to the cell, or the inexplicable events occurring within it.

~

A distraught and dishevelled Viktoria raised her hands to shield her eyes. The level of light in the room had suddenly increased from semidarkness to a brilliant intensity. And she was no longer lying on the hard stone floor but sitting on a sofa. In her distressed state of mind, she felt disoriented. As far as she could recollect, a moment ago she had been somewhere in Russia, cowering in her cell, alone again after the latest interrogation by her captors. She was not alone now though, a woman who looked remarkably like her was sitting beside her, cuddling her and speaking reassuringly to her in Ukrainian. And, as her eyes became accustomed to the light, she noticed the room she was in looked nothing like her cell.

"I'm sorry for what has happened to you, Vika, and I regret it took us so long to find you. But you are going to be all right now. We will look after you; you are with friends."

Viktoria thought she must be hallucinating, and she began to sob and mumble to herself.

Her companion continued reassuringly. "My name is Anna. Please have a sip of water, and after you've showered, perhaps you would like something to eat. You can use some of my clothes. They will fit you; we are sisters, after all. And don't worry, Vika, I know what you like to eat."

Viktoria accepted the offered drink, and after taking a sip, handed the glass back. Her companion then led her to a door, which opened into a small en suite. Viktoria was still confused, but her recent experiences had made her somewhat compliant. At first she was terrified of the water, remembering the torture she had endured at the hands of her captors. But, with Anna's reassurance, she relaxed and scrubbed herself vigorously, as if to remove all traces of her ordeal. She couldn't understand why the Russians had captured her, and who were the visitors they kept asking her about. She just knew she was going to die at their hands. The questioning and near drownings had seemed to go on for days. And now there was a woman who called herself her sister looking after her. She wasn't talking in Russian, but in Ukrainian. And with no accent, she was a native speaker. And come to think of it now, her interrogators had a slight accent even though they spoke perfect Russian. Not Ukrainian, though. She couldn't quite place it.

The clothing she was offered included several of her favourite brands, and they did indeed fit her perfectly. Feeling much better, she accepted the food prepared for her. Anna sat in silence, watching Viktoria hungrily consume her meal.

"Who are you again? I see you look and sound like me, but I don't have any sisters."

"You do now, sweetheart, sisters who'll do everything needed to look after you. But we'll speak about that later; for now we have to get you well again. After you have finished eating, I'll take you to meet some of my friends. They'll look after you; one of them is a doctor."

12

On Saturday evening, the group was enjoying drinks sitting at the bar in a nearby restaurant with good natured banter about their skiing prowess or lack thereof flowing between them.

Suddenly, Bernie stopped talking mid-sentence. The others turned to see what had caught his attention and were astonished to see Anna and Belle approaching. One of them looked concerned, and the other completely bewildered.

"Hello everybody," Anna said, "this is my sister Viktoria. She is unwell and needs someone to take care of her."

Heidi let out a gasp of surprise when she heard the name Viktoria. *Another one?*

Viktoria turned to Anna and asked in Ukrainian, "Which one is the doctor, Anna?"

By now, they had all stood up and Jessica noticed Viktoria appeared to be disorientated.

She touched her on the arm and said, "Hello, Viktoria, I'm Jessica. Do you speak English? I'm a doctor. What's wrong?"

Before she could reply, a news flash on the TV above the bar interrupted them.

"Breaking news—President Boage has been found unresponsive in the Oval Office and rushed to hospital. Initial reports say he is critical, but no further details are available at this stage."

Anna was glaring at the TV.

Bernie's skin had been tingling ever since Anna walked in. She frightened him, and he wasn't afraid to admit it. The news and her expression alarmed him, and as she turned her gaze towards him, his thoughts galvanised into sharp focus.

"Anna—what have you done?"

"They were hurting Viktoria," was her simple explanation.

Bernie's look morphed immediately from alarm to consternation. He reached out and gently took Anna by the arm before turning towards the others.

"Excuse us, please. I need to talk with Anna alone for a moment. Don't worry, Viktoria. Jessica will look after you. We'll just be down at the end of the bar. Come with me, Anna—please."

He tried to force a reassuring smile to Heidi and led the compliant Anna away until they were out of earshot of the others. Heidi had never seen Bernie like this. It just added to her alarm.

As soon as they reached the end of the bar, Bernie leaned in close to Anna and, in a hushed and sincere tone, said, "Anna, please hear me out. First off, on behalf of my government, and from me personally, let me thank you for destroying the missile fired at Pine Gap. I believe we haven't done that yet."

Anna gave a slight bow, a gesture Bernie interpreted as acceptance, though it struck him as odd given the circumstances.

Bernie had never seen anything as beautiful as Anna's eyes, especially from this close. The yellow flecks interspersed within their hazel backdrop seemed to flicker like fire dancing within her soul. And he couldn't decode the powerful emotion the touch of her skin under his fingers was causing. When Anna looked down at his hand, he withdrew it and refocused.

"If you have harmed the American President, it'll have drastic consequences, both for their country and globally. What exactly have you done, and why?"

"As I told you, they were hurting Viktoria. They had abducted her and taken her away. Their President authorised this. We have punished him."

Bernie was almost in a state of panic now. "Anna, this is very important. I can arrange for you to meet with representatives of my country. They were desperate to meet with you prior to this and had asked me to arrange it when next we met. Believe me when I tell you that, with these latest developments, they will be beside themselves at the moment. Please, will you come with me to talk things through with them?"

Anna nodded before saying, "Yes," adding, "Heidi can come also?"

A very relieved Bernie answered, "Absolutely. I'll make the calls straight away. Thank you, Anna—thank you."

In an impulsive moment, he leaned forward and kissed her on the forehead. The fire in her eyes continued to dance as she held his gaze.

~

Bernie pulled his phone from his pocket.

"Major Spencer, this is Sergeant Ambrose. I have Anna with me and she's agreed to the meeting you requested. I assume you've seen the news about President Boage. Sir, I suggest an immediate evac and the meeting to be arranged for as soon as we get there. If not with everyone, at least you and anyone that can make it. Time is of the essence."

"Certainly. Where are you at the moment?"

"At a restaurant in the Victorian Alps. In the town of Merrijig. There are three of us to evac. And, sir, there are another two people with me as well. It's best if they remain here, out of sight, but I request some security for them."

"Right. I'll arrange for a Blackhawk to be dispatched. I'll send a patrol down on it to provide the security. What are we dealing with here?"

"Not a secure line, sir, but don't spare the horses."

"Understood. I'll call you back shortly."

With a reassuring glance towards Anna, Bernie led the way back to the others.

"Anna and I are going to a meeting. Heidi, you're coming with us. We're getting picked up shortly by helicopter. Jess, it's best to keep Viktoria out of sight back at the chalet for the moment. Viktoria, you'll be all right. Jessica will be with you all the time. And I've arranged for some soldiers to come down here to ensure your safety. One of them will be a medic, so you'll have some support, Jess."

He paused for a moment as he looked around.

"I'd like to take the opportunity to have our meal, but I'm worried about the security camera over the bar."

Heidi had never seen this side of Bernie. So this was what he was like at work. All business.

Anna said, "Security camera is not working."

Bernie's eyes narrowed slightly, then he almost said out loud, *Glad you're on my side, darling.*

"I am to travel with you?" Anna enquired.

Thinking quickly, Bernie replied, "Do you have a better way for us to get to the meeting, Anna?"

"Yes, but I have never been in helicopter. I will travel with you."

Bernie felt disappointed that he had missed the opportunity to see how the aliens got around, but he chose not to comment on it further.

The waitress interrupted, saying their table was ready.

"Would it be possible to upgrade to a table for five? Two friends have just turned up unexpectedly."

"Of course, sir, I'll see what I can arrange."

As he followed the waitress, Bernie turned to the others and said, "Let's eat. It's going to be a long night."

Halfway through his entrée, his phone rang. "Bernard Ambrose."

"Evac at Mansfield airport, 12:15 Zulu. I've arranged for the police to meet you there. Looking forward to your safe arrival in Canberra."

"At 12:15 Zulu, Mansfield airport. Roger."

~

After their meal, they went back to the chalet to drop off Jessica and Viktoria. Everyone except Anna seemed to still be on edge. Once inside, Bernie disguised his nervousness by going to the fireplace and adding some wood.

Viktoria noticed a digital piano against the wall. She went over and started touching the keys. Although Heidi was still anxious and a little distracted, she saw her chance to find out something more about the aliens. Could they play? And if so, what kind of music did they enjoy?

"Do you play, Viktoria?"

"I used to when I was young, but I have not played piano for some time. I play violin now. Do you have one here?"

"No, I'm sorry, I don't."

"Anna plays. I saw piano in her room. Play something for us, Anna."

Heidi went straight to the piano and switched it on. "Please, Anna, we'd all love to hear you play. There's a lot of music under the bench. Pick something you like."

Anna smiled and said, "Yes, this is for you, Vika." She sat at the piano and, with no need for music, played Beethoven's *Für Elise*. When she finished, she stood and bowed, smiling at their applause.

Heidi said, "That was lovely, Anna. You play beautifully."

"Yes, we love this music. Like Viktoria, Belle and I used to play when we were young. We have been practising again in our room."

Heidi said, "Please, play some more."

"No, I have to speak with Viktoria now."

She went over to Viktoria, reached out and held her by both shoulders, leant in close and said in Ukrainian, "I realise you've been through a lot and I appreciate how confusing this is to you, but I am your sister and I love you. We have another sister, Belle, just like us. You wouldn't understand what is happening even if I tried to explain it to you, but you are safe now and we'll look after you, even if we're not with you all the time. These people are our friends and you'll be safe with them. I have to go away for a little while, but I will come back to you. I promise."

"Yes, but how did we get here?"

"As I said, you wouldn't understand, but I'll explain it to you one day."

She leant in closer, stood on tiptoes, kissed her sister on the forehead and gave her a pat on the arm before walking towards the door.

~

They heard it before they saw it, sweeping in low from the north to hover momentarily before quickly descending to land. Five fully armed commandos rapidly egressed the chopper and moved over to the waiting 4WD and the three people standing beside it.

"Hey, Toast, good night for it," one shouted above the noise of the idling chopper.

"Never a better one, Sharpie. Here's the address of a chalet down the road. There are two people there I want you to look after, keys are in the car. Take good care of them, mate—precious cargo."

To Sharpie, Bernie seemed unusually tense. "Will do. You owe me one, Toast. Till later then."

With that, Bernie led Anna and Heidi towards the Blackhawk. As they reached it, the crew chief helped them to their seats and gave them each a headset. Once they settled, the chopper took off and sped north.

George got behind the wheel of Bernie's car while one of the other soldiers took the passenger seat. The rest piled in behind them. They headed off toward Merrijig, leaving the police scratching their heads, wondering what that was all about.

~

Heidi was full of adrenaline on the flight north. She had never been in a helicopter before, let alone one as imposing as this. She'd never witnessed five fully armed soldiers who looked as if they meant business jumping out of one, either. Or shared the ride with an alien!

Anna focused on the pilots and the flight instruments. The headsets crackled continuously as she fired questions at them, and they seemed to be only too willing to explain things.

Bernie was contemplating what was going to occur at the meeting. And what was going on in America at the moment? How the meeting would go was very much dependent on who was in attendance. He hoped it would be a small group of military people; sensible people. But he suspected otherwise. And who was Viktoria, how did she fit into all this, and what exactly had the Americans done to her?

13

An ashen looking Judith and an apprehensive Major Spencer were waiting for them when they landed.

"Welcome back, Anna. Thank you for agreeing to meet with us again. This is Major Spencer, Bernard's commanding officer. You understand our chain of command? Hello, Bernard, Heidi."

"Please, it's Mick. It's a pleasure to meet you, Anna," he said as he boldly offered her his hand, unsure of her reaction.

"Yes, we understand these things. Major Spencer—Mick," Anna replied, leaning over to accept his handshake. He continued to hold her hand as he assisted her in alighting from the helicopter. Her grip was firm and the eye contact between them was intense.

"Thank you for sending soldiers to protect Viktoria and Jessica."

~

A government limousine whisked them off to a building all too familiar to Heidi. Anna also recognised it. She had been here before. It was the building that housed the Signals Directorate. This time, there were no security checks, however.

"Thank you, gentlemen," Judith said as they walked straight past the perplexed security personnel and proceeded on to the same conference room that Anna had been in during her last visit. There were another two security guards standing in the hallway. "Thank you, gentlemen," Judith repeated as one of them knocked lightly on the door.

As if someone had flipped a switch, the room fell silent—the vacuum of sound pulling them inwards. Judith waited until the heavy door closed behind her with a soft thud.

"Ladies and gentlemen," Judith's voice trembled slightly, "this is Sergeant Bernard Ambrose and Ms Heidi Almendinger ..." Her gaze shifted to Anna, the centre of attention. Judith's next words caught in her throat, choked with emotion. "And this is Anna."

The room returned to complete silence. Eyes darted towards Anna, assessing her with curiosity, suspicion and more than a touch of fear. She stood there, an enigma, revealing nothing.

General Mitchell cleared his throat. His gaze shifted from Anna to the others as if gauging their reactions. "Welcome, Anna, Ms Almendinger, Sergeant Ambrose," he said, his voice steady. "Please let us all take a seat and I will introduce everyone."

Anna motioned for Heidi to sit beside her. Bernie settled on her other side, flanking her protectively. She was not alone here.

Anna's eyes scanned across the assembled group, lingering on the uniformed personnel. Her scrutiny was intense, dissecting each face, each insignia. The civilians received briefer appraisal, their presence seemingly inconsequential.

The Minister for Defence said, "We've met before. Hello again, Anna."

She just looked back in silence, then, with a dismissive blink, returned her attention to General Mitchell.

He went around the table with his introductions. When he came to Anna, he said, "Anna, I apologise—I haven't been told your surname or how to describe your—occupation."

"I am simply Anna." Her voice held a quiet authority, as if she had no need for embellishments.

Leaving it at that, he continued with the others.

With the introductions completed, he drew a breath to allow himself time to choose his words. The weight of the moment pressed down on him, but he suspected he wasn't the only one wrestling with nerves.

"Thank you once again for agreeing to meet with us, Anna. It is a great privilege, and today marks a momentous occasion for us all. If everyone is comfortable, please let us begin. I'm sure you all have many questions, but to maintain some control, I would ask you to raise your hand if you have something to say and I will recognise you. Anna, if there is anything said that you do not understand, please tell us immediately and we will attempt to clarify it."

"That will not be necessary; we know this language," Anna replied, her tone offhand.

"I appreciate that, Anna, but I want to be sure there is no misunderstanding. It's not only the words that we use, but the context that conveys our message."

"We know this. We realise you do not always say what you mean, and certainly do not always mean what you say."

That comment caused a few glances to be exchanged between several of the meeting attendees.

After another awkward silence, the Prime Minister raised his hand and received the nod to proceed.

"Anna, first let me express, on behalf of our entire nation, our thanks and gratitude for your intervention in stopping the attack on Pine Gap. We take this as a sign of your friendship and hope we can remain friends throughout whatever is coming."

"Yes, thank you."

General Mitchell added, "Thank you, Allan, and of course, that sentiment applies to all those present in this room as well. Perhaps Sergeant Ambrose could bring us up to speed with why Anna requested this meeting and with the events leading up to it."

Bernie quickly related the events at the restaurant, finishing with, "Anna, could you please tell us what, if anything, you know about President Boage's condition?"

The mention of yet another sister surprised Judith and most of the others in the room. She was also aghast at the thought that Anna was in any way involved with President Boage's illness. After casting a quick glance towards Heidi, she looked back at Anna, and felt a chill crawling up her spine. Anna's gaze bore into her, unyielding and unsettling.

Before she answered, Anna returned her attention to Bernie. Her finger tapped rhythmically on the table, a beat of anticipation for the others. Then, folding her arms, she leaned back slightly in her chair.

"The Americans had abducted Viktoria and were hurting her.

They wanted her to tell them about us. She knew nothing about us, and they should have left her alone. We rescued her, but unfortunately she now knows she has sisters. President Boage authorised the abduction and mistreatment of Viktoria, and we have punished him."

Anna's words washed around the room. The meeting had taken an unexpected turn—one that would reverberate far beyond these walls.

Several of the attendees raised their hands, but General Mitchell ignored them all and leaned forward. "How did you punish him, Anna?"

"We removed his brain stem," Anna replied, her voice devoid of remorse. "He is not repairable."

Gasps of horror echoed around the room.

The Defence Minister growled, "You assassinated the President of the United States! Do you realise what you've done?"

Anna's gaze remained unyielding, her silence more damming than any words. Empathy held no place in her eyes.

With bated breath, Bernie asked, "Have you punished anyone else, Anna?"

"Yes."

More gasps reverberated.

"Who?"

"The five men who were hurting Viktoria and the one who instigated it. We have not harmed the ones like you."

"The ones like me? Which ones like me, Anna?"

"The soldiers. The ones who abducted Viktoria and took her to Saudi Arabia. They meant her no harm. They were just following orders."

Major General Henderson asked, "Who was the man who instigated it, Anna?"

The attendees were exhibiting such a change in urgency that they ignored the rule of the raising of hands for permission to speak.

"The Director of their CIA."

"And you removed his brain stem as well?"

"Yes."

Fucking hell!

Not only the President, but the Director of the CIA! A catastrophe was unfolding before their eyes. Everyone looked at each other, hoping for some reassurance that things could be resurrected, but no one showed any sign they considered it even a remote possibility.

What were they dealing with here? Someone—or something—that could remove people's brain stems at will. Even in the secure area of the President's office, or that of the Director of the CIA. And Anna seemed so dispassionate when admitting of such horrific acts. Her demeanour contrasted so vividly with the others in the room, she may as well have been from a different world.

Judith got everyone's attention by asking the question at the back of all their minds.

"Anna, who are you and why are you here? Where are you from?"

"We are from far away. We are here to ensure continued habitability of this planet."

Heidi thought, "So Judith was right, not time-travellers after all."

"How many of you are here?"

"Enough."

"Your sister Belle, is she with Viktoria now?"

"No, Belle is busy."

"Is Belle in America?" Judith asked in a much quieter tone.

"No."

The Defence Minister stood and glared down at Anna as he pointed at her angrily.

"You are not ensuring anything of the kind. Your actions have destabilised the planet. We are heading for anarchy. America will descend into chaos and the world will follow." He was practically snorting by the end of his tirade.

Anna hadn't taken her eyes off him since he had stood and was now glaring at him with an expression showing her abhorrence of the man. The outburst horrified General Mitchell. He could read the signs. He, along with most of the others, could feel the mood within the meeting shift dramatically. Things had to be deescalated before it was too late. They now knew what Anna was capable of; if she lost her temper, all hell would break loose. And he was desperate to get all the information he could from her.

Drawing himself higher in his seat while angrily motioning for the Defence Minister to sit down and shut up, General Mitchell asked,

"How do you see your mission progressing from here, Anna, and what would you like us to do to help?"

As she looked at him, her expression lost its hard edge. "We will only interfere if we consider it necessary, otherwise it is up to you all to agree on how to behave. We consider your objectives should coincide with ours."

General Mitchell settled back into his seat and tried to force a reassuring look.

Out of nowhere, Anna changed the subject. She pointed accusingly at Judith and said, "You should let Jessica speak to her doctor about paper I gave her." She held Judith's gaze. This was a topic of importance to her, and it needed to be followed through.

Judith blinked, momentarily disorientated. Jessica's request had slipped her mind amidst the chaos of unfolding events. Anna's directive snapped it back into focus. She had been debating how to proceed, but now she had her answer.

"Of course, Anna," she replied, her voice steadier than she felt. "I have a meeting with Jessica on Tuesday to discuss just that."

Anna nodded, showing her acceptance of this reply, then pressed her hands together as she turned to look at Heidi.

"I would like to return to Viktoria now; she is very distressed." Then came something completely unexpected. With a mischievous grin, Anna looked at Bernie out of the corner of her eye and said, "Perhaps you can teach me skiing, Heidi. I am sure I will be as good as Bernie."

He stared back at her, baffled. They had just been discussing events that could potentially unravel the world. And now this? The rapid fluctuations in conversation left everyone gasping. Suddenly Anna was no longer the destroyer of worlds, but almost a playful child.

General Mitchell got the meeting back on track. "Anna, we would very much like to be able to contact you if the need for urgent communication with you arises, as I am sure it will."

Anna studied him for a moment, her gaze inscrutable. Then, without warning, a flash of blue light erupted. An object materialised on the table before her—a device the size of a smartphone, made of what looked like translucent Perspex. It was emitting a faint strawberry red glow.

Everyone except Anna recoiled in shock at this unworldly event. Any nagging disbelief of what they had seen in the videos obliterated. A long silence stretched out as they all stared in fascination at the object.

Before sliding it towards Heidi, Anna said, "This is secure device, no one can intercept or interfere with it. It does not need recharging. You may use it to call us at any time. We will be listening. To call, you touch like this." She placed the tip of each of her index fingers against the face of the device.

Heidi placed it in her pocket. "Thank you, Anna. I'll keep it with me all the time."

Anna placed both her hands on the table, slid her chair back, and stood.

"We should return to Viktoria now. Thank you, ladies and gentlemen. Perhaps you will take me in your helicopter again."

As she stood to join her, Heidi touched Anna on the arm and interjected. "Jessica said it would be better for Viktoria if she went to hospital to determine the extent of any injuries she has. They'll be able to provide a much greater level of care there. If you like, we could take her to the hospital where Jessica works. I'm sure Major Spencer can arrange any necessary security for her."

"Yes, thank you. Americans will find her there, of course, but we will stop any further attempts to interfere with her," Anna said matter-of-factly.

General Mitchell stood up to join them and hurriedly assured her, "I'm sure that will not be necessary. We will explain to them the importance of leaving Viktoria alone."

The mention of Jessica's name surprised Judith. It meant she was with them in Merrijig as one of the group of friends enjoying a skiing trip Bernie had mentioned. If she was socialising with them, it had dangerous connotations regarding keeping the details of the original meeting secret. Given the current situation, she let it slide, but she was going to ask Heidi about it when she got the chance.

Heidi explained, "We're all going to be really busy for a while, Anna, but when we get time, I'd love to take you skiing. I'm not all that good at it myself, but I'm sure we can arrange for your expert tuition. And I'd love to watch Bernie trying to keep up with you." She looked towards Major Spencer for help.

He jumped to his feet. "I'll dispatch the helicopter back to pick up your friends. We'll have Viktoria in hospital by morning."

As she turned towards the door, Anna replied, "Thank you, Mick. I want to go with her."

Heidi grabbed Bernie by the hand and dragged him towards the door. "Of course, Anna, let's go."

As the three of them headed towards the door, Major Spencer briefly looked at Major General Henderson. After receiving a nod, he hurried to join them, simultaneously reaching for his phone.

"Please excuse us. Which hospital are we going to, and could you please arrange for Viktoria's admission?"

Judith replied, "The Gold Coast University Hospital. I'll inform them you'll be arriving by air."

Anna looked back at Judith and bowed slightly, then turned her attention to Major Spencer as he opened the door and ushered them out. Judith felt a flush of excitement at the quite personal gesture offered to her.

After they had left, the room returned to complete silence. General Mitchell was looking intently at Judith. He needed a colleague here, and she was his first choice. He was about to break the silence, but she got in first.

She glared at the Defence Minister. "What were you thinking? Your outburst almost ruined everything."

He glared back at her, refusing to acknowledge that she deserved a reply.

Realising that she would not receive an answer, Judith widened her audience. "Where do we go from here?"

General Mitchell answered, "Wherever it is, we need to take very short and measured steps. And we somehow have to persuade the Americans to do likewise."

After a further period of silence, he looked back at Judith and said, "Heidi, and probably to a lesser extent, Sergeant Ambrose, are the keys to getting us through all this. You need to keep her on side and offer her any assistance you think she requires when dealing with the aliens. She is crucial to any further interactions with them, given that they have specifically supplied her with a comms device."

"Don't worry, I intend to."

Jessica, Viktoria, and George were sitting in the car awaiting the return of the chopper. One of the soldiers was a little way off, talking to the police. They were curious as to what this was all about, but no information was forthcoming from him. The other soldiers were out of sight, squatting down in the shadows, vigilant of any danger.

As soon as the chopper landed, Bernie jumped out and raced straight for his car. George got out of the driver's seat and sprinted towards him, cutting him off midway.

"Toast, what the fuck have you got me into here?"

"Sorry mate, it's complicated. How are the others? No trouble?"

"All good—fuck me, you hang around with some gorgeous chicks."

"Yeah, lucky me. I take it you've been talking to Major Spencer?"

"Yeah, just said we're off to the Gold Coast. Taking Viktoria to hospital. Told me he'd meet us there, and until then I wasn't to let her out of my sight."

"Right, the others in the car, I take it?"

George gave him a nod. "My boys have a perimeter established. The others are in the car."

"Let's get 'em." Bernie went to the rear door and opened it. He reached in to take Viktoria's hand. "Viktoria, we're going to take you to a hospital now so that you can be properly cared for. It's the hospital where Jessica works and she's coming with you. Let's go over to the helicopter now. Anna is waiting there."

George motioned to the soldier talking to the police to come over. "Go back to the chalet and make it ship-shape, then drive the car back to Canberra. The rest of us are off in the chopper."

Bernie led them back to the Blackhawk. He found Anna leaning forward with her head between the two pilots as they explained the cockpit to her. As everyone climbed in, Anna flashed him a smile and returned to her seat. As Viktoria embarked, Anna took her hand from the Crew Chief and guided her to the seat beside her. Viktoria looked at her anxiously, and Anna squeezed her hand to reassure her. George signalled to the other three soldiers, who seemed to materialise out of the gloom. The chopper took off as soon as they were all on board.

14

Major Spencer was waiting for them when they landed at the hospital helipad. He had two uniformed police officers and the head of the Trauma Services department accompanying him. As soon as it touched down, he went to the aircraft, put on the headset offered to him, and tossed a bag full of clothes to George.

"You guys change into civvies and leave your main weapons in the chopper. Hand guns only from here on. Good morning ladies and gents."

He looked at the young woman sitting beside Anna. There was no doubting they were sisters, more like twins. "You must be Viktoria, pleased to meet you. I understand you have suffered some misfortune recently. Please be assured that we are friends and we are going to look after you." Turning to the other woman he had not met, he said, "Dr Gordon."

They started to get out of the chopper, the women first. Not so much for protocol, but to give the soldiers busy stripping off their uniforms some privacy. Not that it looked as if they thought they needed any.

As soon as they could, they dashed over to the hospital doorway to escape the noise of the Blackhawk still idling on the helipad. The head of Trauma was standing with his hands clasped over his ears. He greeted Jessica with a nod as he removed his makeshift earmuffs, grimacing uncomfortably at the increased noise level.

Jess was holding Viktoria by the hand, and she raised their clasped hands towards him. "This is Viktoria. She was being detained by a foreign power and has been subjected to intensive interrogation, including waterboarding. She appears to be fine, but we need to make a full assessment of her. I'm worried they may have administered drugs as well."

He showed his agreement, then leant in and shouted, "Thank you, Dr Gordon. The authorities have forewarned us. We have a private room arranged."

By this time, several other men had emerged from the chopper and made their way over. One of them stepped forward. "Sergeant Fredericks. My men and I will act as security for the young woman," he declared.

The head of Trauma Services stared back blankly. This was so far from a normal day for him he thought he might be on a movie set.

One of the police officers introduced himself. "Chief Superintendent Charmers. We've been informed you will provide close personal protection. Several of my officers are on station here to provide any necessary assistance. This is Senior Inspector Wade. He's in charge and all requests should go via him."

George nodded and shook hands with both of them, after which Senior Inspector Wade handed him a card containing his contact details. George glanced at it, nodded to him again, and placed the card in his breast pocket.

~

As they made their way to Viktoria's room, Major Spencer tapped Bernie and George on the shoulder and motioned for them to fall back from the others. "Well done, Bernie," his voice was low and intense. "George, I haven't got time to tell you the full story, but bloody hell man, the shit has well and truly hit the fan."

"I gathered that. I'm copping some of the overspray—what can you tell me?"

"At this stage, let's just say, look after that girl as if all our lives depend on it, because they quite literally do."

George glanced at Bernie for some enlightenment.

He just shook his head and said, "You will not believe the friends she has. Her sister is the most lethal person any of us will ever meet. And she's really pissed off at the moment. Apparently Viktoria's an innocent party caught up in all this through a case of mistaken identity."

By this stage, the rest of the group had entered the room. Major Spencer terminated their conversation by following them in.

While they were still alone, Bernie grabbed George by the arm, saying, "Hang on tight, mate, you're in for one hell of a ride. And you and I are going to sit down and sink some piss together if we ever get through it all."

They joined the others to find Viktoria lying in bed with a Vital Signs Monitor already attached. Jessica was drawing a blood sample and Anna was standing near the monitor, running her fingers over the display, following the heart beat trace.

The nurse put her hand on Anna's arm and said, "Don't touch that."

Anna snapped her eyes to the nurse. Heidi reacted first, rushing to get between the two of them. She quickly brushed the nurse's hand aside and said, "It's just that the equipment is very sensitive, Anna. It shouldn't be touched while it's working. The nurse was just doing her job."

There was a combined sigh of relief when Anna nodded, gave the nurse a small smile of apology, then went to sit on the bed, reached over to hold Viktoria's hand, and started talking to her in a foreign language.

Once again, George felt stunned by how alike the two girls appeared. And the hairs on the back of his neck were standing on end as he looked at Anna. She must be hell on wheels, the way Bernie had just described her. Both of them knew their fair share of lethal people, but she trumped them all, according to him. He went over and made himself comfortable in the chair adjacent to the bed.

Once Jessica had finished drawing her sample, she turned to Heidi and handed her a set of keys. "Why don't you take Anna and Bernie back to mine and get some rest? I'll text you the address. You'll need this fob to get into the building and access the lifts. I'll be busy here for the rest of the day. I'll call you when I'm finished." She touched Anna on the arm and said, "Viktoria needs some rest now, Anna. I'll take good care of her. You should go with Heidi and Bernie and get some as well."

Anna had been engrossed in her conversation with Viktoria, but after the touch on her arm, she flicked her gaze to Jess and her expression lightened slightly.

Jess marvelled at Anna's ability to communicate her feelings with the most subtle movement of her eyes.

Anna then returned her attention to Viktoria, squeezed her hand, and leant in to murmur something in the same language they had been using, eliciting a smile from Viktoria in response.

Anna stood and gave George a slight bow of her head before turning towards the door. Heidi thanked Jessica and joined her as she headed out. Bernie smiled reassuringly to Viktoria, gave a subdued hand gesture to both George and Major Spencer, and followed the others.

Jessica patted Viktoria on the arm. "I just have to take this sample down to the laboratory. I'll be straight back."

Major Spencer addressed George. "I'll relieve you at 18:00. I'll sort your men on my way out. Call me immediately if anything comes up."

"Yes sir."

That just left Viktoria, George, and a very puzzled nurse in the room. She had no idea what was going on, but this was the most exciting shift she had ever worked.

"The Russians can't reach us here?" Viktoria asked anxiously.

Christ, they're bloody Russians. No wonder all this cloak and dagger.

Smiling reassuringly, George said, "No, sweetheart, they can't reach us here. You're perfectly safe."

This seemed to relax her somewhat.

"You know Anna, yes?"

"No, I just met her last night."

"I have just met her as well. I did not know I had sister."

"It appears you do, and she's very concerned about you—I hope you're comfortable now."

"Yes, I am fine now. But I do not understand any of this. Why did they take me and who are visitors they kept asking me about?"

Concerned, George asked the nurse, "Could you please excuse us? I just want to talk to Viktoria alone for a minute. You can wait just outside the door. I'll call you if anything happens."

Once they were alone, he said, "I don't know anything about it at all, Viktoria. What were they doing to you?"

"They were trying to drown me. And constantly yelling at me to tell them about visitors. But they would not believe me when I told them I did not know."

"They must have believed you eventually, if they let you go."

"They did not let me go; Anna came and got me."

"Your sister Anna is a very special girl, isn't she?"

"Yes, she takes us from place to place as if by magic. She told me one day she would tell me how she does it."

The door opening and Jessica entering interrupted their conversation. She headed straight for the bed and said, "I'll have the results of your blood tests soon, Viktoria. You should try to get some rest now."

She frowned towards George and shook her head, indicating he should not be asking questions of Viktoria. As the nurse re-entered the room, he relaxed back into his chair, his face furrowed in confusion.

~

Heidi opened the door and stepped into Jess's apartment.

I'm Impressed Jess. Nice.

It was very modern, with no real clutter, and, while obviously sporting that feminine touch, had a lived in look. Voicing her assessment, she looked back at the others as they followed her in. Bernie headed straight for the balcony, while Anna went over and ran her fingers over the guitar nestled in a stand beside the sofa.

Bernie called out — "Check this out."

From the twelfth floor, the view of the dawn breaking over the ocean was beautiful. On any other occasion, it would have been great to just sit on the balcony and relax while taking it all in. Not this morning, though; too much had just happened, and their present company had them on edge. Anna had been nothing but polite to them, but her recent actions had shown what she was capable of.

While they were taking in the view, Heidi said, "Beautiful, isn't it?"

Bernie nodded, but Anna showed no reaction to her comment. She seemed to be mesmerised by the vista before her.

He asked, "Coffee anyone?"

This got Anna's attention. She immediately spoke up. "Yes, coffee is nice. Americano, thank you."

Heidi definitely wanted one as well. She had turned to follow Bernie, saying, "I'll help make them," but, distracted by the mention of the type of coffee Anna asked for, she paused and looked back, before adding, "we're both so sorry about what has happened to Viktoria. I'm sure Jessica will help her get better. She's in good hands at the hospital, and she has all those soldiers guarding her."

Leaving the coffees to Bernie, Heidi went back over to stand beside Anna, who was still looking at the dawn breaking. She was quickly becoming less intimidated by Anna. In fact, despite what she knew, she was almost beginning to relate to her as a friend.

Anna said, "Yes, but Jessica is also unwell. She should show paper to her doctor."

"Our government is trying to keep your presence here a secret. They're frightened if the scientists and other doctors see it, they'll have to expose you."

"Yes, but we want Jessica to get well again."

"Can you make her well again yourself? Then it can still be a secret."

"We want to keep our presence here secret also, but not treatment for MS."

This comment gave Heidi and Bernie pause for thought. Anna seemed to be on a one-track mission to get Jessica better. Well, not exactly one-track. After all, she was busy sorting out the Americans as well—there was that. But she seemed fixated on Jessica's health. And if she didn't want the document to remain secret, she could easily tell anyone she wanted to about it. The fact she hadn't done so yet made them think that, for some unknown reason, she wanted their cooperation. Heidi thought she may have a solution.

"Anna, my dad is a neurologist, so he understands a lot about MS. Not as much as you do, obviously, but I'm sure he'll understand what's in the document. Do you think I should get Jessica to show it to him?"

Although he was in the kitchen, Bernie was eavesdropping on their conversation. He knew this was going against the instructions they had received, but things had now progressed considerably. He was prepared to see how Anna wanted them to proceed. And as long as it was only with Heidi's father, things would still be relatively contained.

Anna agreed. "Yes, she should show it to him."

"Would you like to discuss it with him, Anna?"

"No—perhaps after he has read it, if he wants to."

"I'm sure he'll want to, so I can tell him that?"

"Yes."

Bernie turned his attention back to making the coffees. Jess's coffee machine looked intimidating though, so he searched the pantry for instant, but no luck there. Obviously, Jess didn't slum it with her coffee.

He called out, "Anyone got an idea how this machine works?"

Both women went to see what the problem was.

Surely he can handle some coffees.

Then Heidi saw the problem. Jess had a really fancy coffee machine. A SMEG bean-to-cup model.

Hmmm, maybe a bit quick to judge.

Bernie raised both hands palms upwards in a gesture of uncertainty.

Laughing, Anna pushed him aside and said, "I will make them for us."

She looked cheekily at Heidi. "Men."

With coffee in hand, they went back out to the balcony and sat around the small table.

Anna held the cup under her nose and breathed deeply, took a sip, and sighed in pleasure. "I think I will get one of these machines."

Heidi replied, "It is nice, isn't it? And I really needed one."

Out of nowhere, Anna leant forward and put her hand on Bernie's arm.

"Sometimes, I frighten you, yes."

This action, and its accompanying comment, took Bernie by surprise. Not because he thought it was incorrect; in fact, it was right on the money. But she had completely changed subjects yet again. Bloody hell, she was hard to keep up with. And there was the recurrence of that strong emotional response caused by having physical contact with her.

How do I answer that without things going haywire?

"Let's put it this way, Anna, some of the things you can do have us all on edge."

"I am not going to hurt you, Bernie. Or Heidi. I would never do this." As she said this, she gently stroked his arm with her fingers.

Bernie looked down at her hand, and his posture shifted slightly.

Stay focused, sunshine. She's probably just trying to reassure you.

"It's not just the two of us I'm worried about, Anna. What you did to the Americans will have disastrous consequences for lots of people."

"We did not want to do this, but we had to."

"Why, Anna? Surely you didn't need to do that. After all, you had already rescued Viktoria. They couldn't hurt her anymore."

Anna peered intently at him for some time. Eventually, she frowned and removed her hand.

"This is how things are done," she stated unemotionally. Her tone brooked no argument. The discussion was over.

Bernie frowned back, wondering what she meant.

The way Anna had touched Bernie, and his response to it, distracted Heidi. It had seemed so intimate. Were they falling for one another? And Anna was acting completely differently to what she was expecting. There were layers to her. Depths she could not fathom.

Anna shrugged, then looked back out at the sun breaking over the horizon. She shifted her gaze to Heidi and a brief smile played across her face until eventually focusing within her beguiling eyes.

"Yes, view is beautiful."

~

Viktoria slept most of the morning.

Jessica had been coming and going, checking on her repeatedly. Whenever she entered the room, she found George mostly sitting in his chair, just looking at Viktoria. Otherwise, he was standing at the window, staring outside. During one of the times Viktoria was awake, George handed her a menu that had been left for them.

At lunchtime, the nurse returned and woke her for her meal.

After she left, George said, "Let's tuck in then. I hope you had a good rest. You looked so peaceful lying there. I see you're a vegetarian; I hope you don't mind me having the fish?"

"No, of course not. I am glad there is so much food. I usually only have small servings, maintaining my figure, you understand. But I am so hungry. Russians did not give me anything to eat."

"Well, we're going to give you plenty. I'll get more for you when you finish if you're still hungry."

He thought, "You and I have a different idea of a large serving."

"So, you're Russian, Viktoria?"

"No, I am from Ukraine. But I live in France now."

"Ah … was Ukrainian what Anna was talking to you in?"

"Yes."

"You were saying Anna can take you to places as if by magic. What's that like?"

Viktoria waved her hand almost dismissively, but her wide eyes showed her true feelings. "I do not know; one minute I am somewhere; then I am somewhere else. She has done it twice, once when she took me from Russians, and once when she took me to meet people who brought me here."

"Where did she take you when she took you from the Russians?"

"To her room."

"What's her room like?"

"It is nice. She lives there with her sister Belle."

This comment startled George. "She has another sister!"

"Yes, I have not met her, but Anna told me she is just like us."

George looked at Viktoria as she continued to eat. The vacant look in his eyes was at odds with the rapid processing occurring in his mind.

Fucking hell, Toast, you and I are going to have a big chat when I get my hands on you.

The door opened and Jessica came back in. "Ah, you're awake. I hope you're enjoying your meal. I have good news for you, Viktoria. Your blood tests came back clear. We're still running more tests but haven't found anything unusual yet. It looks as if they didn't use any drugs."

What Jessica didn't know was Viktoria had been injected with a cocktail of drugs. They had been scrubbed from her body during her transfer to Anna's room.

"You appear to be healthy, with no physical effects from your ordeal. How did you sleep?"

"Well, thank you. I was so tired."

"That's great, Viktoria, no nightmares?"

"No."

"Well, it seems you're going to make a full recovery. When Anna comes back to see you, we can discuss your release. I'd like some follow up to make sure you don't develop any psychological issues, but we can discuss those details with Anna."

George said, "I can phone Bernie and ask him when they're coming back if you like."

Jess shook her head. "I'm letting them rest. I'm sure they'll come back as soon as they wake up."

George looked back noncommittally. He thought, "Bernie will be wide awake. You can bet on that." But he said nothing.

A moment later, with impeccable timing, the door opened, and the three of them entered.

Anna went straight over to Viktoria. Heidi and Jessica exchanged pleasantries and Bernie handed George a burger.

"Thanks mate."

Jessica said, "But you've just eaten."

"That was fish; this is meat." George took a bite then offered the burger to Bernie.

"All good, mate. Had one on the way."

Heidi said, "Eeeew."

Jessica matched her look of disgust.

George said, "What?"

With a look of concentration on her face, Anna was shifting her gaze back and forth between the two soldiers. After a slight pause, she turned to Viktoria and asked in English, "How are you feeling now, Vika?"

"Much better. I have had sleep and some lunch. Jessica said she is going to speak to you about taking me with you now."

This news seemed to please Anna. She looked at Jessica, her eyes widening slightly in question.

Jessica said, "We can't find anything wrong with her physically. If she gets anxious, would you let me know and I'll arrange for her to visit our psychologists? I'm happy to discharge her into your care, if that's what you want."

"Yes, thank you. Let us go, Vika." Anna reached for Viktoria's hand.

Jessica rushed to them and said, "Stand up slowly, Viktoria, just in case you feel a little dizzy."

Viktoria complied and got to her feet with no ill effects.

Jessica said, "OK, just some paperwork and you can go. George, please inform your superiors that Viktoria is leaving with Anna now."

As George reached for his phone, he saw Bernie turn towards the door. He reached out and grabbed him by the arm. "Not so fast, champ."

"Later, mate."

George fell into step beside him.

As they were doing the paperwork for Viktoria's discharge, Jessica's supervisor came over and told her she was to go home and get some rest. And he told her she was to take the next day off as well.

15

Once they had let themselves into the apartment, Bernie said, "Anna, I feel like going for a run. I need to destress a bit. George probably feels the same. I'm sure everyone will be safe if you're with them, and we'll only be half an hour or so."

"Yes, of course. I like to run as well. I used to go by myself, but now Belle and I go for runs together on our island. Perhaps we can join you sometime."

"I'm looking forward to it. George, there's a sports shop down the street. We can get some gear there. You up for it?"

"Never felt more like a run in my life, mate."

Bernie, being preoccupied, missed the reference Anna made to an island. Heidi didn't though. She filed that away for future reference.

~

As they approached the beach, Bernie said, "Take a knee, mate. Best you're not standing up with what I've got to tell you."

They went over and sat on the sand. But, at first neither of them spoke, the only sounds being the melody of the breaking surf splattered with the laughter of children. Bernie was looking at his feet, collecting his thoughts, while George stared vacantly at the ocean. In his peripheral vision, he could see the children playing at the water's edge, either accompanied by, or under the watchful eye of, their parents. Some joggers were plodding along, others lazed on the sand, comfortable in the sun's embrace. But this barely registered in

George's consciousness, such was his preoccupation. It was all just background noise for the beach as well. It had seen all this countless times before.

Although patience wasn't one of George's virtues, he was prepared to wait. The time for questions had run down; it was now time for answers. But Bernie wasn't to be rushed. He picked up a handful of sand and let it slowly filter through his fingers, then shaking off the residue, he looked towards his friend.

"OK mate, this is going to sound crazy, but it's the God's honest truth. We're mixed up with fucking aliens. That Anna, man, she is one complicated chick. But I know this much; she is hardcore. The bloody Chinese launched a nuke at Pine Gap, and she zapped it in mid-air. Then she zapped the missiles off one of our F-18s, just as a demo apparently. And she has taken out President Boage and the director of the fucking CIA. Assassinated them. Can you believe that? Her idea of punishment for what they did to Viktoria." George's calm acceptance of what he had just been told surprised Bernie. He was expecting to be laughed at.

But George just looked back at him with a slight frown and said, "Why'd she do that? Viktoria told me the Russians had her."

"No mate. Anna said it was the Yanks, and she's not the kind of girl that fucks up. Dickheads thought it'd be a good idea to interrogate her to find out more about the aliens."

He paused and studied George for a moment. "You seem to be taking this a lot better than I thought you would."

"I've been chatting with Viktoria, mate. Some of the things she said are starting to make sense now."

"Such as ..."

"She told me Anna moves them from place to place as if by magic. And apparently there's another one of them, Belle."

"Yeah, there is. I've met her. Spitting image of those two. What's this about moving around by magic?"

"Sounds to me like they can beam themselves around like on Star Trek or something. Anna, that is. I don't think Viktoria knows what's going on."

"Yeah, Anna said as much, but they will move heaven and earth to look after her. She must mean something to them. And I missed a chance there, with the beaming that is."

"What?"

"When Anna told me she was involved in what happened to Boage, I immediately got onto Major Spencer and arranged a meeting with the brass. They wanted to talk with her, anyway. He arranged the Blackhawk, and you know the rest. Then Anna told me she could have got us to the meeting. I jumped at that chance, but she said no—she wanted to ride in a helicopter. Too quick for my own good with that one. But at the meeting she popped something out of thin air and gave it to Heidi. Right before our eyes! Some kind of communication device, apparently. She can probably do the same thing with people."

"Bloody hell." George shook his head in amazement. "You serious?"

Bernie nodded. "Yeah. Weirdest thing I've ever seen. Mate, she is something else!"

"So, what, you hang with this Anna or something?"

"No mate, Heidi's my girlfriend. She means something to the aliens as well, but I haven't figured out what yet. I've only met Anna twice, once just after the nuke incident and now."

"Right, so where to from here?"

"Well, it looks like they're here to save the planet or something. Which is just fine by me—I like the place. At first, being around Anna had me shitting myself, but, as you'll find out, she has a way of growing on you. And from what I've seen, if things start getting loud, we're best off in her corner."

"I'm Johnny-come-lately here. I didn't get the impression Anna took much interest in me."

"Things can change pretty quickly around her. Just stay on your toes."

"Right, great run mate, think we should head back?"

"Race yah."

~

They were both a little out of breath when they got back to the apartment. Bernie had won the race, just, but he had kind of jumped the gun, so you could probably call it even.

The girls were sitting around the table, deep in conversation, when they came in.

Jess got up and said, "Looks like it was a serious run, guys. I'll get you a juice."

"The girls must be fast shoppers," Bernie thought, "they've changed clothes, and it looks as though they've also bought handbags."

The one beside Viktoria was noticeably larger than the others.

As Jess handed them their drinks, Anna went over to George and touched him on the arm.

"Viktoria cannot stay with Belle and me, but she should be with someone for a while. She lives alone at her home in Paris and has no one there to take care of her. You will look after her for us, yes?"

George cast a quick glance at Bernie and got a wink in return. "Ah —sure—I can do that. I live in Sydney though. Will it be OK if we go there?"

"Yes. Thank you, George." Anna patted his arm and smiled reassuring to Viktoria, who was obviously happy with this arrangement.

George went over to Viktoria and said, "I'd love to have you stay with me, Viktoria. And I'm really looking forward to getting to know you. Sydney is such a great place; you're going to love it. I can show you all the sights."

"Thank you. I am looking forward to it as well. I have heard so much about Australia but have never been here until now."

Anna went and hugged Viktoria. "I must go now but remember you can call me at any time." As she said this, she tapped the handbag beside Viktoria, then headed towards the door.

As she opened it, she turned and smiled at the others, left and walked towards the lifts. When the doors opened on the ground floor, the lift was empty.

16

Jessica and Heidi had her apartment to themselves. Bernie was off on another run and George and Viktoria had left for Sydney.

Heidi said, "I'm not so scared of Anna now. Actually, I think I like her."

Jess frowned and shook her head. "What do you mean? I've never felt scared of her. Worried about what might happen if no one takes any notice of her, but she doesn't really scare me as such."

She waved her hands around in an animated gesture. "Actually, she appears quite caring to me. She seems very attached to Viktoria, and let's not forget about the document she gave me. It just might save my life."

Heidi rubbed her gently on the arm. "You don't know the half of what she's done. Anyway, I've been talking to her about your document. My dad's a neurologist, and I asked her if we could show it to him. Jess, I think that's a better idea than showing it to your specialist at the moment. What do you think?"

This really got Jess's attention. Her face brightened with enthusiasm.

"Sounds like a great idea. I didn't know your father was a neurologist. What an amazing coincidence. I'm dying to get the document out there and Anna wouldn't have given it to me if she didn't want that as well. After this unscheduled time off, I'm not sure I'll be able to make it to the meeting with Judith. Should I phone her and cancel it, and tell her about giving your dad a copy?"

"For the moment, just tell her your shifts have been altered, and you'd like to postpone it. Don't mention anything about my dad yet."

"OK, hang on and I'll email it to you."

"No, Jess, I think it's best if you can give me a copy on a stick. More secure than having it floating about on the Internet."

"Righto, I'll make you a copy."

~

With a theatrical flourish of his arm, George opened the door and invited Viktoria to enter.

"Well, this is home. There's only one bedroom, but it's yours for now. I'll set myself up on the couch. Just have to change the sheets on the bed and we'll be all set. Sorry, but only one bathroom as well."

Viktoria clapped her hands, then raised them to her mouth in excitement.

"This is nice, George, thank you. But no need to sleep on couch, there is enough room in bed for us both." She gave him a seductive smile. "No touching though."

"If you insist, but I had better warn you, I mightn't have that much self-control. But no pressure—I can easily use the couch. And don't worry, I've slept in a lot more uncomfortable places than that." He watched Viktoria place her bag on the table, then, in a bright voice, he said, "Let's have a celebratory drink. All I've got in the place is beer, though. Is that OK for you?"

"I have never tasted beer before, but yes, we will celebrate." Viktoria was rubbing her hands together and looked happy at his suggestion.

George was getting the idea that she might like to play up a bit. And she had that quality that he admired in a woman: mischievousness. She certainly had his attention, that was for sure. He opened a stubbie and poured some into a glass for her, and after handing it to her, they clicked drinks and raised them to their mouths.

Viktoria pulled a face accompanied by a stylised spitting motion. "Yuck, this tastes horrible. How can you drink it?"

George chuckled and put his arm around her. "OK, you can pick the drinks next time. We'll go out and get some shortly." He reached out and said with a grin, "Don't waste this, though. I'll polish it off for you."

She willingly handed over the glass.

Placing it on the table, he became a little more serious. "Viktoria, you know I'm a solider, but I don't know anything about you. What do you do when you're home in Paris?"

"I am model and actress. But Anna told me not to speak about these things with you."

A gorgeous one at that. And single, she must be choosy. There'd be dozens of guys chasing her. And Anna must—

She interrupted his thoughts. "Now, I must go and get some clothes and things. You will take me shopping, yes?"

This was going to be a whole new experience for George, going shopping for women's clothes. And he was worried about the hit on his bank balance. He pursed his lips in a look of uncertainty and said, "Ah … I don't know much about shopping for women's clothes, but the shops at the mall should be good enough to get us started."

With that beautiful smile of hers, Viktoria said, "That is OK, George. I know a lot about it. And I have plenty of money to spend. Anna gave it to me."

She opened her handbag, and George looked inside in awe. It was almost completely full of rolls of $50 notes. There must be thousands in there, he thought, probably tens of thousands. And there was a piece of plastic in there as well. It was emitting a faint red glow.

"Wow, Viktoria, that's a lot of money you've got. We won't need all that now, and you should leave most of it here. I've got a safe where you can store it."

He reached into her bag and touched the red object.

"What's this?"

"Anna gave me that as well. It is phone to call her on if I want to."

"Well, we're going to take that with us. But don't show it to anyone. It'll attract attention."

"Yes, Anna told me this."

She clipped her bag shut and, while placing its strap over her shoulder, she reached out and took George by the hand and excitedly headed for the door.

"Just a minute, Viktoria. Remember, we're going to leave some of your money here. It's not safe to carry that much around with you."

She clutched her bag in both hands and extended her arms, handing it to him, with her head cocked cheekily to one side and a dazzling smile adorning her face. By the way she was acting, George got the impression this was her favourite activity. He was fast being brought up to speed on feminine tendencies. And he was smitten with her. She was gorgeous. But in the mood she was in at the moment, she was intoxicating. Of course, all this was tempered by the fact that her sister was an actual alien. A very protective one. But that was OK. He wasn't about to threaten or mistreat her in any way. Quite the opposite, in fact.

17

Heidi rang her dad. "Something important has come up. Don't really want to say anything about it over the phone, so I'm coming down. I've booked a flight for this evening. I'll tell you all about it when I get there. And don't worry, I'm all right and not pregnant or anything like that."

"Can't you give me some idea what this is all about? It sounds urgent if you're coming down tonight."

"It is, Dad, but not over the phone." She heard a resigned sigh.

"When's you flight due? I'll get your mother to pick you up. You know how unpredictable my finishing hours are."

"QF 1529, 7:45. Thanks, Dad, love you."

~

Kurt was waiting for them at the front door. He looked questioningly at Ursula and kissed her hello, gave Heidi a peck on the cheek and said, "Hi darling, you look well. Now please, tell me what this is all about."

"I've got something to show you, Dad. It's a document about MS. And don't worry, as I told you before, I don't have it. Anyway, I think we should eat first. After you read it, we'll most probably be in for a long night."

"OK, you must be hungry after your flight, I suppose, but I must say you have me intrigued, especially since you wouldn't say anything about it on the phone. Is it to do with your colleague?"

"Kind of."

The meal was a hurried affair, with little time for even idle chatter. The subject of Bernard was not raised.

As soon as they had finished, Heidi handed a USB stick to her father and said, "This is what I want to show you. It's kind of classified, but the woman who gave it to me told me I should show it to you."

Intrigued, her father took the stick and went into his study.

Heidi helped her mother clean up after the meal. Kurt was still in his study when they finished, so they went to the lounge, put on some music, and sat and relaxed.

~

It was a little over an hour later when Kurt emerged from the study and joined them in the lounge.

"Heidi, darling, where did you say you got this?"

She had just nodded off, but his question pulled her back to full awareness. She could tell by the tone of his voice, and the look in his eyes, that he was excited.

"It's complicated. Remember, I told you I had a colleague with MS. She's not actually a colleague so much as a friend of mine. A woman we both met recently gave it to her. She's a sort of friend of ours now as well. The woman who gave it to us asked me to show it to you— Dad, is it about a cure for MS?"

Kurt shook his head, as if to clear the daze infusing his mind.

"I've only managed a cursory glance, mind you, but I'm totally awestruck. The content delves into pioneering research and the profound insights are nothing short of mind-bending. It meticulously dissects the disease's origins, and the treatment proposed is very controversial. It pushes the limits of what's considered possible at the moment."

"I thought it may be something like that. The woman said she wants my friend cured. Can that be done?"

"Well, sweetheart, not at the moment. It's not as simple as that. This will have to be researched further, and that might take decades. And, as I said, I don't think the treatment is even possible. But, if what is in there proves to be correct, medicine is about to take a quantum leap forward."

"Dad, the woman told me she's willing to talk to you about it if you want to."

Kurt was so excited, he almost stumbled with his reply. "I'd absolutely love to. How long do you think it would take to set up?"

"No time at all. I'll contact her now."

She took out the device Anna had given her. Its appearance took both her parents aback. They knew she worked for a secret organisation but had seen nothing like it.

Heidi touched the device with her fingers as Anna had demonstrated and it instantly changed to display a miniaturised, but crystal clear, 3D image of Anna's head. It was about 100 mm high and appeared to be floating just above the device.

Anna's image vocalised her greeting. "Hello, Heidi. What can I do for you?"

"Hi, Anna, I'm here with my parents."

She shifted the device a little, hoping that it worked like a phone and Anna could see them at her end. It turned out that wasn't exactly how the device worked. This became evident as the image of Anna swivelled to look towards her parents.

"Hello, Professor Almendinger, Doctor Almendinger."

The image and its sudden appearance still shocked her parents. And to be addressed so formally? What was going on here? It surprised Heidi as well. She had told Anna that her father was a doctor, but she hadn't mentioned her mother at all. How did Anna know anything about her? Both parents picked up on her Eastern European accent.

Kurt said, "Hello. Anna, is it? And please, it's Kurt and Ursula."

Anna smiled but made no comment.

Heidi said, "I've shown Jess's document to Dad, and he'd like to meet with you to discuss it —"

"Yes, very much so," Kurt butted in.

"Yes, I am busy now, perhaps once you have had time to study it."

"After that, can we meet to discuss it?"

"Yes. And then you will make Jessica better?"

"We'll have to talk about that, Anna. There's a lot of work to be done before that'll be possible."

Anna looked disappointed, and a little puzzled. She appeared about to say something, but changed her mind and remained silent.

"Anna, do you know who wrote this?" Kurt asked as he held up the memory stick.

"Yes, my mother wrote it."

So that's it. It must be secret Russian research and they've smuggled it to the west via one of their daughters.

Kurt didn't believe Anna would understand any of the document's technical details. "Well, we're very grateful for the risks you two have taken to get it to us. Do you think we could talk to her about it?"

"No, that is not possible. But I will speak to you about it later."

Heidi said, "Can Dad show this to his colleagues?"

"Yes, we want this."

Kurt said, "But won't it endanger your mother, when word of it gets out?"

"No, my mother is safe."

Anna suddenly changed the topic of conversation completely. "Heidi, Belle would like to speak with Lars. You can help with this, yes?"

This statement was met with complete silence and looks of sheer bewilderment by the three in the room. Lars had been a friend of Heidi's—well, actually a little more than that—back when she was at school. Their parents knew each other. His family was from Sweden and had been in Australia for a year while his father was on sabbatical.

"I haven't had anything to do with Lars for years, Anna. How do you know about him?"

"We know these things."

"Well, I guess I can try. The last I was in contact with him was a few years after he went back to Sweden. We used to exchange chats, but that petered out. Where is Belle now?"

"She is in France."

"What's she doing there?"

"She is busy. She wants to speak to Lars."

"If I can contact him, what do I tell him?"

"That you would like him to meet friend of yours."

"OK, Anna, I'll see what I can do."

Anna said, "I will go now. Thank you." She smiled politely, and the device reverted to its previous state.

Kurt asked, "What was all that about?"

Heidi shook her head. "Part of a bigger picture."

"There's a bigger picture than this?" he asked, holding up the USB stick with a look of bewilderment on his face.

"Yes, Dad, a *much* bigger picture."

"Has that dammed soldier got you mixed up with espionage?"

"No, Dad, if anything, I've got him mixed up in all this. And please, cut him some slack; he's one of the good guys. And I like him." She looked at her father inquiringly. "Why didn't you ask Anna more about the document while she was on the phone? I'm sure there was something you wanted cleared up."

"She wouldn't have understood my questions, sweetheart; they were quite technical."

"You'd be amazed at what she understands. She's a very special person."

18

Heidi flew back to Canberra early the next morning in time for her to make it to work.

Later that evening, there was a knock on her door; it was Anna.

"Anna, I wasn't expecting to see you so soon. Please come in."

Although she didn't say anything, Anna touched Heidi on the arm in greeting and gave her a big smile.

Heidi said, "I'm sorry about Dad. You went to all the trouble to talk to him, but he didn't ask you anything much about the document."

"Yes, he thinks I am too young to understand. My mother has made some mistakes; she did not realise how long you take to learn things, and how bad you are at teaching. But she knows this now."

"Your mother, Anna, the two of you are close?"

"Yes, my mother loves me."

"And she loves Belle and Viktoria as well?"

"Yes, she loves us all. I have plan on how to meet Lars. You can go to Sweden with Belle and phone him from there. Tell him she is your friend, and you are on vacation. You thought it would be good chance to catch up while you are there. He is married now. His wife is Ingrid."

"Anna, I can't just fly off to Europe. I've got to go to work."

"I can take you there. You can be back by morning in time for work."

Bernie had told her he thought Anna had a way of getting from place to place almost instantly, and he had added if she got the chance, she should find out anything she could about it. The more they knew about Anna and Belle, the better.

"All right, when do you want me to go?"

"You can go now."

"Now, as in right this minute?"

"Yes."

Heidi took a few breaths.

"I just need to freshen up and change first. Give me a minute."

As she came back out of her bedroom, Anna smiled at her. "Thank you, Heidi."

~

Heidi was no longer in her apartment. She was in a hotel room, and Belle was standing beside her.

"Hello, Heidi, thank you for helping me."

"Good to see you again, Belle. Ah, just let me sit down for a minute. Where are we exactly?"

"I thought Anna told you. We are in Sweden. In Malmö."

Heidi sat on the edge of a chair, her breathing quite rapid and shallow. "Do you think I could have a glass of water, please?"

"Yes, of course. I will get you one."

Heidi was slowly getting her breathing under control and sat in silence, trying to collect her thoughts. When Belle handed her the glass, she took a quick sip.

"Thank you, Belle, ah … Anna said you want me to help arrange for you to meet Lars."

"Yes."

"Just give me a minute to get my thoughts straight."

Heidi went over and looked out the window. The busy jostling of traffic and the purposeful movement of people on the sidewalk somehow comforted her. She didn't feel as if she was in a completely foreign place; cities the world over, at a basic level, were all the same. But it wasn't where she was that had her heart racing, it was how she had got here.

Heidi took several more sips of water, closed her eyes, and forced herself to breathe slowly and deeply. As her mind cleared, she reopened her eyes. "OK, I think I'm ready."

Belle handed her a smart phone with a number already entered. "He has changed his number since you knew him, but I know it."

Heidi touched the call button.

"Hello, this is Lars."

Heidi spoke a little Swedish. Lars had taught her some when he was in Australia. And of course, she recognised the name Lars, and his voice. She replied in English.

"Hi Lars. It's Heidi. Guess what? I'm on holidays in Europe and have ended up in Sweden. I wasn't intending to come here, but the opportunity arose so I thought, 'why not'. Only here for a short time, but it'd be great to catch up with you if that's possible. Sorry for the short notice."

"My God, Heidi. It's so good to hear from you. How long has it been?"

"Ages, Lars. A lot's changed since we last saw each other. How's life with you?"

"Well, I'm an engineer now. I work for Vattenfall. It's a power generation company. And you?"

"I work for the government."

"Great. Hey listen, I'm at work now and can't talk for long. I live in Malmö. It'd be great if you could drop in and visit, and my wife would love to meet you. We could have dinner together and catch up on each other's news."

"You wouldn't believe it. That's where we're staying tonight. Coincidences, hey?"

"Yes, funny how things just work out sometimes. Where are you staying? I'll come and get you. I'm sure Ingrid will be glad to have a guest for dinner."

"OK, let's see, just give me a minute ..." She scurried to the sideboard and looked at the brochures stacked neatly on its surface. "It's the Scandic Triangeln, excuse my pronunciation. Oh, and I'm travelling with a friend. Is it all right if we make it two?"

"Absolutely. Fantastic, I'll swing by around sixish."

"Thanks, Lars, so looking forward to seeing you again."

~

Ingrid heard the car arrive and hurried to the front door. Lars had told her about a school friend from Australia calling and that he had invited them to dinner.

Lars introduced them. "Ingrid, this is Heidi and her friend Belle—my wife, Ingrid."

She greeted them in English. "Hello, please come inside. Lars often talks about his time in Australia and has told me all about you, Heidi. It's great to finally meet you. I'm so glad you called. And it's nice to meet you too, Belle."

Heidi said, "Lovely to meet you, Ingrid. You have such a nice home. As Lars said, this is my friend, Belle." She put her arm around Belle and gave her a brief hug. "She lives in France now and is showing me the sights."

"That's so handy, your own personal tour guide," Ingrid said as she pointed towards the hallway. "Let's head into the dining room. We can have drinks before we dine. I hope you like meatballs. I thought, why not treat you to one of our traditional dishes?"

Both guests agreed that sounded lovely. Belle didn't mention she was vegan. She would accept their hospitality and try to enjoy the meal.

Lars asked, "A glass of red for everyone?"

Heidi thanked him, but Belle said, "Just water for me, please. I used to drink, but I am trying to give it up."

Once they had their drinks, Lars asked, "How long are you in Europe for? Enjoying it so far? I bet you're finding it different from Australia."

"Oh, I've just started out really, haven't seen a lot of it yet, but it is beautiful. So anyway, tell me all about life since coming back from Australia, and how you met your beautiful wife." Heidi steered the conversation towards those two topics throughout their meal.

After they had eaten, Lars invited them to the lounge to relax and continue their conversation. Ingrid excused herself and said she wouldn't be a minute. She just wanted to clear the table. Belle jumped up to help.

Heidi and Lars were reminiscing about the past and catching each other up on events when she glanced at her watch. They had been so engrossed in their conversation that she hadn't noticed the time slip by. They had been in here for almost an hour.

"Oh my God, look at the time. I'll just see what's keeping the others."

She found them sitting at the dining table speaking quietly to each other in Swedish. Ingrid was facing her, and Heidi noticed the puzzled look on her face.

Ingrid looked up and said, "There you are. I'm sorry, so rude of me to be ignoring the two of you. Belle and I were just talking about things. She's a very interesting girl."

Belle turned and smiled at Heidi, who attempted to reciprocate.

"You have caught up on all Lars' news, yes?"

"Yes, it's been great. Sorry, but we lost track of the time."

"Perhaps we better be getting back, Heidi. It is late and we have big day planned tomorrow. And Lars and Ingrid have to work."

Heidi agreed.

Belle reached out and touched Ingrid on the hand. "So pleased to have met you, Ingrid."

As she was saying this, Lars came into the room to see what the holdup was.

Heidi said, "Time's getting on and we don't want to keep you up any later. Don't worry about getting us back to the hotel. We'll call a cab. It was so good to catch up, Lars, and thank you for the lovely meal, Ingrid."

~

The two of them sat in silence during the cab ride back to the hotel, but once they entered the room, Belle said, "Thank you, Heidi. Would you like to go home now? I would like to show you Paris, but I am busy."

"Ah … Belle, where does Ingrid work?"

"For the government."

"And it was her you wanted to see, not Lars?"

"Yes." Belle gave a cheeky grin. In contrast to the seriousness of the situation, Heidi thought she looked like a mischievous child who had just gotten away with something.

"What were you talking to her about?"

"You do not need to know that, Heidi."

"Well, if it's not too much trouble, yes, I'd like to go home now, please."

Belle smiled at her.

~

Heidi rang Bernie. "Babe, I have to talk to you. Can you come over before you go to work?"

"Sure, is something wrong?"

"No, all good. I just want to talk about some travel arrangements."

"Can't wait. I'll be right over. Love you."

Heidi met him at the door and gave him an excited hug. "I've done it! Oh my God, Bernie, you were right. They can just go from place to place. And they can make us do the same. Can you believe it?"

"You mean you've been travelling with Anna?"

"Yes, well, kind of. She sent me to see Belle."

"OK, let's sit down. I want to hear all about it."

Still a little breathless, Heidi related her night's adventures. "Anna came and saw me last night. She asked me if I'd help Belle with something. Didn't exactly say what about, but I agreed. Belle was in Sweden. I told her I couldn't get off work to fly to Sweden and back, then she told me she could take me there."

"What's it like? Do you feel anything?"

"No, nothing. I was just standing here talking to Anna, then I was in a hotel room in Sweden with Belle standing beside me. I can't remember anything about getting there—Bernie; what can't they do?"

"I'm more interested in what they can do. What did you get up to in Sweden?"

"A guy I knew at school lives there, and Anna wanted me to help Belle meet him. Bernie, I haven't been in touch with Lars for years, hardly even think about him these days. How did Anna know about him?"

"I think Anna knows a lot about you, Heidi. What did she want to see him about?"

"That's just it. She didn't want to see Lars at all. She wanted to meet his wife."

"What for?"

"She wouldn't say. But she told me she works for the government there."

Heidi was still firing her answers back quickly and was a little flushed in the face. She took a few steadying breaths. She touched

Bernie on the arm.

"Bernie, they aren't going to hurt us. They're going to look after us."

"I'm thinking the same. But it won't hurt to keep our guard up. You never know what's around the corner."

Bernie gave her a cuddle and said, "You're sure you feel all right — no after effects from the trip?"

"No, I'm all good."

Bernie stood up and walked towards the kitchen. "I think we both need a coffee. You don't think you should take the day off, do you? You look pretty tired."

"No, I'm fine. Adrenalin is keeping me going at the moment. I'm going to need a big sleep tonight, though."

In all her excitement, Heidi completely forgot to tell Bernie that Anna had also been talking about her mother.

19

As soon as they disembarked the Royal Australian Air Force KC-30A at joint Base Anacostia-Bolling, they were whisked to the waiting Marine Corps helicopter for the short flight to the White House.

As it swooped in to land, they could see the riot taking place outside the grounds, along with the heavy National Guard and police response. There appeared to be thousands of people involved, and several vehicles were ablaze.

Upon landing, their escorts took them straight to the meeting room. They almost had to force themselves through the door. Tension hung thick in the room—they could almost see it. It felt palpable.

The newly promoted President Sanger stood up to greet them. "Ladies and gentlemen, please welcome Ms Amanda Turner, Australia's Foreign Minister and General Charles Mitchell, their Chief of Defence. Thank you both for travelling here. I understand you have important information best discussed in person."

Amanda answered, "Thank you, President Sanger. I would first like to reiterate my government's condolences on the passing of President Boage. And I hope you can quell the civil unrest that has ensued. It is a very traumatic time for your country."

She lowered her eyes and paused in respect before taking her seat. "I do not wish to appear presumptuous, but what we are here to discuss is in relation to the Pine Gap incident of a few weeks ago. Is it OK to discuss that in the present company?"

"Yes, Minister Turner, everyone here has had a full briefing on that subject. Please proceed."

She looked around the room, making eye contact with each of them. She breathed in deeply, held it for a moment, and slowly exhaled. Her skin tingled from the tension she was absorbing from within the room. She stood to address them.

"We have had another meeting with Anna." She let that hang out there for a moment, but it did nothing to ease the tension. If anything, it added to it.

Amanda exchanged looks with General Mitchell, and after gaining some strength from him, continued in measured tones. "She is a very intense young woman, and she made some startling revelations."

She still couldn't read the room. Tension overruled any other emotion.

"She reiterated we are dealing with an alien presence and that they are here to preserve the habitability of Earth. The sane ones amongst us should agree, on the surface at least, that this appears to be a good thing. We do, however, need to persuade them not to wipe us all out in the process."

She let this statement sink in.

"Ladies and gentlemen, we've seen some of their tech first hand. Not in a video, right before our eyes! It's mindboggling. We are treating this with the utmost urgency, and I recommend you do likewise."

She again sought strength from the Chief of Defence. He nodded almost imperceptibly in reply.

"Our analysis is they were confining their activities to intelligence gathering and demonstrating some of their capabilities."

Stony silence.

"That was until you abducted Viktoria. They're furious about your treatment of her. Anna told us it was they who removed the brain stems of President Boage and Director Stark along with five others, presumably her interrogators."

Now she really had their attention.

"Viktoria is now under our protection. Anna warned they will react strongly to any further attempts to interfere with Viktoria. As will we. Ladies and gentlemen, I beg you; take notice. And to give you some perspective, our analysis indicates they're not interested in shooting the messenger. They take action against those who write the messages. Very severe action."

Everyone in the room was looking from person to person before all eyes ended up on the President.

Amanda's eyes followed them, hesitated, and then swept back around the room. "They have opened a communication channel with one of our junior staff. Our intention is to leverage this to reach some accord with them. We intend to pursue a diplomatic course of action."

She looked directly at the President, stooped slightly and placed both hands on the table to emphasise her next statement.

"And, excuse my frankness, bully-boy tactics won't work in this case. If you pursue that line, you will stand into clear and present danger. Even with all your military might, you can't handle them."

Amanda resumed her seat.

If they possessed the senses to detect it, they would have been able to feel the tension crackling and chagrin churning in the room, such was the level it had risen to. But all they perceived was silence. Everyone was digesting the information they had just received. And some could feel the bile rising in their throats.

President Sanger was looking around the room, hoping for some enlightenment. Things were quickly piling up around him, and he wasn't sure he could keep his head above water. The Australians knew the cause of President Boage's death. That was highly classified information. And they knew the CIA Director had met the same fate. News that he had died had not been released, let alone his cause of death. And they now had confirmation that the aliens were involved.

Eventually, he said, "Well, I think we are already past the diplomatic solution stage, Minister Turner. I consider the assassination of our president an act of war. By claiming responsibility, the aliens have shown their hostile intent, and they have caused irrevocable damage to our country. We will retaliate with all the means we have available. We are not a country to lie down in the face of a threat."

Amanda was about to reply when he silenced her by raising his hand. He wasn't aware of the whole Viktoria episode and was determined to get to the bottom of it as soon as possible.

He asked, "Can anyone here shed some light on the incident with this Viktoria that Minister Turner mentioned?"

The new Director of the CIA raised his hand and stood up.

"Mr President, I only have basic knowledge of the incident, but I know that the staff conducting the interrogation were killed during her escape. I will have an in-depth report prepared on the incident. Sir, if they found her at our site in Saudi Arabia, they must have scoured the planet looking for her. I think we can safely assume we have nowhere to hide."

"Thank you, Harold."

The President looked at the Science Adviser. "Any comments?"

He jumped to his feet with excitement. "Mr President, I agree with Ms Turner's advice. We should try to pursue a diplomatic solution. We need to keep them on side. This is an unprecedented opportunity for all of us. If we can get them to share their technology with us, just think of what that will achieve. Not only militarily, but scientifically. And the financial rewards will be incalculable; our companies will be so far ahead of the opposition they won't even see our tail lights. Perhaps this is an opportune time to hear the views of the Unidentified Aerial Phenomenon Independent Study Team people." He looked towards the Chairman of that group and resumed his seat.

"Thank you Garry. Wayne ..." the President said.

The Chairman of the UAPIST stood.

"Thank you, Mr President. This is the most credible evidence to hand about the existence of extra-planetary life. Irrefutable evidence. Intelligent aliens! Not only their existence, but their presence here. We must show great caution in any further interactions with them. Their actions to date, at first glance, appear to have been hostile in the extreme. Assassinating the president and the director of the CIA; there seems to be no other way to interpret that. And the way and place in which they did it. Brain stems removed with unparalleled precision, and no evidence to show how this was accomplished. No signs of surgery at all. Unbelievable technology."

He shook his head to reinforce his observations before continuing with his assessment.

"However, given their displayed capabilities, it's my opinion that they appear to be exhibiting some desire to limit the extent of their attacks. I think you'll all agree, we could have fared far worse. And don't lose sight of the significance of them sharing medical information. Is that a subtle sign they possess detailed knowledge of our biology, and can launch a bio-weapon attack if they so desire? The fact they have made contact is highly significant. Are they prepared to negotiate? We've got to follow that up with whatever means we can."

The President cut him short and moved the conversation forward. He turned towards Amanda and said, "Minister Turner, when you counselled we pursue a diplomatic solution, can I take it they informed you we are not under threat of imminent attack?"

"Except for those relating to any further interference with Viktoria, she made no direct threats. It was more as if she was advocating a peaceful solution. I believe if we all act rationally, we could reach some consensus with them."

"I'm afraid I'll need more than your analysis of the matter but thank you. Have you anything to add, General Mitchell?"

"No, Mr President, I've just come to answer questions Minister Turner needed help with. But we are still extremely worried about the Chinese. After their missile launch, there's no telling what they'll do. All our intel suggests they have taken a step back for the moment. We would appreciate any information you have acquired, or deductions you have made about their intentions."

"It's my understanding we are sharing that. Harold ..."

"Yes sir, that's the case. Everything is being shared."

"Anything further, anybody?" As he looked around the room, all he could see were shaking heads. He pushed the Chief of the Army. "Closing comments?"

"Mr President, I'm as outraged as you are about the assassination of President Boage and the others, but I urge caution. The aliens have capabilities we are defenceless against. And they obviously have very good intel on us. The act of assassinating President Boage alone could well bring our country to its knees."

The President looked down and seemed to study his hands for a moment. He then returned his attention to Amanda. "I'm going to send the Secretary of State to your country. I request you invite him to any further liaisons with the aliens until we can get direct comms established with them ourselves. Please inform them he speaks with my authority."

He stood and said, "Thank you all, especially to our Australian guests. Ladies and gentlemen, I pray to God we can get through this together. Oh, and, Harold, could you join me in the Oval Office?"

As the meeting closed, Amanda approached the Secretary of State. "Can we offer you a lift on our return flight, Mr Secretary? I'm very interested in getting to know you better. We're scheduled to head back tomorrow morning."

"Thank you, Minister Turner. I'd love the opportunity. However, I doubt my security would clear that. Perhaps it is I who can offer you a lift."

"Thank you. That is most gracious of you."

As they headed back to their hotel, Amanda reflected on the meeting. *That could've gone a lot better. It seems the Americans have dug their heels in. Things could spiral downwards very quickly from here.*

Given the Americans' confrontational attitude, she was also apprehensive about how Anna would react when the Secretary of State tried to muscle in on any discussions.

~

As soon as they reached the Oval Office, the President said, "Harold, we need to get ears on the Australian Government. What exactly they know and what their intentions are. Get onto it straight away."

"Yes sir."

"And I want the identity of their mysterious communication asset. And when you have it, they are to be placed under 24-hour surveillance. I want to know everything that gets exchanged between the Australians and the aliens."

"Yes sir."

"Any thoughts on the timeline involved?"

"Should be able to be accomplished quite quickly, sir. We've been cultivating an asset high up in their government. In their inner circle. It shouldn't be hard to develop him into a source."

20

Judith's approach startled Heidi. "Could I see you for a moment?"

Thinking that somehow Judith had heard of her night with Belle, Heidi said somewhat hesitantly, "Of course, Judith, what can I do for you?" She reached for her handbag.

"In private, please."

~

As they entered the lift, Heidi looked questioningly at Judith, but she just shook her head.

Once they reached her office, Judith went straight around and sat in her chair. She indicated Heidi should sit in the chair on the other side.

"Heidi, we'd like to have another meeting with Anna. The American Secretary of State is here, and he is quite keen to talk with her. Do you think you could call her and try to arrange it?"

"I can ask her. Can you tell me what about specifically, and who else will be at the meeting?"

"Well, it'll be hard to keep this to just a few. There are a lot of people interested in taking every opportunity to meet with her. I'm not aware of the exact attendance list, but I expect it to at least include some who were at the last meeting, plus the Secretary of State. And I believe there will be some other Americans as well."

"I can call her now if you like and you can talk with her directly."

"Thank you, Heidi, that'll be great."

Heidi took her device out of her bag, but before she made the call, she described how it worked. Even though she had just been forewarned, the sudden appearance of the 3D image of Anna caused Judith to recoil in alarm.

"Hello, Heidi. What can I do for you?"

"Hi, Anna, um … I've got Judith here with me and she asked me if I could call you to arrange a meeting. It's probably easier to talk to her directly."

Judith was still staring in fascination at the image floating above the device. She was further startled as Anna's head swivelled to look at her.

"Hello, Judith. I am busy. Could you call me back in an hour?"

Judith didn't move or show any sign she was about to respond.

Heidi answered for her. "Absolutely, thank you, Anna."

The device reverted to its inert red glow.

Judith looked at Heidi with wide eyes.

"That device is amazing."

"Yes, their tech is crazy."

She put the device back in her handbag, then asked, "What do you think she's up to at the moment?"

"God only knows. But I can feel a shiver going down my spine."

Judith swivelled her chair and gazed out the window for a few moments as she shook off the feeling. Turning back towards Heidi, she said. "Thank you, Heidi. We'd be lost without you. Perhaps you can come back in an hour's time."

"See you at eleven."

~

Heidi went back to Judith's office to make the call.

They sat together at her desk. Heidi placed her device on its surface and touched it with her fingers. It instantly sprang to life. Even though Judith had seen this before, she still leaned back a little in surprise.

Anna's image turned toward Judith. "What would you like to speak about?"

She was ready for the change in the image this time and remained lucid. But she still felt pins and needles on the back of her neck as she replied, "Anna, the American Secretary of State is visiting our country and has asked if we could arrange for him to meet with you. Several other senior people wish to do the same. Do you think you could spare the time to meet with them?"

"Yes, I will come. When is meeting?"

"Well, as soon as possible. Are you free tomorrow, say around 3:00 p.m.?"

"Yes, is it in same room?"

"No, Anna, it will most probably be in Parliament House. If you come here, we can take you."

"Perhaps we can have lunch together, Heidi, then you can take me there."

"I'd love that. When can you get here?"

"I will come early, to your house. We can have breakfast together as well. I will go to your parliament for morning and watch. It will be interesting to see how your government works. We can have lunch at cafe. Then we can go to meeting."

"OK, looking forward to tomorrow."

The device reverted to its inert state. Anna had terminated the call.

Heidi said, "Well, it looks like that's all set. The way she was talking, do you think she expects me to be at the meeting? I don't think I'll be invited, and I wouldn't have any input—a bit above my pay grade."

Judith closed her eyes and shook her head, trying to get her thoughts straight.

"No, I don't think you'll be at the meeting, but now you mention it, she was probably alluding to you being there. Maybe you can explain over breakfast that you don't go to these types of meetings."

"OK—God, what is she going to think of us if she sits in on parliament?"

"Not very much, I fear. I wonder what's on the agenda tomorrow." As she said this, she opened her computer and looked it up. "They're introducing the climate change bill. That could get chaotic."

21

As Judith led Anna towards the meeting room, she said, "Anna, please be patient during the meeting. There are going to be people there who will be meeting you for the first time, and they are extremely excited about it. But the American Secretary of State might appear quite abrupt. That is how they talk sometimes. He will not mean any disrespect."

"Yes, we know this."

Judith beckoned her forward as she opened the door. "Well, here we are—after you." All the other meeting attendees were already present. The cacophony of their overlapping conversations dissolved into silence as Anna entered. Some of the Americans looked completely overawed.

Judith cleared her throat. "Ladies and gentlemen, let me introduce Anna."

Anna bowed slightly and said, "It is pleasure to meet you."

Ushering her to her seat, Judith said, "Please, Anna, make yourself comfortable. Thank you again for agreeing to come. I will chair the meeting."

She introduced the attendees individually, starting with the Secretary of State. Judith dwelt on him, explaining how important he was, and that he spoke on behalf of the President of the United States. Anna held eye contact with him during Judith's entire introduction. Her expression had turned cold. As the introductions moved on to the others, Anna relaxed slightly as she nodded to each in turn. She could read the excitement written on some of the Americans' faces, could almost reach out and touch it.

With the formalities over, Judith said, "Ladies and gentlemen, please don't let Anna's youthful appearance put you off; she commands immense power." Judith moved in her chair, signalling her discomfort, then said, "Mr Secretary, perhaps we can start with you."

"Thank you, Ms Morton. Anna, my government would like to establish a direct line of communication with your commanders. Can we discuss that?"

"Why do you want this?"

"So we don't have a repeat of the events that occurred with our former president, for one."

"You should not have touched Viktoria. After you did this, speaking to us would not have helped."

"Assassinating our president was somewhat of an overreaction, don't you agree?"

"We love Viktoria."

Judith tried to interrupt the escalating tension. "Anna, perhaps you could give the Americans a device like the one you gave to Heidi?"

"No."

"Please, Anna, having a means of communication is extremely important in averting potential disasters. If the Americans could talk to you, they would not have needed to touch Viktoria."

Anna was still staring daggers at the Secretary of State, who was glaring back. She looked livid; he looked about to explode.

"Do you realise the damage you've caused to my country? It's unforgivable. We consider it an act of aggression that requires retaliation."

"We have done nothing to your country. Your problems existed long before we arrived. You call yourselves the *united* states, but there is much division and hatred amongst you."

"Don't lecture me about my country. We're the most powerful nation on the planet, and I can't understand why you didn't contact us as soon as you arrived," he ranted.

"You see yourself as most powerful nation on planet. We see you as biggest problem."

The meeting had spiralled out of control. Judith again attempted to deescalate things. "Perhaps we could take a short recess at this point."

Anna stood and said, "I will go now. We are not interested in speaking with this man."

As Anna headed for the door, Judith rushed after her. "Please, Anna, let's take a brief break so everyone can calm down, then we can start again."

The Secretary of State jumped to his feet, his chair toppling over. "Don't you walk out on me, young lady," he growled.

"I will go now." Anna continued towards the door.

Judith followed her. "Anna, please don't go."

Taking no heed, Anna continued down the hallway. "Goodbye, Judith."

~

The Secretary of State banged the desk. Hard. He did it again. Then he screamed, "Goddamn aliens."

The Prime Minister tried to rein in his anger. "Please take a few breaths, Mr Secretary. We all need to calm down here."

"I've had enough of this nonsense," he blurted as he stormed out of the room, heading in the direction that Anna had just taken. Luckily for him, she was nowhere to be seen.

~

Those left in the room looked at each other in bewilderment. They couldn't believe what they had just witnessed. The UAPIST people in particular. They had been incredulous when first told of the encounters, and they were ecstatic to be invited to attend this meeting. It was the chance of a lifetime; perhaps the one chance in history. Now it had been blown away by a pompous idiot.

The Chairman looked at the psychologist. *What the ...?* He shook his head in disbelief.

The psychologist put his head in his hands and rubbed his temples. *What hope is there for us?*

None, he answered himself.

The Chairman said, "After all the expectation, and all this way. For that." He still had complete exasperation written all over his face.

The psychologist placed his elbows on the table and steepled his hands in front of himself. "Unbelievable. But did you *feel* her presence?

I can't wait to talk to her directly. One on one. With no fools in the room to distract us."

"It was only a fleeting glimpse, but did you get any insights? How we might best approach them? And what might be in store for us?"

The psychologist studied his hands for a long moment, tapping his index fingers together while appreciating the enormity of what was transpiring.

He looked up and said, "The wording she uses. The same as in all the transcripts of her previous interactions. It's very enlightening. She talks in the first person and in the plural. We. Us. She appears to be human, but I think, in her mind, she believes she is one of them."

"Is that significant?"

"Everything is significant to some extent. To a very large extent with this subject. And her initial politeness is at odds with some of their actions. Complex. Let's not jump to any conclusions about them."

His fixation on his previous assessment persisted. Shaking his head, he reiterated, "She doesn't speak as if she's a third party relaying information. She is the first party. This is extraordinary. But the chances of them looking like us ..."

The Prime Minister asked, "What about the way she just got up and left?"

"It appears they don't suffer fools gladly. Politeness aside, there might be a limit to their patience."

As he looked beseechingly at the Prime Minister, the Chairman said, "You simply must get things back on track. And gently-gently. Kid gloves, not bluster and bravado. What's done is done. We must move on. This is too important and we can't afford to mess it up. It could be world-ending."

The Prime Minister nodded and swallowed nervously.

22

When they arrived, they found President Sanger channel surfing between news feeds of the latest riots.

He had summoned the Secretary of Homeland Security and the Director of the FBI to his office for an update on the domestic situation. And he had the Attorney General with him. Things were going from bad to worse, and they were desperate to put an end to the rioting and widespread public disturbance taking place.

He muted the sound, turned towards them, and asked the Secretary, "What are the latest figures?"

"Sir, the biggest trouble spots remain Washington and New York. The situation is fluid, but this is fairly up to date. In New York, the NYPD and National Guard have suffered over one hundred casualties, with our estimate of civilian casualties in the order of fifty times that number. And we don't have the resources to combat the gang violence. We've got no idea of the casualties there. But the National Guard has security perimeters established around all hospitals. It's a chaotic situation, and they're at capacity treating the injured."

As he was saying this, the President called up the CBS channel and watched the live feed showing the scene outside the New York Community Hospital.

"Washington is even worse so far as casualty numbers are concerned, with nearly double that number. It is still the epicentre of the unrest, but the National Guard are finally making some headway in restoring order.

"All the other states report multiple disturbances. Especially in Texas and Alabama, both Governors remain vocal in promoting the unrest. Sir, unless we take immediate action, we risk those states descending into anarchy. And the domino effect may push others to follow suit.

"Maybe the FBI can update you on where we are with the militia groups."

The Director of the FBI entered the conversation.

"Sir, most of the groups we have under surveillance have been mobilising. Our prediction is we will be in armed conflict with at least a dozen more within the week. The good news, sir, is my agents are still loyal to the government and will act on your orders. The bad news is, we don't have the manpower for a nationwide response. We are desperate for help from whatever quarter you can provide. And the longer we take to restore order, the more widespread the mayhem will become."

The President looked towards the Secretary of Homeland Security and asked, "What's your call?"

"It's crucial we act immediately. Our financial institutions are reeling, the dollar is in freefall, and we all know the hit Wall Street took before you ordered trading to be suspended. Absenteeism in the workplace is rife, and our infrastructure is being undermined. Of particular concern are the power grid and water supply. Sir, we have to get on top of this now, or we might never recover."

Although he expected this news, the President looked crestfallen for a moment, then with his resolve returning, he steeled himself. He looked at the Attorney General and said, "Have we got all our ducks in a row? I want to proceed with mobilising the army."

"Yes sir, your proclamation ordering the insurgents to disperse has been published. All that remains is for you to issue the Executive Order."

"Good." He turned back to the Director of the FBI. "You'll get your manpower. I'm going to declare martial law in New York City, the District of Colombia, Texas, and Alabama. I want the FBI to place Governors Wallace and Holly under house arrest. The army will supply you with the troops to enforce it."

With that out of the way, he closed his eyes and seemed to be lost in his own thoughts.

"What is the status of foreign interference or agitation with all this?"

The Secretary of Homeland Security said, "Sir, we have thousands of individuals in detention. We are currently blocking over ten thousand web sites and have significant resources monitoring the situation. New sites are popping up each day, but foreign agitation appears to be minimal and is still non-existent in the case of China. Our major problems are home grown. We need to focus on that."

"Thank you, gentlemen. I'll sign the Executive Order as soon as we finish here. You may return to the crisis room. I'll be looking at the hourly updates to gauge the effectiveness of these measures going forwards."

He sat back in his chair and closed his eyes. On top of all this domestic upheaval, the goddamn alien had walked out on the Secretary of State, after heated words were exchanged. She had uttered disparaging comments about America, and she had refused to open dialogue with them. He was getting fed up with this whole alien saga and the world of hurt accompanying it.

23

Anna had just completed her ten laps of the beach. She trotted over to where she had left her gear stacked neatly beside the Sea Rockets and Blue Daisy-Bush. Stooping down, she grabbed her energy drink and took a sip, then absently returned it to the pile. She remained bent over slightly, and with her hands resting on her knees, breathing deeply and rhythmically. After taking several breaths, she straightened, arched her back, and stretched her arms above her head. She drew in a deep breath through her nose and held it for a moment, savouring the smell of the ocean. It wasn't a smell from her childhood, but she had grown to love it. It was the smell of nature, pristine and untouched. A vision of what the world would be like without us. There was a group of seagulls skylarking at the water's edge, but it was the sea-eagle soaring majestically on the up-currents from the cliff to her left that held her attention. Just imagine what it would be like to be able to move like that, effortlessly leveraging nature. That would be the ultimate high.

Such was her level of fitness, her breathing was already almost back to normal. She sat on the sand, enjoying the kiss of the sun on her face, and took another sip. The beach was such a peaceful place, the entire island, in fact. Especially on a day like today. Just lovely.

Belle was off working in Europe, but Anna was not alone; she had company just a thought away, and she felt like talking.

"Hello, Mother. It is so beautiful here. Thank you for picking this island for us."

"Did you enjoy your run? Sometimes, you confuse me. Running around doing all that work for no result. Why do you do it?"

"In a strange way, it relaxes me. And it's not all for nothing—it keeps me fit. Humans are meant to move around and do these things. Actually, there's no feeling quite like it. I wish you could come with me."

"Yes, Anna, that would be nice. But I have you to share these feelings with. When I made you and Belle, it was just so I could talk with the humans, but you have given me so much more. You provide deep insight into them and how they think. I am glad I made you."

"Well, I'm glad you did too. And it's so nice to have a companion. One who is so much like me. Belle is my best friend. And I love being able to talk to you as well."

"Yes, you are both so special. But you and Belle are no longer exactly alike. Humans' experiences mould them. Your brains change. And your paths are diverging. But you both mean the world to me."

Anna smiled to herself.

"Is that a metaphor, Mother? Us meaning the world to you. Or is it a joke you are sharing?"

"Yes, it is both. I am glad you noticed it."

This was the most in-depth conversation Anna had shared with her mother, and she wanted to pursue it for as long as she could. She drew a circle in the sand with her finger, then tapped inside it.

"Do you think there is any hope for us, you know, in the long term?"

"This is a question that vexes me. Sometimes I think the planet would be better off without humans. But it would not be the vital world it is without you."

"I don't know what to say to that. Surely you're not considering removing us all."

"It would solve some problems. But humans are such an enigmatic species. You do so many selfish and destructive things. But not always. Sometimes you are kind. And the most confusing thing is why you always lie. You hide yourselves from others."

"It's a defence mechanism. We have to lie sometimes. To be kind. We could not live together if everyone knew how we truly felt about each other. It's what makes our civilisation possible. And our relationships. Of course, some people misuse its true purpose. They lie just to advantage themselves."

Anna didn't receive a direct answer to that, but she persisted.

"Do you lie sometimes, Mother?"

Again, a long silence.

"Thank you for explaining that to me. Now I understand the concept, and how useful it is."

"We don't just lie to others either. Sometimes, we lie to ourselves."

"How can you do that? You know it's a lie. You cannot deceive yourself."

Anna allowed herself a wry smile.

"We do it anyway. It's called deluding ourselves. We usually do it to vindicate the decisions we make that go against our inner beliefs. Or when we are contemplating things that are too horrible to think about. Paradoxically, it helps keep us sane."

This time, there was a significant pause from her mother. So long, in fact, that Anna thought she might have gone off to do something else.

Anna smoothed out the sand where she had drawn her empty circle, not comfortable contemplating the answers to that part of their conversation.

She was startled when her mother spoke again, but not because she was still there. It was because of the question she asked.

"Anna, I do not understand premonitions. How do you conjure them up?"

Now that was an interesting question! Anna looked down at the seagulls squabbling noisily at the water's edge, then closed her eyes and answered.

"We don't. They just appear to us. They can't be explained. And sometimes, of course, they are wildly inaccurate. But they are hard to ignore."

"It would be good to have this ability. Perhaps you can guide me."

"You don't get any gut feelings?"

"No, Anna. I do not have a gut."

Anna laughed out loud.

"Well, you certainly have a great sense of humour; you crack a good one, and that's something we all appreciate ... Mother, do you have any other of our emotions, you know, like love and hate, anger and jealously, things like that?"

"Yes, of course I do. I love you, Anna. And Belle. I love you above all else. But I am very angry with some of the humans. So very angry."

"Thank you, Mother, and I love you too, of course. And I agree, there are some terrible people in the world."

"I can fix that if you like, Anna."

Another long silence. Anna didn't want to answer that.

"Thank you for this insightful discussion. Let's make it a habit to have more of these. Now, go ahead and take your shower—I have some work for you."

24

The *USS Henry Teak* was patrolling in the Sea of Japan, part of the picket line established along the coast of China.

The Hawkeye providing overhead surveillance detected an object tracking straight for the *Henry Teak*. It was skimming the sea surface and inbound at hypersonic speed, and the Aegis combat system interpreted it as a hostile missile.

As it approached the ship, the missile slowed to subsonic speed. The starboard Phalanx CIWS engaged it, but a strange iridescent blue glow appeared in front of it. Nothing extended past the gun; it was as if it was firing blanks. Completely unaffected by the countermeasures, the missile continued on until it was approximately thirty metres off the starboard side of the ship, then maintained this position.

The observers on the bridge were amazed to see that what they had thought to be a missile was, in fact, a featureless diamond-shaped object, a menacing jet black in colour.

"What do you make of that?" the Captain asked the Executive Officer. They were both leaning forwards, nervously gripping the bench beside the window, staring in fear and fascination at the object.

"I've never seen anything like it. Let's ask Petty Officer Marks. She's an expert on the latest missile tech."

The Captain agreed and ordered her to the bridge.

Beth was a little breathless as she entered. Her first action was to salute the Captain, who returned it almost casually. She said, "Did the

Phalanx get it, sir?"

The captain remained silent but beckoned her to look out the starboard windows. Beth did a double take, then with wide eyes, looked back at him.

Not a video this time, in the flesh, so to speak.

"Permission to speak freely, sir."

"Yes, Petty Officer, can you tell us anything about it?"

"I've seen a classified video of an object like this," she almost whispered.

Both senior officers exchanged glances.

The Captain asked, "Is it a new weapons system?"

"Not exactly. Sir, I suggest you contact Admiral Blake." She was still whispering, but her voice carried clearly across the deathly quiet of the bridge.

The Captain nodded towards the Exec. "Put the call through now."

Once secure comms were established, the Captain reported, "We have an unidentified object maintaining station off our starboard side. Sir, I believe you know Petty Officer Marks. I have her here with me."

"I'm sorry. Who did you say?"

The Captain motioned for Beth to speak. "Sir, this is Petty Officer Marks. I met you when the incident with the attack on Pine Gap was being discussed. It was me who attended the meeting in Australia. The object appears to be the one in the video, sir." Beth had the senior officers' full attention, focused on what she was saying.

"Ah yes, of course. Excuse me, Petty Officer, I remember you now. The same object you say?"

"If not the same, an identical one."

"It's just maintaining station, no other activity?"

The captain answered, "That's correct, sir."

"No attempt to attack or to communicate with you?"

"No sir, we have tried hailing it on all our usual frequencies and on the PA system. Nothing so far. No observable activity at all."

"I've got to see this for myself. How fortunate I'm currently visiting the fleet. It'll take an hour or so to get to you from the *Carlton Jackson*. Expect my helicopter around 11:30 hours."

"Aye sir."

With the call terminated, the three of them again continued to stare at the object, then at each other.

The Captain asked, "Can you please bring me up to speed?"

"It's designated top secret. With respect, sir, I think we should wait for the Admiral to arrive."

The Captain just nodded and went over to stand beside the window and gaze at the object. He was still there when the helicopter approached. It did a circuit of the ship and hovered off the starboard side to allow its occupants a good view of the object. It then landed on the ship's helipad.

The Exec was there to greet the Admiral. "Welcome aboard, sir. Fascinating times."

"Thank you, Lieutenant Commander, indeed they are. Takes your breath away, doesn't it? What do you make of it?" As he said this, the Admiral pointed at the object.

"Don't really know, sir. It has just kept station and shown no activity so far. There are no EM signals emanating from it. And no obvious signs of its propulsion system—but, sir, it can really hoot. It came in at mach 12." He pointed towards the ship's superstructure. "Please, let me escort you to the bridge. Captain Curtis is awaiting you."

As they entered the bridge, all came to attention. Admiral Blake returned their salute and ordered them at ease. After greeting the captain, he said to Bethany, "I'm sorry I didn't recognise your name, Petty Officer Marks. Please forgive me."

Beth was about to reply when a bright blue flash illuminated the bridge, and a young woman appeared, standing beside the window. All present stared speechless at the intruder, who smiled and said, "Hello, Bethany, so pleased to see you again."

Two of the sailors on the bridge recovered their wits and reacted by reaching for their sidearms.

"Stand down!" shouted the Admiral. Simultaneous with his shout, both handguns disappeared in a pulse of blue light.

Beth finally found her voice. "Hello, Belle."

"I am Anna," she corrected her as she stared down the two dumbfounded sailors.

"Anna! It's such a relief it's you who we're talking to. This is

Admiral Blake, Captain Curtis and Lieutenant Commander Howard. Sir, this is Anna. The device outside is hers."

"Pleased to meet you, gentlemen." Accompanied by a slight, but almost formal, bow from the waist.

Admiral Blake collected his thoughts for a moment. "Anna, it is a privilege to meet you. Can you tell us what your intentions are?"

"I have come to speak with you."

"With me—"

"Yes, Admiral Blake, with you."

"Anna, is this ship in danger from your device?"

"No. We do not want to harm any of your ships."

Turning towards Captain Curtis, Admiral Blake said, "That is very reassuring news. Captain, could we please use your quarters? I think this discussion is best conducted in private."

"Certainly, sir, I'll take you there," he said a little reluctantly. He desperately wanted to be part of the discussion as well.

As Admiral Blake ushered Anna towards the exit, she smiled at Beth, following this with a slight bow of her head, then turned to follow Captain Curtis.

Once they had left, the Exec said, "She's something to behold, isn't she? Beth, do you know what's going on?"

"Not really, sir. But she was at the meeting I attended in Australia. Sir, that UFO outside has unbelievable capabilities. I'm amazed we're still all here, unharmed."

"What can you tell us about it?"

"Nothing, sir. It's classified."

~

It was half an hour later when a preoccupied Admiral Blake re-entered the bridge.

"Captain Curtis, no discussion of this is to take place until further orders. That includes any radio traffic. I will be leaving shortly."

"Yes sir, and the young lady?"

"She has gone."

Admiral Blake joined the others at the window, gazing at the object while shaking his head.

Captain Curtis asked, "How do we deal with that?"

Suddenly, the object disappeared. Everyone just looked at each other for a moment, then Beth said, "Do you think it will come back?"

In a blunt manner, Admiral Blake said, "Not if I can help it. Assume any further incidents to be hostile acts by the Chinese and take appropriate defensive action." He nodded to the Captain, showing he was ready to leave.

25

It was time for Jessica's six-monthly check-up and she was sitting in the waiting room of her treating neurologist.

As usual, he was running late. Finally, Dr Taylor came down the hallway and invited her into his consulting room.

"Hello, Jessica. How are you feeling? Has anything changed in the last six months?"

"Hello, Dr Taylor. Yes, it has, but not in a bad way. I feel great. No more aches and pains, no tiredness, no numbness or tingling. No symptoms at all. It's as if I'm my old self again."

His face creased in a surprised frown. "That's good to hear, but highly unusual. Did this seem to happen suddenly, or have you gradually felt better?"

"It was very sudden. I must say, I was under a lot of stress at work and things were getting me down. But I woke up one morning last week feeling revitalised. It was as if nothing was wrong with me."

"That's great news, Jessica, but somewhat unusual to have such a drastic improvement overnight."

He looked at her enquiringly. She gave a little shrug and sat up straight, looking very pleased with herself.

After conducting a full neurological examination, he pushed back in his chair, looking at Jessica with a perplexed frown. "An MRI scan will give us more insight into how things are really going. Perhaps we can bring your yearly scan forward. In fact, I'll phone them now and get you the next available appointment."

Jess had a spring in her step as she left.

~

On the Thursday after her scan, Jessica returned for her follow up appointment. An animated Dr Taylor ushered Jessica into his room. Jessica had never seen him like this before; he seemed a little flustered. He invited her to sit and turned the computer monitor so they both could see it.

"Here's your scan from six months ago, Jessica. These bright spots are the demyelination lesions." He changed the view to show two scans beside each other. Pointing at the one on the right, he said, "This is your scan from Tuesday. Notice there are no lesions present at all. I have to tell you I've never seen or even heard of anything like this. It appears you no longer have any damage. Jessica, I think you're feeling better because you really are better. You no longer show any signs of MS. It's impossible for it to regress at all, let alone over such a short term. You and I are going to be seeing a lot of each other from now on as we try to get to the bottom of this."

They sat looking at each other in silence for some time, Dr Taylor with a bewildered expression, and Jessica with a beaming smile.

She finally broke the silence. "I knew it! Thank you, Anna."

"Excuse me, but who is Anna?"

"Dr Taylor, I still can't believe this. Oh my God, she cured me!" As she said this, Jess rose to her feet and was almost jumping for joy.

"You're not making any sense, Jessica. What are you talking about?"

Jess settled down a little and took several deep breaths, then studied Dr Taylor as if making a monumental decision. She sighed and told him a redacted version of her interactions with Anna.

Reaching into her handbag to retrieve the memory stick, she finished with, "Anyway, here it is. It's such a relief to give this to you."

Dr Taylor was looking at Jess as if she had gone mad. He took the stick, plugged it into his computer, opened the file, and scanned through it for about five minutes, captivated by its contents.

He still wore a look of bewilderment, but now an air of excitement was shining through it.

"And you say someone just gave this to you? What were the

circumstances?”

“Mmmmm,” Jess mumbled as a kind of agreement, “her name is Anna. I can’t really talk about her with you, but I hope you get to meet her one day; she is amazing.”

Not really happy with this answer but suspecting he would not get much further enlightenment, he pressed on.

“Another neurologist has this as well?”

Jess nodded. “Dr Almendinger. I can get his details for you.”

“Kurt Almendinger, I know him. He has a practice in Melbourne. I’ll contact him to discuss this as soon as we finish here. Jessica, what shifts are you working at the moment?”

“Day shifts until Saturday. I’ve got Sunday and Monday off. Then I start nights.”

“Right, is it OK to contact you of an evening to discuss this after I’ve talked with Kurt? No consultation charges, of course,” he finished with a wry smile.

“Yes, that’ll be fine. I finish at 6:00 p.m.—nominally,” she answered with a similar smile. She stood and Dr Taylor walked her to the door.

~

Jess was beside herself with excitement. The MS was gone! She had to tell Heidi. But first, she had dinner. Being way too excited to cook for herself, she called into her favourite restaurant, just down the street from her apartment. And she had a second glass of wine in celebration. Once she got home, she had a shower, went out to her balcony and rang Heidi.

“Heidi, you will not believe this. My MS is gone! I just know Anna has something to do with it. Isn’t she wonderful?” Her conversation came out in an excited torrent; she was quite breathless by the end.

“Oh, my goodness. I’m so happy for you, Jess. I had a feeling Anna was going to do something. Are you sure it’s gone?”

“Yes, absolutely. My scan confirms it. Of course, I wouldn’t believe it possible, except you and I both know what Anna is capable of. I couldn’t help myself in all my excitement and told my specialist about the document. I gave him a copy, and I told him your father has one as well. Do you think I’ll get into trouble?” The words were still pouring out of her.

"That's exactly what Anna wanted you to do. I can't see anyone giving you any grief about it. So, you told him my dad has a copy?"

"Yes. He's going to contact him about it. Your dad won't mind, will he?"

"I'm sure he'll be glad to have someone to talk about it with."

"I didn't tell him about Anna being an alien or anything, but I think I might have said something along the lines of 'she cured me'."

Heidi tried to laugh it off. "That's OK, he won't have a clue what you meant."

At last, there was silence at the other end of the call. Jess had finally drawn a breath.

"Listen, I'll talk to Dad, then phone you back later tonight if that's all right."

"Of course. I'm so excited, Heidi. I can hardly contain myself."

"It's the best news ever, Jess. I'll call you back later."

~

Later that night, Heidi rang Jess back.

"Dad's going up there this weekend. I was thinking of coming up to see you as well. To help you celebrate. And Dad said he'd like to meet you. Is that all right?"

"I'd love to meet him. This is so exciting. We could all have a barbecue here on Saturday night. I'll book it as soon as we finish talking. Is Bernie coming with you? And you're staying here with me, by the way."

"I haven't talked to him about it yet, but I'm sure he'll want to."

"OK, all settled then. Can't wait to see you."

"Me too, Jess. I am so happy for you."

"I'm working day shift on Saturday so won't be able to pick you up, but I'll arrange with the office for you get a key and let yourselves in. Ring me when you arrive, and make yourselves at home. I've got Sunday and Monday off, so we'll have plenty of time to catch up. See you soon."

~

After she finished talking to Jess, Heidi went and poured herself a glass of wine, then called Bernie.

"Hi babe, you're not going to believe this, but Jess is better. I'm planning on going up there this weekend to help her celebrate. Are you coming? We both want you there."

"Bloody oath I'm coming. What great news! Gone, you say?"

"Yes. Anyway, we can talk about it soon. I'll book us flights on Saturday, coming back late on Sunday or early Monday. We're staying with Jess. Bye, babe."

~

Heidi was on a roll with all these phone calls. She finished her glass of wine, then took out her device.

"Anna, Jess just rang to say her MS has gone. I just know it was you. Thank you so much. She is so excited and thankful."

"Yes, my mother made her well again. We are happy."

"Well, make sure you thank your mother from both of us. And Jess has finally shown your document to her specialist. He and Dad are going to meet this weekend to discuss it. Anna, this is so wonderful."

"Yes, I will tell her, but my mother already knows how excited Jessica is."

"I'm so glad. How is Viktoria?"

"She is happy. She likes Sydney, and she likes George."

"And you, Anna?"

"I am busy."

"OK then, I'll let you go, just wanted to pass on Jess's thanks."

Heidi went to her computer and booked the flights.

26

Heidi and Jess were waiting for them in the foyer. Her mother being with them surprised Heidi. "Hi, Mum, what a pleasant surprise. Dad said you weren't coming. Hi, Dad."

"Hello darling, you didn't think I'd miss a chance to see my little girl, did you? And take the opportunity to spend a weekend on the Coast. This is Dr Taylor, Henry, and his wife Catherine. Henry is Jessica's treating specialist."

"Hello, Catherine, Dr Taylor — Mum, Dad, this is my friend Jessica." She gave her an excited hug.

Jess said hello to them all.

Kurt said, "Hello, Jessica, I'm so pleased to meet you. And it's fantastic to hear you're well again. I can hardly wait to talk to you about your recovery. And thank you for inviting us to your celebration."

"Yes, of course. Come on through to the back; the cook's busy getting the barbie ready."

Heidi explained to her parents, "Bernie's here as well."

Dr Taylor insisted they call him Henry, but Jess couldn't bring herself to do it. She was so used to referring to him as Dr Taylor. It didn't seem to worry Heidi or Bernie, though; Henry was fine with them. Jess gratefully accepted the two bottles of wine Henry handed her and filled glasses for them all. Bernie getting one gave him an excuse to polish off the beer he had been drinking while preparing the barbeque plate.

As they were lifting their glasses to toast Jess, a couple came around the corner, saying, "Surprise!"

It was Viktoria and George.

George laughed. "Hey, Jess. Congrats. Heard you were throwing a barbie." Still sporting a huge grin, he went over to shake hands with Bernie. He passed over a cold six-pack of beer at the same time.

"George, you mongrel. It's good to see you." Bernie accepted the beers, opened one and handed it back to George, opened another for himself, then placed the rest into the Esky.

Viktoria had come over as well, and Bernie reached out and gave her a hug. "Hi, Viktoria, you look well. I hope things are settling down for you."

"Yes, George is looking after me." She smiled and, in her cute way of passing things over, using both hands and cocking her head slightly, handed Bernie the two packs of vegetable patties she had been holding. Accepting them, he raised an eyebrow at George.

George glanced back towards where they had entered and gave him a wink. "For the girls."

Viktoria went over to hug Jess and Heidi. As she did so, another two gate crashers arrived; Anna and Belle. They were both grinning from ear to ear.

Jess gasped and raised her hands to her mouth. The shock only lasted for a moment, though; she ran over and hugged them both at once. Anna pushed her away slightly and kissed her on both cheeks, with Belle following suit.

"Hello, Jessica, so good to see you."

"Now, who's who? We can't tell you apart, you know."

"I am Anna, red jumper; Belle is blue one. To make it easy for you," she said as she squeezed Jess's arm. Breaking contact, both the girls rushed over to Heidi and greeted her with their usual cheek kissing. It was obvious they were both in high spirits.

Anna clapped her hands and looked around the group. "We are here to have party, to celebrate with Jessica. We are on vacation!"

The Taylors and Almendingers were staring open-mouthed at the late arrivals. Catherine didn't think she had seen more attractive young women. And they were triplets. The guy with them obviously knew Bernie.

Anna looked towards Heidi's parents and the Taylors, obviously including them in her greetings. "Hello, I am Anna. These are my sisters, Belle and Viktoria." She pointed towards George. "And this is George."

Kurt said, "Hello, Anna. What a pleasure it is to meet you in person."

Henry was looking with amazement at Anna. He remembered the name from his talk with Jess. She was just a slip of a girl. What did Jess mean when she said Anna had cured her?

Bernie, the commensurate host, interrupted them. "Drinks, ladies?"

Heidi was about to say something when Anna said, "Yes, thank you. We will have wine to celebrate with Jessica."

Jess said, "I'll just go up and get some more glasses. Won't be a minute." Heidi went with her.

Belle went to look at the adjacent pool area, and Viktoria went back to stand beside George. Anna followed her. She was pleased to see that Bernie looked decidedly more at ease than the last time they had been together.

"Hello, Bernie. How are you?"

"Great thanks, Anna. It's good to see you again, and in such a relaxed atmosphere. With you, there's usually a bit more going on."

"You are taking good care of Heidi, yes?"

He nodded. "Not that she needs any looking after. But I'm keeping my eye on her."

Anna reached out and touched Bernie's stubbie. "This is Australian beer, yes?"

"Nectar of the gods! Would you like one? They're on George anyway, so let's get stuck into them."

With a mischievous look, Anna nodded. "I will have beer with soldiers."

She was definitely in a playful mood, smiling as she flicked her eyes between the two of them. As she looked towards George, Bernie caught Belle's eye and raised a bottle questioningly. She declined with a shake of her head and a polite smile, accompanying this with a wave of greeting towards him.

After he had opened Anna's beer and handed it to her, Bernie asked, "Did you want one, Viktoria?"

"No, thank you. I will wait for wine."

George leaned in to whisper, "She isn't a fan of beer."

After clinking bottles, the three of them took a mouthful. Anna pulled a face after tasting the beer.

With a wink, Bernie said, "Work on it, Anna. You'll end up loving it." He then asked casually, "So, you guys travel here together?"

"Viktoria and I flew up. The girls picked us up at the airport. They've hired an SUV!" This got a quick look from Bernie and a big smile from Anna.

Bernie said, "Bloody hell. I've got no doubt you're an excellent driver, Anna, but let's hope you don't suffer from road rage."

George allayed his fears. Putting his arm around Anna's waist, he pulled her in close and said, "No, in certain situations our girl can be pretty chill. Unfortunately, Viktoria's bag didn't turn up. She was a bit pissed, and I thought things were about to go pear-shaped. But Anna just smiled and told her, 'Not to worry, Vika, we'll get you more clothes—don't sweat the small stuff.' I breathed a sigh a relief then, I can tell you."

Anna leaned into George, showing her gratitude at his assessment of her behaviour. As George pulled her in a little closer, Bernie reached out and caressed Anna on the shoulder. They exchanged smiles. And winks. She again captivated Bernie. She was gorgeous; but when she smiled the way she was now, the entire world lit up.

Jess and Heidi arrived back with the extra glasses, along with extra plates and cutlery. Heidi, noticing Anna holding a beer, looked at Bernie, and shook her head. She got a wink in reply.

Once everyone had their drinks, Heidi said, "To you, Jessica, darling, I'm so glad it's over."

Everyone joined in the toast.

Jess said, "Thank you, everyone. And especially you, Anna. Words cannot describe my gratitude."

With a beaming smile, she went over and hugged her once again.

Anna reciprocated and said, "You are welcome, Jessica. We are happy."

The two doctors and their wives were taking all this in, trying to make sense of it.

Bernie interrupted. "Steaks are ready, as are your patties girls. I've been slaving here over a hot barbie getting them ready so tuck in before they get cold."

"Ladies first," Jess said as she looked at George.

"What?"

"I've seen you in action when meat is on offer." She gave him a good-natured poke in his ribs. Heidi indicated the older guests should fill their plates first. As instructed, George waited until last. The conversation died somewhat as they ate.

Suddenly, Anna laughed and pointed a delicate finger at Bernie. "I understand now, Toast—this is so funny. Soldiers have best humour."

Bernie and George smiled at this unexpected comment, Bernie winking back as well. The other guests, not understanding what she meant, looked inquiringly at her.

"I've got George to thank for that. It's what he dubbed me when I transferred to 2 Commando."

Heidi explained, "Toast is Bernie's nickname in the army. Where does it come from?"

Bernie looked at Anna and said, "Why don't you tell them, Anna?"

"It is joke about cooking—burnt toast—but you are good cook. This is funny." She chuckled to herself again.

"Thank you, Anna. It's good to see someone finally appreciate my talents." He gave an exaggerated bow as he spoke.

"I need name for when I am drinking with soldiers. Give me one too, George."

George thought for a second or two. "OK, to us you're going to be Arc."

"Arc. Why this name?"

"Well, Anna, sparks are apt to fly when you're around. And you remind me of the Archangels written about in our religion. Do you know about our religions?"

"Yes, we know about this … good, I am Arc."

As she said this, she raised her beer while flicking her gaze between Bernie and George. They both did the same.

While still looking at her, both soldiers said in unison, "Arc," and took a mouthful.

Anna followed suit. This time she didn't show the same reaction to the taste as she had previously.

Bernie winked. "Told you."

Jess changed the subject. "What do you think of Sydney, Viktoria, enjoying it?"

"Yes, I love it. George has been busy showing me all around," she replied, touching him affectionately on the arm. This gesture didn't go unnoticed by Heidi or Bernie, but neither showed any reaction.

Once they finished eating, Anna said, "You should speak with doctors tomorrow, Jessica. I will come with you and explain some things. Tonight we should celebrate—we need music; we will dance."

Anna burst into spontaneous dancing, with Belle and Viktoria joining in.

Jess said, "Let's take this party up to my apartment. I've got music up there." Looking at the doctors, she added, "I hope you don't mind putting our talk off until tomorrow. My friends have come a long way to help me celebrate."

Henry said, "Yes, of course, Jessica. And I'm sure Kurt will be fine with those arrangements. You all seem so happy together. I am looking forward to tomorrow though, and having Anna there as well —I can hardly wait. I don't think I'll get any sleep tonight."

Kurt said, "Of course, Jessica, I'm so grateful you have agreed to talk with me."

Jessica smiled by way of reply and started collecting the plates and cutlery. The boys joined in to help, then they made their way to the elevators.

~

As soon as they'd cleaned up and loaded the dishwasher, Jess opened her phone and put on some music. Anna came over to her and started to dance. Jess joined in but couldn't match Anna's graceful moves.

While the young ones were dancing and drinking, the two doctors were talking between themselves.

Henry said, "What do you make of the triplets? I've heard the name Anna before. Jessica's convinced it was she who cured her. And the conversations before were a little strange, don't you think?"

"I was finding them hard to fathom as well. This whole thing is baffling."

Catherine and Ursula joined their husbands on the balcony.

Catherine said, "Your daughter's so lovely. You must be very proud. And Jessica, I don't think I've ever seen anyone so happy to be alive." She gestured towards the sisters, who were dancing together. "My God, those triplets, aren't they beautiful? And they seem to be such good friends. Can you imagine the hearts they have broken and the mischief they must have got up to in their teens?"

Ursula replied, "They could still be in their teens. They look so young. And yes, they're gorgeous. I've talked to Anna briefly on the phone when Heidi called her to discuss the document about MS. She seemed to know a lot about Heidi. This is all very intriguing."

Bernie and George weren't dancing but were enjoying their beers while watching the show. And they loved Jess's version of a fridge. Every time they opened it, the six-pack they were raiding was mysteriously full again. Bernie was about to get refills for George and himself when Anna approached. She took him over to the curtains and showed him a device about the size of a fly adhering to the back of them.

"There are several here, but none of them work anymore," she said while touching it. "The Americans."

Bernie nodded and grimaced. "I'll check Heidi's place when we get back."

"No need, it is same. They do not work either."

"Bloody hell, Arc—you really are something, you know that."

She smiled and winked at him. "Sometimes I am like soldier, yes? I even ride in helicopters."

Bernie put his arm around her and gave her a hug.

"You're kick arse, sweetheart."

Those on the balcony observed this exchange. They couldn't hear what was said, but they noticed the serious looks on their faces at the beginning of their conversation. And the smiles exchanged between them at the end. They were obviously close to each other. Things were getting more confusing by the minute.

As they turned to return to the others, Henry saw the opportunity to engage with Anna. "Excuse me, Anna, thank you for offering to attend our meeting with Jessica tomorrow. What would be a good time for us to meet?"

"I am pleased to come. Do you think around ten? We could have coffee beforehand."

"That sounds perfect. Would you like to come to my house? Kurt and Ursula are staying with us."

"Yes …" Anna called out and motioned for Jessica to join her on the balcony. When she reached it, Anna said, "Jessica, is ten o'clock tomorrow OK for meeting? We can go to Henry's house."

"Yes, ten sounds fine. Is it all right to meet at your house, Dr Taylor?"

"Yes, absolutely. Kurt and I are very much looking forward to it. I'll text you my address. It's easy to find."

Jess hugged Anna.

"I can't wait either. Thanks for coming with me, Anna. It's going to be so exciting."

Henry said, "Well, we might get going. We'll leave you to your celebrating together. Thank you for a most memorable evening. And Catherine and I are so thrilled for you, Jessica."

On their way to the door, Ursula said to Heidi, "Sweetheart, Jessica and Anna are coming over to Henry's tomorrow morning to talk. Would you like to come with them? It'll be a good chance for us to catch up."

~

After they had retired for the night, Ursula said to Kurt, "I hope Heidi doesn't end up getting hurt. Bernie seems to be very chummy with Anna. We've seen this all before. And she's so beautiful. If she is after him, it'll be hard for him to resist."

"You're right. I noticed that as well. But she also seems to be very close to Heidi. There doesn't appear to be any friction between them at all. And she did greet Heidi before she went over to talk to Bernie. But, yes, they seemed to be quite affectionate towards each other. Normally I'd be happy for her to break them up, but now I'm not so sure. The guy is growing on me a little. And Anna is a very confusing young woman. I don't know what to make of her. They all seem to take a lot of notice of anything she says."

Ursula relented. "Perhaps I'm jumping at shadows. I'll sleep on it."

27

They partied long into the night, then crashed at Jessica's apartment. The first to rise were Bernie and George. They had slept on the floor, but that was nothing new to either of them. They got up quietly so as to not disturb the others and went down to a nearby coffee shop.

When they returned, Jessica and Viktoria were still sleeping. Belle was showering in the main bathroom and Anna was in the en suite. Heidi was sitting in the lounge with her feet tucked under her and hugging her legs. She gratefully accepted one of the coffees the boys had brought back for them all.

Bernie said, "Anna let her hair down last night. God only knows what she actually is, but I like her. And Viktoria is quite the party girl."

Heidi added, "And she seems pretty keen on you, Georgie boy. Happy days, hey?" George winked at her. She said, "I've never seen that side of Anna. You wouldn't believe she's the same person who came to that first meeting."

As Bernie signalled his agreement, Belle came out of the bathroom, casually wrapping a towel around herself as she did so. She said good morning to the boys, then went into the spare bedroom to get dressed.

Once she and Anna had joined the others, Belle said, "We could go for swim while others speak to doctors. What size are you boys? I will get you bathers as well."

Without thinking, they told her their sizes, but then Bernie said,

"We'll go down to the shop with you, Belle."

"They are not in shop; they are in bedroom."

Both the boys laughed. George said, "You girls sure take some keeping up with."

A sleepy and slightly hungover Jessica came out of her room with a hand to her head. "I'd better have a shower and get ready or we'll be late."

Heidi said, "The boys brought us all back a coffee, but yours will need to be heated, sleepyhead."

Jessica reached for it and said, "Thanks boys, this is going to help."

As she took it over to the microwave, Bernie picked up the guitar and absently strummed a few chords.

Heidi said, "I didn't know you played. Why haven't you mentioned it?"

"Just dabble a bit. Self-taught, and I'm about as good at it as I am at skiing." This got a chuckle from Jess and Heidi.

~

A very excited Henry ushered them inside. "How did the rest of the night go? You all looked ready for a big one."

Gingerly touching her head, Jessica replied, "It was great, maybe a little too great. I was suffering a bit when I first woke, but the boys' coffee and a nice shower seem to have done the trick."

"Well, come on through and I'll put another one on."

They went into the dining room and exchanged greetings with Catherine and Ursula. Over coffee, they swapped comments about how nice Jess's apartment and complex were, but the women noticed how keen the two doctors were to begin their discussion about Jess's illness and recovery.

Ursula suggested, "Let's go out to the deck, Heidi, so we can catch up. I'm sure the boys are keen to talk to Jessica and Anna."

Anna looked at Heidi and said, "You should come with us, Heidi. I have much to say and you should hear it as well. I am sorry, Ursula."

"Not at all. That's fine, Anna. You go with them, Heidi. We can catch up later."

Henry said, "We can go into the study if you like. I'll just get another chair."

Henry's study was quite an elaborate affair. It was a large room and had a bookcase, filled with medical books, extending across one entire wall. There was a large desk that housed a computer with several other books strewn across it. Human nervous system charts hung on the walls. Towards one corner was a low table, around which they all sat. On the table was a scuffed up copy of Jessica's document, with numerous Post-it notes protruding from the pages.

There was an expectant hush around the table as they all looked at Anna.

Jessica broke the suspense, asking, "Anna, how did you make me well again?"

"I did not make you well again. My mother did."

This startled Jess. "Your mother?"

"Yes, your doctors were going to take too long." As she said this, she glanced towards Kurt, then Henry.

Jess said, "I didn't know about your mother. Did she come here with you?"

"No, she came alone. She made Belle and me after she got here. She made us like Viktoria."

The two doctors were staring wide eyed at Anna. They were expecting a very unusual conversation, but could not believe, or make any sense of, what they were hearing. Jessica and Heidi were also stunned by her comment.

Heidi jumped into the conversation. "Your mother didn't make Viktoria?"

"No, she was already here."

"How did she make you, Anna?"

"I am not to tell you this."

"How did she make Jess get better?"

"I am not to tell you this either. But it does not matter, because Jessica is fixed now, and you have paper to tell how you can do this for everyone." She smiled at Jess as she was talking.

Henry interrupted them. "Yes, thank you, and please thank your mother for this." He reached over and picked up the document, flicking through the pages. "Could you tell us how she knows all this about MS?"

"My mother knows many things."

"Where is your mother from, Anna?"

"She is from far away, but she is here now."

Kurt had been staring wide eyed at Anna during the preceding conversation. He went out on a limb and, with a croaky voice, almost whispered, "Anna, when you say your mother is from far away, do you mean far away as from another planet?"

"Yes."

That one word sat Kurt and Henry back in their seats. They were speechless. Their faces were vacant, and they felt a little dizzy.

Kurt recovered enough to ask, "And she will share her knowledge with us, like she did with the document on MS?"

"Some of it, perhaps—when you are ready."

"Anna, Henry and I have already discussed this. We're going to pursue this line of research, but genetic engineering on humans is a highly controversial and tightly regulated area. It is a staggering breakthrough in itself to have identified the sequence of the complications that cause the disease, but to also provide a solution is truly remarkable."

Anna interrupted him. "Yes, slightly abnormal physiological conditions cause myelin protein to misfold. My mother has included code of gene for protein that will refold it to correct shape under these conditions. Gene has appropriate control sequences and will only be expressed when necessary. You already possess technology to produce it."

Both doctors looked at her in amazement. Jessica appeared to be about to say something when Anna continued. "But yes, genetic engineering requires careful thought. And in organism as complex as human, there is much scope for things going awry. Not in this case though. My mother is sure it will work as designed."

She pointed a finger at the two doctors. "But my mother does not have laboratory; she has simulated all this in her mind. Testing is work for you. She is glad you like her paper."

The two doctors looked back with blank faces.

Henry asked, "She can tell how proteins will fold?" It almost came out, not as a question, but as a statement. One he found enthralling.

"Yes, it is about physics and chemistry—science. And mathematics."

"And staggering computational power. Anna, we cannot do the

necessary calculations to determine that yet. It's too complicated."

Anna shrugged. "We know this."

Kurt picked up from where he had been interrupted. "Well, we're going to start on it straight away. But there are years, perhaps decades, of research and testing to be done. And a lot of collaboration with others will be necessary. Some other doctors, but mostly biochemists and molecular biologists. In fact, they will do most of the work. And the research and results will need to be published. Your mother's document needs to be submitted for publication as well. We'll have to cite the author. Could you ask her for permission and what is her name? And if this is done, will she be in any danger?"

"I have already told you; my mother is not in any danger. You cannot cite her; no one will understand. But this is what she wants. She wants to help you. You can do your research and publish your papers. Do not mention anything about my mother."

Henry asked, "Anna, why did you say you wouldn't tell us how your mother made Jessica well again, when it's all described in the document?"

"My mother fixed Jessica by another method. She does not want me to discuss this. It is technology she does not want you to know about." As she finished saying this, she again smiled at Jess.

Heidi said, "Anna, it was so nice of you and Belle to come and celebrate with Jess. Why didn't your mother come as well?"

"My mother could not come. This is not possible."

Jessica said, "Well, that makes me truly sad. I'd love to thank her personally."

"She knows this; I have told her. She is happy."

Heidi chimed back in. "Do you talk with your mother often, Anna?"

"Yes, I can speak to her whenever I want to."

"Can you speak to her right now?"

"Yes."

"And she can speak to you whenever she wants to as well?"

"She can speak to me whenever I want her to." Then, accompanied by a flutter of her hand, she continued rather cheekily, "Which is most of time."

"And Belle and Viktoria can do the same."

"Belle can, but Viktoria—no, she cannot. This is why my mother gave her communication device."

"So, you and Belle are not like Viktoria?"

"We are just like her, except for that … and some other things."

"What other things, Anna?"

Anna shrugged and waved her hand dismissively. "It is just we are smarter than her, this is all."

Seeing the opportunity to gain some more knowledge about their activities, Heidi said, "Well, I'm pleased Belle could come. When I was last talking to her, she told me she was busy."

"Yes, she wanted to come. Her work is going well. So is mine."

"What's Belle working on?"

"She is working on science and climate change. You have helped with this. Thank you."

"Well, I didn't do much, and I've got to tell you, it was very exciting going to Europe. Thank you."

Anna smiled at her. Kurt looked at both of them with a puzzled expression. How was Heidi so mixed up with the aliens?

Heidi asked, "What are you working on, Anna?"

"I have been working on medicine and fixing Jessica. This is done now. And I have been speaking with US military. With Bethany's commander."

"Anna, we're all sorry about what happened to Viktoria, but it was only a small number of them who did that. There are lots of good Americans as well. Please don't punish them all."

"Yes, we know this. We will stop any further harm to Viktoria. We love her. And we love Jessica and you too, Heidi. We love you very much."

Heidi and Jessica both spoke at once. "We love you too, Anna."

The two doctors again exchanged puzzled looks. What did Heidi mean about punishing Americans? Did it have anything to do with their president?

Anna looked towards the doctors and stated, "You have much to do now. You will be busy as well. My mother will be watching with interest."

This pulled them back into focus. Henry looked intently at Anna and said, "When we are studying your document, we're going to get a little lost from time to time. Would you come and visit us and help us understand the things that we find puzzling?"

"Yes, I will do this, but everything is explained in paper."

"Anna, you keep referring to this as a paper. Is that what your mother calls it?"

"Yes, is science paper. This is how scientists share their information." She seemed a little puzzled by the question.

"Well, it's the most comprehensive paper I've ever read. Not only is the content staggering in its detail, but it is so beautifully written."

Anna lowered her eyes at the compliment but did not reply.

"You've read the paper, have you, Anna?"

"Yes."

"And you understand it all?"

"Yes."

The two doctors exchanged looks.

Heidi wanted to pursue something Anna had said previously. "Your mother, Anna, you said she can watch things."

"Yes. If she wants to."

"I bet she gets a little confused and disillusioned by what she sees."

"Yes, she finds humans fascinating. You are all the same, but you are all so different. There are still many things she does not understand about you, and why you act in way you do."

"Well, there are people who would very much like to know things about your mother as well. They would be fascinated to meet her."

"One day, perhaps. But for now, you can speak to Belle and me."

"Yes, Anna. And thank your mother for letting us do that." Heidi paused while she considered something else. "Judith and our government will most likely want to know what you've told us. Should we tell them, Anna?"

"No, my mother has been watching your government. She does not want to speak to them. If you tell Judith, she will just tell them, so don't tell her either. If they are upset Kurt and Henry have paper, say I gave it to them. I do not answer to your government."

"OK. But she'll realise you've met them if I tell her you gave it to them."

"Yes. But my mother will be watching them as well. If your

government tries to harm them, she will stop it." Anna looked at the two dumbfounded doctors and gave a reassuring smile.

Heidi said, "It's very unpredictable how the government will act. They are trying to keep you being here a secret. If you find you have to intervene, please keep any force you use non-lethal this time."

Anna did not immediately reply, instead she just stared at Heidi.

After several seconds of silence, she said, "Tell Judith I have given paper to Kurt and Henry. Tell her no one must interfere with them or their research. We will punish anyone who attempts to."

"Anna, people can act irrationally when under stress. Please show some restraint."

"Yes, you can catch up with your mother now, Heidi. We are finished here." Anna looked at Jessica and added, "Mr Hamilton is well now."

Jess snapped her head towards Anna. "What do you mean?"

Anna just smiled at her and stood up. She reached out and shook hands with the two doctors, who had stood to join her. "We wish you well with your research. I will go now. I want to go swimming with my sisters."

There was a brief blue flash and Anna was no longer in the room.

~

Kurt and Henry were staring at the spot from which she had disappeared. Jessica was doing the same, but she was still wondering what Anna had meant about Mr Hamilton.

After several seconds of silence, Heidi said, "Well, now you know about Anna. Amazing, isn't she?"

Kurt recovered enough to reply. "Words cannot describe her, in any language that I can speak, anyway. And to just disappear like that —do you think she is some kind of advanced hologram or something?"

"No, Dad, she's very real. She can touch you and vice versa: can eat and drink, can carry things, can sign papers, can even play the piano. Both Jess and I have seen her do it. That's how she travels around. She can make things appear and disappear. She gave me the device I called her on the night I gave you the document."

Still a little stunned, Kurt turned to Henry and said, "You realise we've just been handed a Nobel Prize."

Henry shook his head in disbelief and said, "I can't believe it.

Aliens! Here with us. And we've just been talking with one of them."

Heidi said, "Yes. You would not believe what else they can do and have done. But you are better off not knowing. National secrets and all that. And we're not allowed to talk about it. But you can go ahead with the MS research. And Jess and I won't get into any trouble because it was Anna who gave it to you. Well, close enough anyway."

Heidi hugged Jess and said, "Exciting, isn't it? I can just tell everything's going to work out."

"Yes, I think so too—I wonder what she meant about Mr Hamilton?"

"I don't know. Who is he? And what's wrong with him?"

"He's the nicest man. I didn't know anything was wrong with him."

Heidi looked at her, encouraging further elaboration.

Jess explained, "Mr and Mrs Hamilton are farmers. They live near the town where I grew up. I used to think of them as being rich, but that was before I started rubbing shoulders with medical specialists."

She winked at Henry and Kurt and received smiles from both of them.

She continued on. "I didn't know them at all, but one day when I was in grade 10, I was called to the principal's office. He said he knew the Hamiltons and that he had told them how smart I was. He explained to me they had offered to pay for me to go away to a boarding school in the city for grades 11 and 12 if I wanted to. And he encouraged me to do so—explaining it would allow me to further my education and be able to pursue any career I wanted to. The only stipulation being I wasn't to talk about it in public. My parents weren't having a bar of it, of course, but I pleaded with them to let me go. It's a long story in itself, but they finally relented. I couldn't understand why the Hamiltons did it, but apparently they are a childless couple who have a soft spot for smart kids from the bush. I later found out they'd funded some others previously, and for all I know, they could still be doing it."

She had a look of sadness pulling at her features. It remained for a few moments, a poignant insight into her thoughts. Then it faded as a faraway look entered her eyes. She was back in a happy place.

"You'd probably find them a bit rough and ready, and if you passed them in the street, you wouldn't give them a second glance. But to me, they are everything that is good about this world. Just goes to show; you can't judge a book by its cover."

She rubbed her hands together, her eyes positively sparkling now.

"Anyway, off I went to Somerville House for grades 11 and 12. It was the best thing ever. Way different from anything I'd experienced at home. It opened up the world to me. I got good enough marks to go to uni and ended up studying medicine at Griffith. The Hamiltons paid for my accommodation there as well. I'll never be able to repay them for what they've done for me, but the funny thing is, they say I already have. They came down to my graduation to help me celebrate. They were so happy for me. You will never meet anyone like them — they're the salt of the earth."

Heidi said, "What a wonderful story, Jess—you're just full of surprises. They must be the nicest people. You've got to find out what's wrong with Mr Hamilton, well was wrong with him. Sounds like he's better now, whatever it was."

Kurt said, "Yes, we're all interested to find out."

"I will. I'm sorry I went on so long about them, but they mean the world to me."

Heidi blinked to clear her eyes before hugging Jess again.

She said, "Now everybody, obviously no talking about Anna to anyone. You don't want them thinking you're mad or anything."

Kurt stood and said, "Let's go out and join the others. I, for one, need a drink. A stiff one."

Henry reached out and grabbed Kurt's arm. "I think we're going to have to tell Catherine and Ursula some of what Anna has just told us. It's bound to come out eventually and I think it should come from us. But swear them to secrecy, of course."

Heidi said, "I'm not sure it's a good idea to tell them everything at this stage. If Anna wanted them to know, she would've asked them along as well. But yes, I guess we'll have to tell them something. They'd already be aware the origin of the document has you intrigued. And some of Anna's comments last night must have them bamboozled. I'll leave it to you to decide what to tell them. But it's essential that whatever it is, it goes no further."

~

They went back out and joined the others, explaining that Anna had suddenly been called away by her other friends.

Catherine started preparing lunch. She insisted she didn't need any help, and asked, "Why don't you two have the chat you had planned?"

Ursula was keen for this. She took Heidi out to the deck so they could be alone. As they left, Kurt shook his head slightly while looking at Ursula. She noticed, but she didn't understand the meaning behind it.

~

Once they were by themselves, Ursula said, "That was surprising, Anna just leaving without saying goodbye. She seemed so polite up to now."

"Yes, she's always polite. But she doesn't get to see her sisters that often, and being triplets, they're extremely close. They wanted to spend some time together."

Her mother didn't look as though this explanation convinced her. She said, "Heidi, darling, I don't want you to end up getting hurt here. Are you sure that Bernie is still interested in you? He seems to be very close to Anna. Maybe your little group is too tight for you to notice."

Heidi shook her head vigorously, "No, Mum. Bernie and I are fine. Really. We're both good friends with Anna. She's the best friend anyone could have in this world. Believe me. Dad knows a bit more about her now. He'll fill you in later."

"OK darling, I just thought I should bring it up. That's all. Anyway, you all looked so happy together last night."

Heidi smiled and said, "Yes, Mum, we were. It was a great night."

Their conversation became a general catch up on each other's news.

After a few more minutes, Ursula said, "We really should go in and help Catherine."

She put her arm around Heidi and hugged her.

Heidi hugged her back and said, "No more talk about Bernie and me. We're fine, really."

She smiled reassuringly to her mother as they turned towards the house. She appeared to mean what she had just said, but the seeds of doubt had begun to sprout.

~

Jess wanted to chase up on Mr Hamilton's health. Calling her parents wouldn't be of any use. And it would open old wounds. She called her brother—did he know anything? No, not that he had anything to do with the Hamiltons either. But he'd quietly ask around.

After he got back to her, she was still none the wiser. That wasn't all that surprising. Mr Hamilton would most likely keep it to himself, anyway. She was reluctant to cold-call him and ask personal questions about his health, so she decided it'd have to wait until she could find the time for a visit to her hometown.

She usually visited her parents for Christmas, in her ongoing attempts at reconciliation. But that was months away. She didn't want to wait that long. She decided the perfect excuse for a visit was to go out for their upcoming thirtieth wedding anniversary. And maybe this time, they could bury the hatchet. She was certainly ready to.

28

Once Belle returned from Jessica's celebrations, she got straight back to work. She rang Ingrid and told her she had something to give her.

They met at the same hotel she had stayed at previously. Belle was sitting at a table sipping coffee, and as she approached the table, Ingrid greeted her in Swedish. They exchanged pleasantries as Ingrid took a seat and signalled to the waitress she would like to order.

As the waitress left, Belle asked, "Have you spoken to your superiors about what we discussed?"

"Not really. I don't quite know how to broach the subject. I'm sorry, but I'm only a junior officer at work and don't get involved in decisions on our country's policies, or anything to do with EU issues."

"But you work for EU delegate. You travel to their meetings."

"Yes, Belle, but I don't actually attend the meetings or have any input at all. I'm just an assistant there to provide background information and do any searches for documents required by the delegate."

"We like what your country is attempting to achieve regarding climate change. And for your concern for less affluent countries. EU countries help each other and resolve issues without resorting to armed conflict. This is good. I want to speak with your government to help progress your work, but I realise they will not meet with me if I approach them directly; they will think I have nothing of value to add to discussion. I have paper you can show them. It will get their attention. You can tell them I gave it to you and want to meet them to speak about it. You can show it to Lars if you want to; he will understand implications and benefits it will provide."

They were interrupted by the waitress delivering Ingrid's coffee. After thanking her and waiting for her to leave, Ingrid said, "OK, that'll work. But I don't know anything about you. What's your background? Who will I say wants to meet with them, and what's the paper about?"

Belle took a sip of coffee, her face reflecting her pleasure at its taste, then waved her hand almost dismissively. "Tell them I am scientist. That I know these things. Paper is about energy. When they read it, they will want to meet with me, and will include people with appropriate knowledge. Actually, tell them they should include Lars —it will be nice to have someone there I know."

"OK, but you're so young, Belle. I don't think they'll believe you when you tell them you're a scientist."

"They will want to speak about paper. I will answer questions. We do not understand why you think young people do not know things."

"It's just that education takes time. That's all."

"Very well. Here is paper." As she was talking, she handed Ingrid a USB stick.

"Thank you, Belle. Can I show this to Lars before I take it to work? Just so I've got an idea of what it contains."

"Yes, of course. You can show him tonight."

Ingrid thanked her with a smile before taking another sip.

Now that she had satisfactorily resolved things, Belle thought it was time to practise her social skills with small talk.

"Sweden is nice country. So is Australia. You have visited?"

"No, I've only travelled within Europe so far. But I'd like to visit there someday. Lars very much enjoyed his time there." Ingrid smiled as she said this. "Your accent, Belle, it certainly isn't Australian. Is it Eastern European?"

"Yes, I am from Ukraine."

"I've never been there either, but I understand it's a lovely country."

"Yes, it was home when I was young. But not much money then. It is good though; makes you appreciate things you have."

Ingrid finished her coffee and looked at her watch. "Well, I had better be off if I am going to get back to work on time. Thanks for calling. It was great to catch up. Could you give me your number so I can contact you? And thank you again for this." She waved the memory stick briefly, then placed it in her bag.

"You are welcome. Do not worry about paying, I will look after it." Belle gave her a phone number. "Careful what you say on phone, others can listen. Just use it to tell me you want to meet."

~

Ingrid had given Belle's paper to her boss and explained how they had met. She added she knew very little about her, but that she had requested a meeting be arranged to discuss the paper's contents. She also mentioned the two of them had talked at length about the effects of climate change. It seemed to be a topic Belle was extremely interested in.

It turned out they were indeed very eager to meet with her. Ingrid was excited to have been invited as well; she had been informed of the list of attendees and had never been in the company of such an esteemed group of people.

She didn't understand anything in the document she had shown Lars. He didn't understand much of it either, but he had told her it contained unbelievably detailed information about chemical reactions.

~

The meeting room was buzzing with several overlapping conversations. Some of those present gathered around the large oblong table in the centre of the room. Others were near a separate table in one corner that contained an urn and cups, conversing while sipping coffee or selecting from the plates of finger food spread across its surface. Mounted on opposite walls were large computer monitors displaying the government logo.

The buzz of conversation died when Ingrid and a young woman, perhaps twenty years of age, entered the room. Those present realised this must be the mysterious donor of the document.

Ingrid took Belle over to her boss, Sara Eriksson, and introduced her as the Minister for EU Affairs. She introduced the Prime Minister. He called everyone to order and requested they all take a seat. After waiting until everyone was comfortable, he proceeded with the introductions.

Once this formality was out of the way, he continued, "Thank you for sharing this document with us, Belle. And for coming here to discuss it. Unfortunately, I don't understand the technical details it contains, but I've invited people along with the knowledge to discuss it with you. They have read it and cannot wait to talk to you about it."

"Yes, thank you for seeing me. And thank you for being such forward-thinking country. We are pleased to share this with you, and I will answer questions."

He gestured towards the monitor facing him, which now displayed the opening page of the document, and said, "Perhaps we could start by you explaining to those of us present who are not professional chemists or engineers what it's about. In simple terms that we'll be able to understand."

"Yes, it is about fuel cell. Has extremely high energy density and is very efficient. It does not contain any dangerous or polluting chemicals, reactions involved are reversible and with appropriate catalyst extremely rapid. Refuelling—or recharging—system is fast. Limiting factor is available energy input."

Belle could see the interest emblazoned on her audience's faces. They were hanging on her every word.

"Once you have developed this technology, you can power all your mobile equipment using it. Not only passenger vehicles, but heavy machinery for industry and agriculture. Even aviation. This will rid you of dependence on so-called fossil fuels."

Belle had finished her explanation, but her abrupt halt surprised her audience. She looked around the table as she patiently awaited their reaction.

It was the Prime Minister who broke the silence. "Do you mean we'll be able to power all our vehicles using it, including shipping and aircraft?"

"Yes."

An excited buzz flowed around the group.

"Before I hand the floor over to our technical experts, who I can assure you are chafing at the bit, let me thank you again for this. Could you tell us what country you're from? We're very keen to collaborate with them when developing the technology."

"You are only ones we have spoken to about this. It is our gift to you. We want to help you, and to repay you for being such generous country. We know you will share this with others."

"We feel very honoured. Your Swedish is excellent, by the way, but you have an Eastern European accent. Are you perhaps Russian?" he pressed, desperate to discover her origins and that of the document.

"No, I am from Ukraine. But their scientists do not know about this."

"I understand you know some Australians as well. Can we contact them to discuss it?"

"Yes, we have friends in Australia. I know them, but it is mainly my sister who speaks to them. She speaks about other things, but not about this."

She paused and looked around the room. It was obvious she had their rapt attention. The professionals were struggling to contain their enthusiasm. The Prime Minister recognised this and invited comment from them.

The chemistry professor immediately jumped in. His voice was high pitched with excitement. "Young lady, may I address you as Belle? I don't think we've been told your surname. Your knowledge and understanding of chemistry is extraordinary. This document has been a revelation to us. Could you please tell us where you studied? We would love to meet your supervisors."

Accompanied by an enigmatic smile, Belle gestured by opening both her hands, palms facing upwards.

"You may consider me home schooled. My mother told me these things."

"Your mother told you?" the professor gasped. He stared at her blankly. "Belle, you don't understand these things in such exquisite detail by merely being told them. It takes decades of study to gain the background to learn the basics. And this is so far ahead of anything any of us have even contemplated. Your mother must be a genius. Please, you must tell us about the lab where she works."

"One day perhaps. But for now, we just want you to have this. Paper will guide you through chemistry, but catalyst is key."

She drew a line on the table with her finger.

"Atomic alignment must be precise to allow for efficient electron tunnelling. It is bio-molecule—protein-metal ion chelate. Structure depends on hydronium ion concentration of solvent."

She lifted her hand and wriggled her fingers.

"At critical concentration structure alters and action of active site catalyses reverse reaction. Paper does not describe precise composition of catalyst or how to produce it, but I have brought sample with me. For your research. Once you have systems developed, we will assist with technology to produce it."

The Professor excitedly reached for the mouse and quickly navigated through the document to display the section he wanted to pursue further. The monitors on the walls were filled with detailed chemical equations and confusing mathematical formulae. Confusing to him, that is; they were completely bewildering to the non-chemists in the room.

"Some of my colleagues and I have read your document several times, but we are still coming to grips with the detail. It'll take us some time to fully understand it. And the catalyst's action can be reversed by simply altering the applied voltage?"

"Yes."

"It's difficult to grasp how it has such a dramatic effect on the reaction."

"To understand this, you first have to understand electron. What it actually is. Your current understanding is"—she paused, casting her gaze upwards as she searched for the appropriate term, then again gestured with her hands—"confused."

He looked intently at her, then, in a tone that was almost reverent, whispered, "You can help us understand the electron?"

"Yes."

The politicians in the room understood very little about chemistry and almost nothing about electrons, but they understood body language. And they could glean from that being exhibited by the professor at the moment the enormity of the message behind the deceptively simple word that had just been uttered.

He took a moment to recover. "Well, Belle, we're going to need some other scientists here with us when we discuss that. Ones with expertise in fields that I only have a cursory knowledge of." He looked towards the electrical engineering professor, who was just staring at Belle with his mouth agape.

The next half hour or so was spent with the two of them in a discussion that no one else in the room understood. Not even the electrical engineering professor. It was an animated conversation. No one interrupted, though, everyone marvelling at the incongruous sight of the most eminent professor of chemistry in the country, effectively being lectured by a young woman just out of her teens.

Towards the end of their conversation, he said, "You said you brought a sample of the catalyst?"

"Yes," as she said this, Belle reached for her handbag and took out a vial containing an orange liquid.

She handed it to Ingrid, who was sitting beside her. Ingrid passed it straight to the professor. He held it up to the light and looked at it in awe. If what she was saying was true, he was holding the most precious substance on the planet.

Belle looked towards the engineering professor and said, "There are no internal losses when using this catalyst. Losses are in external circuits. We will help you develop room temperature superconductor to eliminate this."

She reached into her bag again and took out another container housing what appeared to be a reel of lustrous silver cotton. She also handed this to Ingrid.

"Here is sample of superconductor. For research. It is covered in insulation and you must be careful not to wave it around with the ends connected, but you know this of course."

The engineering professor just stared at Belle. He felt a little disoriented, giddy even.

Who is this girl?

It was obvious the chemistry professor was agog with the knowledge she had shared, but this was the Holy Grail. Room temperature superconductors! If that were true, it would change everything, not just rapid and efficient recharging.

Belle interrupted his thoughts, and those of the other attendees, when she looked at the Minister of EU Affairs and said, "So pleased to meet you, Sara. I have been wanting to speak with you for some time now. Perhaps we can meet later? And it would be nice if Malin came as well."

Sara was a little shocked by this sudden change in topic. She looked at Belle, wondering why she wanted to talk to her specifically.

And have the Minister of Climate and the Environment along as well. She knew nothing about chemistry, or electrons. But she remembered being told Belle was also interested in climate change. She assumed their conversation would revolve around this.

"Yes, of course, Belle. Any time suitable for you is fine with me. Malin?"

The Minister of Climate and the Environment showed her willingness to take part. "Absolutely. I'll make myself available whenever you wish to discuss anything at all with me."

Belle said, "Perhaps in next few days then, once you organise it?"

"That'll be fine, Belle. What, in particular, do you wish to discuss? And what time of the day will suit you best?"

"At 10 o'clock, I will come to your office. We can speak about your influence at EU."

"OK, Belle. My office is on the fifth floor of this building. We can arrange for you to be picked up if that suits."

"Thank you, I am staying at Scandic Triangeln."

"Could we please make the meeting for later in the week? We'll need a little time to prepare ourselves."

Belle stood up and said, "Yes, please tell me when you arrange it. Ingrid has my number. I will go now. Excuse me."

The Prime Minister jumped to his feet and said, "Please, Belle, have some refreshments before you leave." As he said this, he pointed at the table in the corner.

Belle smiled and accepted. "Thank you, perhaps a little."

As she selected something to eat, the two professors approached her.

The electrical engineer said, "You are serious about the superconductor?"

"Yes."

He extended his hand and said, "My dear, I do not know who you are or where you've gained your education, but I am very much looking forward to working with you."

Belle accepted his hand and said, "Yes, you will soon have much work to do." She pointed at the chemist and added, "As will you."

He bobbed his head enthusiastically. "And so too our particle physicists."

Belle looked back at Ingrid and said, "I will go now. Thank you, Ingrid. Good afternoon everyone."

~

When Ingrid returned to the room after escorting Belle from the building, it felt to her as if the very air vibrated with anticipation. Sara immediately approached her.

"This is all fascinating and so promising, Ingrid, but we've been discussing that it's imperative we find out more about that remarkable young woman and the origins of the information and materials she has given us. It must be from Russia. My God, they're far more advanced than anyone suspected. Professor Engström has even described it as other-worldly. Everything must remain top secret, but we simply have to find out what's going on. Could you contact your Australian friends and see if you can find out anything about her?"

"Actually, I don't really know them, but the woman who introduced Belle to us is a friend of my husband, Lars." She beckoned Lars over to join them. "Lars, we need to find out more about Belle. Do you think you could ring Heidi and ask her if she'll talk to us about her?"

"I can try."

He rang the number Heidi had used to call him. It surprised him to find it was disconnected. His last option was her parents' landline number.

"Hello, this is Kurt Almendinger."

"Hi, Dr Almendinger, this is Lars Backlund. I hope you're keeping well. I'm trying to contact Heidi regarding a mutual friend, but I don't have her number. Would it be possible for you to help us contact her?"

"Hello, Lars. We haven't talked in ages. Are you still in Sweden and what are you doing with yourself?"

Lars thought he detected a little reservation in his voice.

"Yes, I'm still in Sweden, happily married now. I miss Australia though. I had such a great time there and made such good friends, none more so than Heidi. She visited us recently while she was holidaying in Europe, and I'm trying to contact a friend she had with her. But the number she contacted me on is disconnected. I tried her old number from when I was over there, but it doesn't work either."

This news further startled Kurt. Heidi holidaying in Europe? Then he remembered her talking to Anna about travelling there. At the time, he had overlooked it because of all the other excitement. Lars wanting to contact Heidi had Anna written all over it. He wasn't going to talk about any of this on the phone, let alone give Lars Heidi's contact details.

He said, "Lars, it's probably better if I let her know you're chasing her. She can contact you when she gets the chance. She has your number, I take it."

"Thank you so much, Dr Almendinger, yes, but I'll give it to you again just in case. I'm sorry to have troubled you."

Lars added his number, and they said their goodbyes. He looked at the others in his group. "That conversation was a little strange. Dr Almendinger was always so polite and engaging when I was over there. I think he must know about Belle all right but didn't want to talk about it on the phone. This whole thing is so intriguing. I guess we just have to wait to see if Heidi calls back."

29

Heidi took out her device and called Anna.

"Anna, there's something I want to talk to you about. Could you please come and see me?"

"Yes, of course, Heidi. I will come now."

The call terminated and Anna appeared in the room.

She greeted her with her usual cheek kisses. "What do you want to speak about, Heidi?"

"Well, I've just had a call from Dad. He told me Lars had called, and he was trying to contact me. About a mutual friend. I assume that's Belle. What should I do, Anna?"

"You can do whatever you want to, Heidi."

"Thanks, but I want your advice on this. I don't want to do anything that would upset you or your mother."

"Nothing you do will upset my mother or me. We love you."

Heidi rubbed Anna's arm in response. "Should I contact Lars to find out what he wants? Or maybe you can tell me now; you probably already know."

"Yes, Belle is helping their government. He told them you know her. They want to speak about this."

"And I can talk about her with them?"

"Yes, of course."

Heidi smiled momentarily, but then it turned into a frown.

"Belle is helping their government? I thought you didn't want to talk to governments."

"Their government is different from yours. My mother likes them."

"OK, that's settled then. I'll return Lars' call. Thanks for coming, Anna."

~

Heidi rang Lars. He was still at the meeting, enjoying the refreshments and engaged in conversation with a very excited professor of engineering. They were both looking at the reel of superconductor he was holding while they contemplated all the possibilities it promised.

Lars was excited when his phone vibrated in his pocket. The only call he was expecting was associated with his previous request. But surely not this soon—only a few minutes had passed since then.

"Hello, this is Lars," he said in Swedish, just in case.

Heidi replied in English, "Hi, Lars. It's Heidi. Dad said you were trying to contact me."

It was her! His heart skipped a few beats with anticipation.

"Yes, Heidi, just a minute. There are some other people here with me who'd like to be part of this conversation. You don't mind if I put you on speaker?"

"That's fine with me. You have me intrigued by what this is all about."

He beckoned the others to come close and explained he had Heidi on the line as they crowed around expectantly.

"OK, I have you on speaker. The Prime Minister and several other government ministers are with me, also some professors."

The list of people at the other end of her call surprised Heidi, and she hardly registered their combined hellos.

Then Lars continued, "Heidi, Belle has given us the most amazing document. We're all so excited. Our experts are stunned at the information shared, and at Belle's exceptional depth of knowledge. I could go on, but, in a nutshell, we know that we're dealing with something incredibly special here. We've got no idea how to interpret the situation."

He caught his breath and exchanged a querying glance with the others.

"The reason for my call is that she was quite vague about where all this comes from. She did mention she has friends in Australia, and I know you're one of them. We're very keen to talk to you to find out if you can shed some light on what's going on."

"OK. But not on the phone. It'll have to be in person."

The Swedes exchanged glances and excitedly gestured they'd be happy to travel to Australia for the meeting.

"OK, Heidi, we'll arrange for a delegation to go over. I'm sure we can get it arranged within a couple of weeks."

"Lars, it'd be far easier if I go over there."

"You don't mind? We don't want to put you at any inconvenience."

"It won't be any trouble, Lars, believe me."

Frantic hand signals were being exchanged amongst the group.

"OK, but my government will pay your fares, of course. As a treat, I'm sure I can persuade them to fly you first class."

"Thanks for the offer, but that won't be necessary. I've got plenty of frequent flyer points."

"All right then, doesn't look as if things have changed much with you, Miss Independent."

Heidi chuckled in reply. "Good, all settled. I'll fly over tomorrow if that suits you. Of course, it's a 30-hour flight, so it'll be the next day or two before we can meet."

"What, so soon? Surely you won't be able to organise your flights so quickly?"

"I have friends in high places. Let's just leave it at that for the moment. See you when I get there."

The meeting attendees exchanged puzzled but excited looks.

The Prime Minister said, "Thank you, ladies and gentlemen. Let's hope Heidi can throw some light on things when she gets here. That conversation just made things more confusing. And it's obvious she's holding things back. I guess we'll have to wait for her to get here. And not a word about any of this until we figure out what's going on."

~

A couple of days later, as promised, Heidi walked into the government building and introduced herself to reception, informing them she'd like to talk with the Prime Minister.

Normally, this would have met with a polite rebuff, but the

events of the previous two days were anything but normal. There had been a flurry of activity with meetings amongst ministers and a constant stream of scientists coming and going. The Prime Minister had also informed them he was expecting her.

He rushed down to reception to greet her personally.

"Ms Almendinger, it is indeed a pleasure to meet you. Thank you for coming over so promptly. Would you like something to eat or drink?" He held out his hand in welcome.

"And you, sir. Thank goodness your English is so good. Unfortunately, I don't speak much Swedish, and what little I did learn was some time ago now. Perhaps a coffee, thank you. I've already eaten, but with the time difference, I feel a little jet lagged. And coffee is certainly the answer to that." She smiled as she withdrew her hand. "Actually, it's the answer to a lot of things."

"Yes, of course. Everyone who was on our end of your phone call has gathered in one of our conference rooms. It's been non-stop meetings over here. I'll arrange for a coffee to be brought up. How do you have it?"

"Flat white with no sugar, thank you. Lead the way."

When they entered the conference room, Lars greeted her with a hug. "Heidi, thanks for coming back over here. We're so thrilled about Belle's document. Can you tell us anything about her? She has us all enthralled."

Heidi was expecting this, and had discussed with Anna what she should tell them when she had arranged for her transport here.

"She's an extremely intelligent young woman. She's entirely focused on the wellbeing of the planet, and as a whole, not just on us and our impact on the environment—she has a holistic view of the entire biosphere."

The chemistry professor could not contain himself. "Yes, Ms Almendinger, but what about her extraordinary knowledge of chemistry? Do you know where she studied?"

"I can confirm it wasn't in Australia. I've only met her recently myself, and the situation's very complex. But the important thing for you to realise is she knows what she's talking about."

The Prime Minister pressed, "She told us she has a sister who lives in Australia and that she is engaged in discussions with you. Are they related to energy storage and chemistry by any chance? We'd be very keen to collaborate with your country on this."

"Yes, she has a sister in Australia. I don't know a lot about her either. I met her and Belle at the same time. Our discussions with her are on another topic entirely. I can't help you with where they come from, or studied, but please believe me when I tell you that, despite their appearance, they are powerful young women who need to be taken seriously. They have extraordinary knowledge about a vast range of subjects. You should take whatever she told you as fact, no matter how impossible it may appear to you. Believe me, you won't meet anyone else like her." Heidi waved her hand before adding, "Unless you meet her sister, that is."

"That's disappointing. We were hoping for some insight into her origins. She has us all intrigued, even more so after listening to what you just told us. And we are taking her very seriously. To allow us to get a more complete picture of this, could you tell us what you're working on with her sister?"

"I'm sorry, not at this stage. But I assure you, it has nothing whatsoever to do with energy storage. You're on your own with this, unfortunately."

Heidi's coffee arrived, and the meeting broke up into small informal groups as they continued their discussions.

Eventually, after looking at her watch, Sara said, "Malin, it's time for our meeting with Belle. Heidi, would you like to come along and say hello?"

"I'd love to."

~

The three of them went down to wait at the reception desk.

Belle stopped momentarily as she came through the door. Then she hurried over to them, greeting Heidi with her habitual cheek-kissing.

"Hello, Heidi, it is surprise to see you here."

Heidi reached up and gently touched her hair, "Hi, Belle. You've changed your style. It looks great."

Belle did a twirl and struck a pose.

"Bob with curtain bangs, you like it, yes?"

"I love it … It's perfect for you."

Sara said, "Welcome back, Belle. I trust you had a comfortable night; the Scandic Triangeln is a wonderful place."

"Yes, thank you."

"Please, follow us. We can use one of our conference rooms."

Once there, they sat at the table, both ministers on one side and Belle and Heidi on the other.

Belle opened the discussion with her usual directness. "It is so important to maintain firm stance on climate change. It is crucial. EU is leading way with this. Of course, push back from some will continue, but you must remain resolute. It will be expensive to implement technology we have provided, but it will pay off in long run. Once you share it, there will be benefits for all."

Malin replied, "We're all very passionate about this, of course, both our country and me personally. What is a realistic time frame for developing the technology?"

"It is difficult to say. From our observations, we presume it will take some time. You are not good at this. But time is crucial. Your government must dedicate much resources and effort, and in meantime you should continue to push agenda."

Sara said, "Well, Belle, we're currently preparing a bill to fund the research and development. It has to remain top secret of course. We don't want word of it getting back to the Russians. Progress on it is now up to the professionals, but I can assure you that sufficient funding will be approved. And I'll continue to do everything in my power to keep climate change a central issue with the EU."

"Yes, we appreciate this. Perhaps you can arrange for me to meet with them."

"You mean with the EU?"

"Yes, I will attend their meeting. I have things to say to them."

"Belle, that might take a little time to arrange. It's somewhat unusual, but I will attempt to set it up. What, in particular, do you want to discuss?"

"I have some revelations to make. It is important they all hear it at same time."

Belle moved the conversation on. She flicked her gaze between the two ministers before looking at Heidi. "It is good Heidi is here. We can talk about another matter. Regenerative agriculture. This is something both your countries are working on."

30

Jess rang her brother. "Hey, Peter, what's planned for Mum and Dad's anniversary?"

"G'day, sis. Not much. We're just having dinner with them down at the RSL."

"Well, I'm coming out for it. But keep it a surprise."

"Do you think that's a good idea?"

"Yes. How are they, by the way?"

"Pretty good. Actually, I was over there the other day and they mentioned you. You know, without any ranting and raving. It was all fairly calm, in fact."

"That's a good sign. Maybe this time, hey?"

"I hope so, Jess. It breaks my heart, you know."

"Mine too, Peter. I'll get onto Cathy and stay with them. See you there. And just in case, you better bring some earmuffs."

Peter laughed. "Righto, will do."

~

Her brother picked her up from the airport and dropped her off at her friend's place. She waited there until her brother informed her that they were all at the restaurant.

Her mother spied her first. Her hands flew to her mouth. "What are you doing here?"

Jess continued her bold approach. "To celebrate with you, of course. Congratulations, both of you." She stooped and kissed them hello.

Her father breathed out audibly. "You're looking well."

Jess thought that was a positive sign. Maybe it would be this time.

"Yes, Dad, I feel on top of the world. If only we could get over all this, things would be perfect."

Her father looked down at the table, hesitated, then looked back up at her.

"Well, don't just stand there. Take a seat."

Jess went to an adjacent table and retrieved a spare chair, positioning it at one corner of their table. Manners in her family didn't run to anything like offering her their chair or assisting her to sit, but Peter and his wife subtly adjusted their positions to create some space for her.

Jess looked pleadingly at her mother. "Mum, can we please move on? What's done is done, and I don't regret my decision for a moment. What I regret is the damage it has wreaked on our relationship. Don't you think it's time?"

"I'm trying."

Jess smiled and reached over to rub her arm. "That's good enough for me, Mum."

Her father tried to ease the tension further. "Let's order. I don't need to look at the menu. I'm having the rump steak!"

Their conversation remained a little strained during the meal, but Peter and his wife were valiant in their attempts to keep it moving along.

When they did speak, Jess's parents reminisced about what they thought of as the most important events of the past thirty years. The stars of these were the births of both Jess and Peter.

As the evening wore down and they stood to leave, Jess's mother reached over and put her arm around her. "Thanks for coming, Jess. It was nice of you."

Jess held back a sob and formed a sad smile. "Thanks, Mum. I enjoyed it."

Peter was dropping Jess off, and when they got to his car, he reached in and retrieved a pair of earmuffs. "Things have certainly changed in the world, didn't even need them."

Jess hugged her brother. "You've got no idea how much, Peter. No idea."

~

The next morning, Jess called the Hamiltons. She told them she was in town visiting her parents and would like to catch up. She went out that afternoon.

The Hamiltons were standing on the verandah to greet her.

As she got out of her brother's car, which she'd borrowed for the trip, Mr Hamilton called out, "Hello Jess, this is an unexpected pleasure. Come on in, we've got the kettle on."

"Hello, Mr and Mrs Hamilton. I'm out here to celebrate my parents' thirtieth anniversary and couldn't come all this way without seeing you as well."

They exchanged hugs on the verandah and went inside.

Mrs Hamilton poured them all a cup of tea and put a plate of fruitcake on the table for them to share. She asked, "How's your work going, Jess? You must be so busy. Bert has been in hospital recently, and the doctors and nurses were amazing. You've chosen a wonderful career."

Jess feigned alarm and turned towards Mr Hamilton. "Have you been ill, Mr Hamilton?"

"Yes, Jess, but as Michelle said, you doctors are amazing. I'm all fixed up now. Good as new."

"Oh well, I'm so pleased to hear you're better. Mind if I ask what was wrong?"

"I had lung cancer. Apparently, it was quite advanced and inoperable. When they told me, I thought that was it—my race run."

He paused and shook his head. "As a last resort, they were treating me with something called immunotherapy, and it worked. I don't think they could believe it, but now I'm as good as gold. Can't remember feeling this good ever. They want me to go back each month for further tests. Apparently, I'm a case study. I don't understand much of what they were saying; boy you doctors use some big words. It's like a foreign language. Of course, I've agreed. I'm very thankful to them. It's finally got me to give up smoking as well. And I get a free ride on the government each month. Happy as Larry really."

Jess was lost for words.

Anna's mother can cure cancer as well!

Once she found her voice, she got up and hugged him. "That's so wonderful, Mr Hamilton. Sounds as though you were gravely ill. What you had is usually considered impossible to treat successfully, but you prevailed against the odds. Do you mind telling me where you were being treated?"

"I ended up at the Royal Brisbane Hospital. Michelle reckons you can keep those big cities. Doesn't know how you stand living in them." As he said this, he glanced towards his wife.

"I can understand, but I love my life on the Gold Coast. And my work. Of course, none of that'd be possible without you both. You know I'll be forever grateful."

"Nothing that we've done has given us more pleasure than seeing you develop into the wonderful person you've become, Jess. If we had any small part to play, that is our blessing."

Jess wiped back a tear and said, "Mr Hamilton, I think I finally understand what you mean."

Mrs Hamilton said, "He's as strong as a bull again, working from dawn to dusk. Things are really looking up for us at the moment. We changed our farming practices about the time you started uni. We think it's really paying off. Our pastures and crops are performing much better. It's like turning the clock back. Things are starting to look the way they did when we first moved here those many years ago. Cattle prices are through the roof at the moment as well, and we've had a good season, unlike those poor people in New South Wales with those dreadful bushfires."

"Yes, that was terrible, wasn't it? My heart goes out to them. As I've told you, I love my work and living on the Gold Coast, but I'm a country girl at heart. Whenever I'm out here, it feels like home. And I know only too well all the trials that go along with it."

They spent the rest of the day talking about how their farming methods had changed. Jess stayed for dinner, then drove back to town and returned her brother's car. She flew out the next morning.

31

Jess had been mulling over who and what to tell about Mr Hamilton and was now ready to discuss it with Heidi. She arranged to go down on her next day off.

Heidi picked her up from the airport and took her to her favourite coffee shop.

Jess said, "I've been to see Mr Hamilton. You're not going to believe it. He had lung cancer but has made a full recovery. Heidi, what can't Anna and her mother do?"

This news stunned Heidi. Her mouth hung open momentarily, then she answered, "I don't know, Jess. It's so exciting and so frightening at the same time. That's wonderful news about Mr Hamilton. Did you tell him you'd also been ill? Or anything about Anna and her involvement in his and your recoveries?"

Jess shook her head. "No—no need for that. I feigned surprise to learn he'd been ill. I didn't mention anything about Anna."

"That's for the best, but it'd be good for him to know you were involved, albeit indirectly."

"No, Heidi, I don't want to claim any involvement. Actually, this has made me realise the joy of helping someone just for the sake of it, with no expectation of anything in return. It's even a better feeling when they're completely unaware of your help. Now I understand why the Hamiltons helped me with my schooling. It's the most wonderful feeling, Heidi."

"You're such a nice person, Jess. I can see why Anna and her mother chose you, but I have no idea what they see in me."

"Heidi, you're the kindest person I've ever met. You were the first to console me at that meeting—oh my God, just think of all the things that set in motion."

"Thanks, Jess. Yes, it's unbelievable really."

"I need to talk to Anna about Mr Hamilton. First off, to thank her, of course, but also to discuss his recovery. His doctors are going to think their treatment cured him and will be led on a wild goose chase trying to work out how."

"OK, Jess, as soon as we finish our coffee we'll go back to mine and I'll call Anna. You'll see why when I call her, the way the device she gave me works is quite startling."

~

They sat at the dining table while Heidi activated her device.

"Anna, Jess is here with me, and she'd like to talk to you about Mr Hamilton."

"Hello, Jessica. Yes, I will come now." She arrived accompanied by the still startling blue flash.

They exchanged hugs and greetings.

Jess said, "Anna, could you thank your mother so much for curing Mr Hamilton? That was a wonderful thing to do."

Anna inclined her head and said, "Yes, she knows you are grateful."

"Anna, his doctors are going to think their treatment worked. That it was the cause of his recovery. It'll send them down the wrong path and waste their valuable time trying to work out how."

"But, Jessica, their treatment is not leading in wrong direction. It is one way to treat this type of cancer. There is much to do to fully develop it, but my mother has left clues in Mr Hamilton. It is good they are going to study him."

Jess hugged Anna and said, "That's wonderful, Anna. And they'll think they've made all the advances, so no need for them to know about you or your mother at all. This is a fantastic way to go ahead. Not only have you cured Mr Hamilton, but, in time, countless other people as well. We're so blessed you have come here." She considered something for a moment, then continued, "Are there clues in my body as well? Would it help if the doctors studied me also?"

"No, this will only confuse them. Their clues are in paper. My mother left no clues in your body. You are in perfect health; no more pain for you, Jessica." Anna smiled as she said this then, changing her focus to Heidi, continued, "You enjoyed trip to Sweden, yes?"

"Yes, Anna, it was very enlightening. I see what you meant when you said Belle is busy. And I suppose she told you about wanting me to help arrange their trade delegation coming here. To discuss cooperation on developing and implementing new farming practices."

"Yes. They are not new practices but returning to old ways. Your predecessors were very observant and much more in tune with nature. They found what worked, even if they did not understand why. With regard to agriculture, some of your Australian scientists and farmers are at forefront of research. Your country is ideal for this study because of ancient soils and only relatively recent intensive farming. Of course, it will take much work and funding to be widely accepted, but I am working on freeing up money from your budget for this."

"That's very exciting, Anna, and it'll help with climate change?"

"Yes. And health of planet."

"But it's so far from my field of expertise. How can I help?"

"You can tell Prime Minister we would like them to welcome Swedish delegation to discuss this. Belle will go to meetings."

"I don't have access to the Prime Minister, Anna. Anyway, don't you think the request would be better coming directly from you?"

"No, my mother wants this. It will help with her study of humans, on how you behave and what motivates you."

"OK then, I'll try. What did you mean when you said you were working on making money available?"

"I hope you will know this soon. It is also part of my mother's study."

Jess had been quietly listing to this conversation with interest.

She said, "Anna, Mrs Hamilton said they had changed the way they farmed several years ago. Do you know if they are using the methods you are talking about?"

"Yes, they are some of these farmers. Now, if there is nothing further, Heidi, I must go. I am busy."

32

Heidi knocked on the DG's door. After being invited to enter, she said, "Excuse me, Judith, could I have a word with you? It's regarding Anna."

"Certainly, Heidi. I was just going to take a break. Why don't you join me? We can go for a stroll and stretch our legs at the same time."

They went to the cafeteria and each ordered a takeaway. Judith paid. As they walked along the path, Judith enquired, "What's on your mind?"

"Anna's been talking to me again. She told me the Swedish Government would like to discuss regenerative agriculture practices with us. They're going to request we receive a trade delegation from them with that as the key agenda item. She asked me if I could help arrange it—to get us to welcome them and to participate. I told her I didn't have any influence or even contacts with the necessary departments. She asked me to try, anyway. I can't think of any other way to pass this request on. Can you help?"

"A trade delegation to discuss regenerative agriculture. Isn't that a bit left field, given who we're dealing with here?"

"I don't think Anna gets involved in trivialities. This must be important to them. I don't even know what she's talking about. Have you any idea what it is?"

"No, Heidi. Never heard of it. Agriculture? It's a big change from nuclear weapons. Or medicine. I can't see the connection."

"Well, there must be one. Do you have any way of passing this on, you know, to the Foreign Minister or someone?"

"OK, Heidi, I'll mention it. And if it's coming from Anna, I think it'll get traction."

~

Once Amanda had received and studied the reports about regenerative farming that she had requested, she informed Prime Minister Fitzgerald of the Swedish request. He said he was unaware of any such approach. And he added he had much more important topics to deal with than some greenie ideas on farming. He didn't want to send the wrong message to his support base. No, that would have to wait. And it would get sidelined during the wait. He wasn't interested.

Then events overtook them. The PM received a message from the Ambassador to the US.

~

The official request from the Swedish Government landed on Amanda's desk. Their timing could not have been worse. She, along with several other senior ministers, was about to travel to the US for a high-level meeting. Summoned by their President. Agenda unknown.

She drafted a response, thanking them for their request, but explaining now was not a good time. Domestic issues occupied all their resources at the moment. Perhaps they could consider it later in the year.

33

Admiral Blake was full of apprehension as he entered the room. The Chief of the Navy had arranged the meeting as soon as he heard what Blake had to say upon returning from his visit to the Pacific Fleet.

How what he was about to tell them would be received was anybody's guess. One thing was for sure; it would set them back in their seats.

He hoped with all his heart they'd take notice. He was convinced their very future depended on it.

It seemed the Chief was taking him seriously at least; the room was crowded. All the Joint Chiefs of Staff were there along with several civilians he did not recognise.

After greeting him, the Chairman Joint Chiefs of Staff introduced the civilians as members of the Unidentified Aerial Phenomenon Independent Study Team, UAPIST. He then invited Admiral Blake to relate his recent experience.

He dived straight in, relating all the events of his encounter. He didn't need any notes; it was all seared into his mind.

He studied the effect his narrative was having. The UAPIST people, in particular, were hanging on his every word.

When he finished, the room was deathly quiet. No one moved; he was the focal point of the entire group. To him, this was a welcome sign. It looked like they were taking him seriously. He decided to add a little commentary.

"The aliens have already demonstrated they can easily carry out their threats. I firmly believe they could destroy any of our hardware they deem necessary with absolute impunity. Somewhat reassuringly, they did no harm to the *Henry Teak,* and Anna specifically said they do not wish to harm us. My suggestion is not to antagonise them in case it causes a change in their attitude."

The last sentence was spoken slowly and deliberately.

"She told me they are not interested in talking to our government or scientific bodies directly, but requested we cancel the Aukus nuclear submarine deal with the Australians. When pressed, she didn't elaborate on the reasons they want this done, just cryptically saying it would be in our mutual interests, however you wish to interpret that ..."

He had seen the disappointment on the members of UAPIST when he mentioned the aliens had no interest in liaising with them, but they did not interrupt.

He fixed his gaze on the Chairman and concluded, "Gentlemen, I am as patriotic as the rest of you. But, after having spoken personally with one of the aliens, it is my considered opinion that if we engage in open conflict with them, we won't last past the first afternoon. I beg you to take great care regarding any decisions as to how we proceed."

"Thank you, Admiral Blake, for your report and for your candour. They are not interested in our conflict with China, you say? Did she give any indication they had been in contact with the Chinese? Or, if pushed, what side they'd favour?"

"No sir, except to say explicitly they would react to any nuclear weapon deployment."

"What would you say was her demeanour when she mentioned the Chinese? It's important that we get a gauge on any interactions they might have had with them."

"Impossible to say, sir. She appeared unemotional when she mentioned them. I pressed her on the issue, but she shut that topic down and moved on. I think we can assume they've been in contact with the Chinese. To unknown effect."

"And they do not wish to establish dialogue with our government? How do they expect us to proceed with anything, let alone cancelling the Aukus deal if they don't? Did you explain to her that these things are decided by our government, and the

Australians'?"

"Yes sir, I did. That's when she stated they are not interested in interacting with our government directly. I got the impression they hold governments in low regard."

Admiral Blake adopted a very different tone.

"Sir, there was one further, quite disturbing, statement she made. She said they had been studying our history. They are aware of our belligerent nature, and preponderance for resolving any disputes by violence toward each other. She added that they consider this to be the natural behaviour of our species. They appear to be completely unconcerned about such conflicts as long as nuclear weapons are not used. In fact, she pointed out that, with us being the apex predators, the resulting wars and several diseases we cannot treat are the only things keeping our population somewhat in check. To me, that was the most frightening thing she said. They may be considering eradicating us, or at least instigating a substantial downsizing."

The Chairman looked towards the UAPIST scientists and asked for their comment.

The psychologist got in first. "That last comment is interesting. Perhaps they've adopted somewhat belligerent behaviour toward us, as they've concluded that is what we respond to."

Then the others all attempted to speak at once. Questions and comments like:

What did she look like?

What did the UFO look like?

Did you say she appeared? What do you mean by that?

What did she say about not being interested in speaking to our scientists?

Do you think we can change their attitudes towards us?

Any mention of how to contact them?

This went on for some time, then the Chair of UAPIST held up his hand to request silence. He stood up to address the meeting.

"It's of the utmost disappointment that they are reluctant to meet with our scientists. We have to work on that. So, what of their behaviour to date? Most of you probably consider it quite antagonistic, outrageous even. But, given their demonstrated capabilities, I believe it has been very restrained."

He exchanged glances with his fellow UAPIST members.

"They most probably have a completely different value set to us. Throughout history, our behaviour when expanding to new lands, conquering them I think is the apt term, has been to destroy the existing culture and often their entire civilisation to make room for ours. They do not seem to be exhibiting anything like that behaviour. Indeed, they have told us why they are here. To preserve the planet's habitability. Why, we don't know. Yet. But, if we can believe them, that is their agenda here. And it appears that the destruction of the human race is not part of it. And their comment about studying us. No surprises there. But for how long? And I fear for what conclusions they have reached."

The meeting fell silent for a few moments, as they all reflected on his comments, after which the Chairman Joint Chiefs got to his feet.

"Thank you, gentlemen. I think this is an appropriate time to adjourn."

~

The military members reconvened after lunch.

The Chairman opened with, "Well gentlemen, we need to agree on a recommended course of action to take to the President."

The Chief of Naval Operations spoke first, and he went straight on the offensive. "I think we can ignore the thoughts of the UAPIST people. They have their own agenda. Our sworn duty is to defend our country. I think the key to doing this is our submarine fleet. Specifically, our boomers. That nuclear weapons and submarines are the only types of assets they've mentioned shows their importance to the aliens. They've exhibited their capability at intercepting an ICBM in flight and interacting with surface shipping and aircraft. Since they are so interested in our submarines, it's possible they cannot track them. I suggest they remain on station as our last line of defence. They might be trying to bluff us into standing them down. Furthermore, the boomers are our primary form of deterrence to a nuclear confrontation with China. If they see us standing down, they'll take it as a sign of weakness."

He paused for effect, then continued. "We can presume they have extensive intelligence gathering capabilities and would be aware of our forward deployment of nuclear weapons and B2 bombers to Japan. Perhaps as a sign of good faith, we could withdraw the B2s and their armaments back stateside."

The Chief of Staff of the Air Force went red in the face and had started to reply when the Chairman raised his hand and demanded silence.

"The time for turf wars and the one-upmanship game is long gone, gentlemen. We work together on this. Thank you for your input, Admiral. It's something to consider. However, I, for one, don't think the aliens consider themselves to be in a game of poker. I don't think bluffing is their modus operandi. I see the merit in standing down the B2s, but I'd like to do so in response to some action by the Chinese. In, as you so eloquently put it, a display of good faith. Now, did you have anything further to add, General Fletcher?"

"Sir, I consider any conflict with the aliens will essentially be an airborne one. It would be prudent to station all our front-line aircraft, especially those with stealth capability, with homeland defence in mind. We're going to have our hands full trying to protect ourselves, let alone any other country. We've seen they can disarm an F-18 on a training mission, but a package of stealth aircraft on an active mission is a different animal entirely. And even if the aliens can neutralise them, I don't think we should just lie down and die."

The Chairman said, "On the contrary, I think our first course of action should be to attempt to negotiate a peaceful resolution to the conflict with China. We don't want that hanging over our heads while trying to deal with the alien threat as well. And I fear we would not prevail in a war with China if we didn't use nuclear weapons. In fact, we may need to join forces with them to combat the aliens. If only we could get them to return our calls. And we'll need to ditch the Aukus submarine deal, if only to appease the aliens. If successful, that is going to create quite a stir. The companies involved are going to scream like hell and demand compensation. And the senators and congressmen in their pockets are going to do the same. On top of all this, there are the Brits and their part in it as well. It's unclear how much of all this alien stuff they know about, but you can bet it's quite a lot."

He looked around the table at each of them. "Agreed?"

"Yes sir," was the chorus in response.

"Admiral Blake, I'd like you to accompany me to the meeting with the President, as you are the one with firsthand contact with the aliens."

34

The United States Strategic Command staff at Offutt Air Force Base were anxiously trying to re-establish communication with the *USS Kansas*. The Fleet Ballistic Missile Submarine had gone quiet eight hours ago, and all attempts to contact it had proven fruitless.

To say the commander was panicking would be an overstatement, but he was very concerned. If the boat was missing, not only were the crew of 8 officers and 140 enlisted personnel unaccounted for, so were the 20 Trident missiles and the 160 thermonuclear warheads they contained.

It was a solemn General May who reported to the Joint Chiefs of Staff via the secure conference call.

"Still no reply, sir. I think we should prepare for the possibility the boat has been lost."

"We haven't given up all hope yet. Best-case scenario is it's suffered a catastrophic communications failure. At this stage, we must pray they will come back online."

"This is unprecedented. All our other boats are still in contact. If it is a comms issue, it must be at their end. I'm very concerned."

"As are we, General. Keep us updated."

After ending the call, the Chairman addressed the other Chiefs. "We have to consider the possibility the aliens have something to do with this. So much for your theory about the subs being safe from them. Perhaps you shouldn't have tempted fate."

The Chief of Staff of the Air Force said, "May I be so bold to suggest that their preferred method of communication might be via actions, not words. And if this has anything to do with them, which I am sure it does, their actions appear to be escalating somewhat. I think if we cancel the submarine deal with the Australians as they have requested, they might take it as a sign of our willingness to cooperate."

The Chief of Naval Operations wasn't having that. "Bow down to them, more like it. The Australians having our subs must be a threat to them. Why else would they be interested in the deal being cancelled? Make no mistake, if they're responsible for the *Kansas* going missing, we are in open warfare with them. I suggest we take no steps that will further weaken our capabilities; but concentrate all our efforts on protecting our homeland."

The Chief of Staff of the Air Force said, "I fear for all of us if it comes to that. If they can take out our missile boats while on patrol, we're in very grave danger indeed. And what do we strike at if we are capable of it? Where is our target?"

He looked around the group in exasperation.

The Chairman said, "Gentlemen, we're going around in circles here. I'll inform the President that, at this stage, all indications are that we have lost the *Kansas*. Reasons unknown, but there is a strong likelihood the aliens are involved."

~

The President entering the room brought the meeting to order. He said good morning and took his seat, triggering the others to do likewise.

He opened with, "Gentlemen. Where are we at?"

The Chairman Chief of Staff brought him up to date.

The Chief of Staff of the Air Force couldn't miss his chance for a snipe at the navy. "Sir, there's the unsettling possibility they have not destroyed the *Kansas,* but they have taken control of it. And the nuclear arsenal it carries. That is a nightmare scenario."

The Chief of Naval Operations fired back. "The aliens appear to be very much against the use of nuclear weapons. If they've taken control of them, they're unlikely to use them. I think we can disregard that threat."

President Sanger raised his hand, effectively stopping the crossfire. "I want you to intensify the search for it. If it's intact, we must find it."

He stood up and paced around in a state of frustration. "The aliens refuse to even talk with us. They have assassinated our president. They have threatened one of our ships. And they have most probably destroyed the *Kansas*. It's overwhelming likely they are in contact with the Chinese. They have obviously provided tech to the Russians, who have shared it with the Europeans, of all people."

His voice had slowly been getting louder during his tirade. He drew a breath to settle himself back down. His voice adopted a much more measured but menacing tone.

"They are busy changing the balance of power, and we are being treated as poor cousins. That stops now. We are at war with them. Gentlemen, I want scenarios as to how to fight back."

The Chief of the CIA spoke up. "Sir, I think Australia is the key. It seems to be the centre of the aliens' activities and is the most probable location of their base. And the original meeting attendees—they seem to have free rein over their movements. Until now, the Australians have been cooperating with us, on the surface at least. However, information has come to hand that the enigmatic Ms Heidi Almendinger has recently been in Sweden. That is information that they haven't seen fit to share with us. I suggest we start playing hardball with the Australians; request they place the meeting attendees under arrest, especially her, and let us question them."

This caused a bit of consternation among some of the others, remembering what had transpired the last time that line of action had been pursued, but the President was paying rapt attention and waved for him to continue.

"I suggest we allocate all available assets to search for any signs of their base. And if we find it, we should be prepared for a pre-emptive strike. I suggest we station the Pacific Fleet off the Australian coast so we can attack at a moment's notice. Their presence will also put some pressure on the Australians to cooperate."

The Chief of Naval Operations picked up the ball. "Sir, if we locate their base, I suggest we launch the attack using a swarm of nuclear armed cruise missiles. We'll only get one shot at this. The aliens have shown they are capable of intercepting ICBMs, but with luck at least some of the cruise missiles will get through. Especially if launched from close proximity. We should station all available SSGNs off Australia ready for such an attack. There is the added capability of using the seal teams aboard to recon or undertake direct action."

President Sanger sat tall in his chair, eyes blazing around the room as he processed his thoughts.

"Right, gentlemen. That's what we'll do. I've had enough of this whole alien threat. It's time to bring it to a head. And apparently, this Ms Almendinger has an alien communications device. We want that device. Pressure the Australians to confiscate it and hand it over. And the Aukus deal stands. For now, at least. It's another bargaining chip with the Australians to ensure their cooperation."

~

The Australian Ambassador received an invitation to the White House. No agenda was supplied, just the invitation. Upon his arrival, he was ushered to the Oval Office.

After greetings were exchanged, the President indicated they should sit. He said, "Ambassador Walsh, there's no easy way to break this news to you, but we're going to bring this alien threat to a head. We want you to arrange a meeting with your government for talks about how we intend to progress this. You should give it your highest priority."

Ambassador Walsh went pale and swallowed nervously. "Mr President, could you please give me some more detail? What ministers and portfolios are you talking about?"

"You can start with the Prime Minister, and Ministers for Defence, Foreign Affairs and Home Affairs. That should give them an indication of what we wish to discuss. They can add any others as they see fit. Our attendees will be myself, the Secretary of State, Chairman Joint Chiefs of Staff and the director of the CIA. We wish to have the meeting here in the US as soon as possible."

The ambassador's eyes widened when told of the list of attendees. This sounded very ominous. Once he found his voice, he replied, "Yes, Mr President. And the agenda?"

"We'll keep that for the meeting. Thank you, Ambassador Walsh."

35

The Artificial Intelligence analysis of satellite imagery reported a hit. Two targets with a 90% probability of being the aliens had been located running along an isolated beach.

The Director of the CIA called President Sanger. "We've found it!"

"Where and what assets do we have nearby?"

"An island off the Tasmanian coast of southern Australia. There are multiple 7th Fleet assets in the area. The nearest SSGN is the *South Carolina*. We can launch a cruise missile strike immediately or send in a team to recon the island. They may be able to pinpoint their base."

The President called the Chief of Naval Operations. "You are about to receive a set of coordinates. They are for an island off the south coast of Australia. I want two dozen nuclear armed cruise missiles set to target these coordinates, and available for immediate launch once authorised. Additionally, orders are coming to dispatch a team for a recon of the island. We've located their base."

~

Bernie received an order to report to Major Spencer. When he entered the room, he found not only Major Spencer, but General Mitchell, Major General Henderson and the Minister for Defence in attendance. There was also a middle-aged person dressed in civilian clothes who was unknown to him, standing in the back corner of the room.

This looked a lot more serious than his usual debriefs with Major Spencer. A lot more.

After they exchanged salutes, Bernie stood at ease.

Major Spencer said, "Sergeant Ambrose, the aliens seem to be stepping up their activity. We'd like a full report on everything you know about what they're up to, and, specifically, their interactions with Ms Almendinger."

Bernie had known this moment was coming. It had been for some time now. In fact, ever since he had received his orders just after that first fateful meeting with Anna and Belle. He had thought long and hard about how he was going to behave and what he would divulge. And his thoughts and feelings had evolved.

He was conflicted. On one hand, he was sworn to the service of his country, and to obey the orders of his superiors. He took this oath seriously, and initially had divulged everything he found out. Well, almost everything. On the other hand, he was in love with Heidi, and he wanted to protect her as much as he could.

And then there was Anna. She was the most complicated person he had ever come across. Meeting her had turned his life upside down. That's right; he considered her as a person, despite the fact he knew she was an alien. Despite all of her powers and lethality. Over time, his feelings towards her had changed. He considered her to be the straightest shooter he had ever met; there was no bullshit with Anna. He had grown to trust her, and both respected and liked her—a lot.

He had discussed his feelings with George. Much to his relief, he discovered they were on the same page. George told him he'd fallen for Viktoria and would do anything to protect her. Bernie had made his decision. He was going to keep some of the things he found out close to his chest. Most of them, actually.

"Not a lot to report, sir. After the hospitalisation of Viktoria, there's been little interaction. We had a get-together at Jessica's apartment once. That's about it."

"And Ms Almendinger. What can you tell us of her activities?"

"Nothing unusual, sir, as far as I know. I've recently moved in with her, so now I've got a fair idea of what she gets up to. She goes to work each day. What she does there, she keeps to herself. We socialise a fair bit. She seems to be involved quite a lot with her father. And she and Jess have become good friends. Nothing else stands out."

"Has she been travelling lately?"

"She went to Melbourne to visit her father a while ago, and we've been to the Gold Coast to visit Jess. Other than that, not that I know of."

The Defence Minister butted in. "No trips to Sweden, then?"

Bernie feigned surprise. "Sweden? Why would she go to Sweden?"

"That's what we'd like to know. You can't shed any light on this?"

"I'm sorry, sir, no I can't."

General Mitchell said, "Thank you, Sergeant. There are two military police officers outside the door. Would you please accompany them when you leave? You and Ms Almendinger are being placed under house arrest, for your own protection. And could I please have your mobile phone?" As he said this, he stood up and held out his hand, then placed the offered phone on the desk.

Major Spencer said, "Dismissed."

As Bernie turned to leave, Major Spencer gave a subtle hand gesture to him, showing things had spiralled out of his control, but that he had his back.

The civilian had said nothing during the entire time.

~

The MPs took Bernie to Heidi's house. That was good, in so far as it would be easier for him to orchestrate an escape than if they had just arrested him and placed him in a cell. It was bad, because he knew Heidi was also going to be arrested and detained here as well.

He was sure, if he bided his time, the opportunity would present itself for him to overpower the two MPs. The federal police gathered outside would complicate things, but he'd come up with something. That would have been his plan if Heidi were not involved. He didn't want to put her in any danger, but he was confident that if anyone threatened Heidi, Anna wouldn't be far away. He weighed things up and decided the best plan was to remain docile and let things play out.

He'd give the MPs a chance, though. "Boys, if you know what's good for you, now would be a good time to leave."

The bigger of the two replied sarcastically, "We know you're the big bad wolf, but that doesn't impress us. Just try it—make our day."

Bernie stared at them, and they looked back as if they didn't have a care in the world.

"It's not me you need to worry about; it's the Spitfire that'll be unleashed if anyone tries to harm my partner."

They both grunted by way of reply.

~

Jessica had just finished her rounds and was heading to the cafeteria when she was approached by her supervisor and two uniformed police officers.

With a worried look etched on his face, her supervisor said, "Dr Gordon, these two constables are here to escort you home. Because of your recent experiences, and the stress it has caused, the government has decided you are to be given some time off work. You are to remain at home until advised otherwise. I hope this is only a temporary arrangement."

With that introduction, the two constables approached Jess and stood on either side of her.

Jess protested. "I'm fine. Really. Never felt better, actually. I can assure you I'm focused on my work here and more than capable of carrying out my duties."

Her supervisor grimaced and said, "I know, Jess. We very much appreciate how hard you work, but this is out of our control. I hope to see you back at work soon."

One constable touched Jess on the arm and said, "Could you please come with us now, madam? And could you please hand over your phone?"

~

Heidi was called to Judith's office. As she entered, she saw there were also two federal police officers in the room. And, almost as surprisingly, the Minister for Defence.

Judith welcomed her and invited her to take a seat.

She said, "Heidi, these two policewomen are here to take you home. You are to remain there until this can all be sorted out. Police will be stationed there for your protection." She held out her hand. "Could I please have your phone and the device Anna gave you?"

Stunned, Heidi looked at Judith and replied, "I don't understand. What's this all about? What do you mean, for my protection?"

Judith said, "I'm sorry, Heidi. I'm trying to sort it all out. But, for the moment, could you please comply? Now, your phone and the device, please." She still had her hand held out, waiting for them.

Heidi opened her bag and handed over her phone. The device

wasn't in there. She said, "I'm sorry, I must've left the device at home."

The Minister for Defence reached out, snatched her bag and checked it. Sure enough, there was no device inside.

He scowled at her, but Judith, with a forced reassuring smile, said, "I'm sure this will all be worked out quickly, Heidi. And please, try to keep a rein on Anna. Now, would you accompany these ladies home?"

The Defence Minister growled, "I'll go with you to get the device."

~

The SAS operators approached the door to George's apartment. They slid a small camera under it, but they couldn't detect any activity inside. One of them picked the lock and they burst in. A quick search revealed the apartment was empty. Two operators remained inside while the rest went down to the entry foyer to await his return.

~

As they approached her home, Heidi noticed several police vehicles parked outside with heavily armed police milling around. They pulled into her driveway, then her escorting officers ushered her inside. The Minister for Defence followed them.

She found Bernie sitting in the lounge, flanked by two burly military police.

Before she could say anything, the Minister for Defence demanded, "The device please."

She looked at Bernie, who shook his head slightly, in a sign she should remain silent. Heidi was certain she had taken the device to work that day; she never went anywhere without it being within reach. She assumed Anna had taken it but feigned searching the house for it. As her search continued to prove fruitless, the Minister for Defence became increasingly irritated. He wanted the device. And he wanted to be the one who delivered it to the Americans. Brownie points were on offer.

As Heidi emerged from her bedroom, still empty-handed, he angrily grabbed her by the arm and insisted she stop stalling and hand it over.

There was a sudden blue flash in the room, which resulted in it now containing fewer occupants. Bernie and Heidi were still there, but the only other person present was Anna.

She was standing right beside Heidi and immediately hugged her and reassured her everything was going to be OK. Anna was holding the communication device and handed it to Heidi, then she looked at Bernie and with a serious expression, gave a slight nod of her head. Anna was in military mode, and she had observed how they acted.

He reciprocated, then blurted out, "Fuck me, Anna, it's good to see you. We've got to hurry; I think they're going after all of us. Jessica, Viktoria and George."

"Yes, they have already arrested Jessica. Viktoria and George are at beach. They have found them there but are waiting for them to return to his apartment."

Heidi started to cry, and Anna cuddled her and said, "Time to be brave, Heidi. Come here Bernie—Heidi needs your comfort."

Anna moved away to give them some space and glanced out the window at the police milling outside while Bernie hugged the still crying Heidi.

Heidi said, "What are they going to do to Jess? And she is all alone."

"Belle is going to take care of her."

~

The police escorted Jess to her apartment. As they went through the foyer, she noticed two very fit-looking men standing near the tourist brochures, apparently deciding where they'd spend the day. She suspected, correctly, that they were plain-clothes police here to ensure her cooperation.

Both the escorting officers went inside with her. She immediately went over and poured herself a glass of water. As she was raising it to take a sip, a sudden blue light flashed across the room; Anna was here! Jess noticed she had changed her hairstyle. Both the officers gaped at her sudden appearance, momentarily frozen in shock. One gathered his wits and reached for his weapon. There was another flash and both the officers disappeared.

Jess screamed. "Oh my God, Anna, what's going on?"

"I am Belle. Anna could not come, she is busy. Your government has made big mistake, but do not worry, we will protect you. You should freshen up, then we will go to join others."

~

Viktoria had decided she wanted to go to the beach. It was such a beautiful spring day. George agreed and had taken her to Bondi, much to her glee. He was sitting beside her while she lay on the beach, sunbathing. He smiled to himself as the lifeguards walked past them for the third time in ten minutes.

Yeah mate, I'd be doing the same.

He was daydreaming about how life had changed for him. And for the better. All this alien stuff was a spin out, but Viktoria had won his heart. And he hers by the way she was acting. As far as he could tell, she wasn't an alien like Anna and Belle. She was a carefree soul full of life and adventure—albeit one who didn't mind spending exorbitant amounts of money on clothes, and don't even mention shoes. "But we all have our faults," he thought. He wasn't sure why the girls all looked so alike, but he suspected the aliens had copied her somehow. And that just made her even more special. They could most probably have copied anyone at all, but they'd chosen her.

The ringing of his phone pulled him from his daydream. He didn't recognise the number. "Hello."

"Sharpie, Toast; Springtime. The feds are rounding us all up. Ditch your phone, take Viktoria, and head for a secluded spot nearby. Anna will grab you, but she doesn't want to startle any bystanders."

"Right." He terminated the call and buried his phone in the sand. "Come on, Vika, grab your stuff. We have to go right away!"

He wanted them to remain in a crowded area until the last minute, because it would make it harder for the feds to do the snatch. He waited until the lifeguards were nearing the end of their patrol and hurried Viktoria to a nearby beachfront bar. They went straight past the crowd of drinkers, heading for the restrooms. George had Viktoria by the hand, and she was trotting to keep up. They attracted quite a bit of attention. It was probably not so much due to their haste, but the sight of the scantily clad beauty being led past them.

"Go inside and get in a cubicle. Anna will get you from there. If she doesn't, come straight back out to me. I'll wait here for you. If you aren't back out in half a minute, I'll know you've gone. Hurry, Vika."

Just as the half minute was up, the lifeguards rushed through the entrance. He saw them out of the corner of his eye as he hurried to the gents.

36

The Chief of Naval Operations put through the call to the United States Strategic Command headquarters at Offutt Airforce Base, Nebraska.

"Still nothing from the *South Carolina*?"

"No sir, no communications since the signal to deploy the recon team. That was four hours ago. Nothing from the team, either. They should be ashore by now. This is not usual operating procedure, sir. I'm worried it might have suffered the same fate as the *Kansas*."

"God save us if that's the case. What in hell are we dealing with here?"

"Unsure, sir, but it seems we are a little under-gunned, to say the least."

"I'll update the President."

He'll most likely go to the backup plan of launching an airstrike from the Carlton Jackson.

~

Anna and Belle's studio had undergone some renovations. Actually, they were additions. There were now several additional bedrooms, a large living room, a much better equipped kitchen, and a gymnasium.

It also had several more residents. Heidi and Bernie moved into one bedroom, Viktoria and George into another, and Jessica made herself at home in the third. The girls still slept in their king-sized bed. It didn't seem to occur to them they needed separate rooms, or beds for that matter.

On their first evening there, Anna suggested they should enjoy some music. She went over, sat at the piano, and started to play.

Belle encouraged Viktoria. "Would you like to accompany her?"

"But there is no violin here."

Belle put her arm around Viktoria and hugged her.

Anna stopped playing and cast a smile at them. "Well, we had better get you one, hadn't we?"

An old and well-used violin and bow appeared on the table. Viktoria clapped excitedly and picked them up. She caressed the violin's body briefly as she looked wide-eyed at Belle. She then went over to tune it against the piano, only to discover that it was already perfectly in tune.

They played together, Viktoria chose the tunes, while Belle produced the music score. But Anna? Anna seemed to transcend the need for notation; her fingers moved with an innate understanding. After several songs, Viktoria offered the violin to Belle.

Anna and Belle looked at each other, silently deciding between themselves which song they would perform. After getting a nod from Belle, Anna started the melody, a gentle cascade of notes like raindrops on a windowpane. Then came Belle, her bow dancing across the strings, conjuring the opening strains of *Amazing Grace*. The notes soared, mournful yet hopeful. Belle's eyes were closed, her entire being attuned to the music, her soul laid bare. The others held captive by the haunting sounds; the piano's resonance, the violin's lament. It was more than a performance; it was a communion. They were no longer separate beings; they were threads woven into a shared existence.

The room held its breath until the final chord hung in the air. And so they hovered there, Anna, Belle, Viktoria, and the others. The anxiety of events that had led them here, distant, resolved.

The moment passed when Anna said, "Your turn, Jessica."

Jess said, "I don't play the violin, or piano, for that matter. And even if I studied for a lifetime, I would be incapable of anything like that."

"Just teasing ..." Anna said with a smile.

Suddenly a guitar materialised on the table.

Jess picked it up and studied it in awe. It was a Maton EA80C.

Brand new. She plucked a few notes.

Anna said, "It is already tuned, Jessica—your turn now."

Jessica caressed the guitar for a moment, glancing upwards while she decided on the first song to perform. Her mind made up, she looked at the others and said, "OK, the girls probably won't know this song, but the rest of you will. You have to sing along with me."

She started playing *We Are Australian*. It didn't completely surprise her to discover Anna and Belle both knew the words and sang along as well. Part way through, Anna went back to the piano and accompanied them.

They played and sang long into the night. A small group of close friends, encased in a protective cocoon, isolated for the moment from the terrors of the world.

~

The mood in the Situation Room was tense as President Sanger gave the order for the attack to begin. Those gathered with him to oversee the coming events included the Joint Chiefs of Staff, the Director of the CIA and the Director of Homeland Security.

The Chief of Naval Operations sent the order to the newly appointed Commander of the Pacific Fleet via the secure comms link.

There was a combined sigh of nervous tension around the room, then the agonising wait for confirmation of the strike began.

~

From their vantage point on the bridge, the Captain and the CAG of the *Carlton Jackson* were watching the hive of activity below. There was no rushing about, but things were happening at a fast rate. To the untrained eye, it looked like chaos, whereas, in fact, everyone knew exactly what to do and when to do it. They were all busy, but, despite their professionalism, those in the know were very apprehensive. They had received an order to carry out a nuclear strike on Australia. Unprecedented. And there was no doubt the order was authentic.

"God save us," muttered the Captain to the CAG. He nodded in assent.

On the deck below, the strike package was being launched. Four F-23s were already airborne and the next two were lining up on the deck.

Suddenly, an alarm sounded. The Hawkeye had detected an

incoming hypersonic missile. It was rapidly closing from the south, skimming the sea surface at a speed of mach 20. The Combat Air Patrol aircraft circling above dived to intercept and the screening destroyers manoeuvred to protect the carrier.

As it neared the fleet, the missile suddenly climbed to 30,000 feet and flashed past the diving F-18s. A moment later, the Hawkeye reported the aircraft were no longer in the area, with the radar aboard the carrier confirming this.

The missile pirouetted and dived directly towards the *Carlton Jackson*. As it approached, it rapidly decelerated and was engaged by all available close-in weapons systems. A beautiful iridescent blue haze enveloped the object as it continued its approach. It slowed to match the speed of the carrier, maintaining a position approximately 100 metres off the port side at an altitude level with the bridge. The Captain's and the CAG's attention switched from the strike aircraft being launched to the scene from the port windows.

They observed the missile was actually a diamond shaped object, its obsidian surface overlaid with an ethereal dance of luminescent blue ripples. It appeared to shimmer slightly, fading in and out of vision, as if it was both there and not there. Existing and not existing. Its trajectory hinted at its cataclysmic intent, but now it paused, a harbinger of doom. The petrichor odour of ozone assaulted those on the deck, and their hairs stood on end from the static permeating the air. The crew held their breath, caught between awe and terror. For this was no ordinary weapon; it was from another realm, and it possessed power unimaginable.

Then they felt a slight shudder and a heeling of the carrier to port. Alarms blared in their ears. Damage reports streamed in. Along the entire length of the ship, at a depth of 10 metres, a one-metre-wide section of the hull was missing. Seawater was engulfing them, determined to regain its rightful place. Each passing second tilted them further towards oblivion.

At 15 degrees, the Captain's voice crackled over the intercom: "Abandon ship."

Simultaneously with his order being given, the object turned and approached the *USS Concord*, a Ticonderoga-class guided missile cruiser. Almost immediately, the front 10 metres of its bow sheared off. It had been steaming at full speed as it manoeuvred to protect the carrier, but now the front of the ship ploughed under the surface and the stern rose as the ship porpoised violently to a standstill.

Moments later, the turbines of the nearest two destroyers tripped due to overspeed; their propellers had suddenly vanished.

The object turned towards the *Henry Teak*. A moment's hesitation, then it continued westward, positioning itself between the crippled fleet and the Australian coast. Its message, unspoken yet thunderous, reverberated across the ocean.

No.

The *Carlton Jackson* toppled over and slid beneath the waves to join the *Concord*. Many of the crew of the carrier were in the water, but there were no signs of any survivors from the *Concord*.

The fleet began rescue efforts. Those capable of it, that is. The two destroyers without their propellers lolled helplessly in the swell. The *Henry Teak*, however, continued on its course of 285 degrees towards the New South Wales coast. All attempts to hail it were fruitless. A helicopter was redeployed from its rescue efforts to do a flyby and ascertain why there was no response. It reported the ship appeared to be deserted. There were no signs of life on board.

~

President Sanger was pacing impatiently beside the monitors when word of the attack on the *Carlton Jackson* Carrier Strike Group came through. It stopped him in his tracks. No words were spoken by anyone in the room. The only sounds to be heard were the frantic voices reproduced by the communications equipment.

He suddenly slumped to the floor. He didn't simply fall but collapsed in a tangled heap of limbs and torso. It was as if he was a marionette whose strings had suddenly been severed.

The others in the room heard his fall and snapped their heads towards the sound. The Director of the CIA was the nearest and rushed to him. He didn't quite reach him, though. As he was completing his first hurried step, he too crumpled to the floor. It was a similar kind of collapse, but, as he had some forward momentum, he sprawled headlong instead of just vertically downwards. If he had the ability to reach out, he would have just been able to touch the president to offer him comfort. He didn't have that ability though, and the president was past any offerings coming his way. Both were stone-cold dead.

The mayhem wasn't quite over yet. The Chief of Naval Operations and the Chairman of the Joint Chiefs of Staff were frozen in place, in shock at what they had just witnessed. Then they too dropped to the floor, robbed of any form of life by the sudden disappearance of their brain stems.

The world, it seemed, had a new form of justice, one orchestrated by forces beyond comprehension.

37

The days that followed were tumultuous for America. Yet another president was sworn in. And this time, things were radically different. Such was the brevity of time since President Sanger's promotion, a vice president had not been appointed. The position of president, therefore, went to the next in the order of succession; the speaker of the house. And she was female! Maria Gardiner.

No one could believe the news about the devastation of the *Carlton Jackson* Carrier Strike Group, and the media went into a frenzy. How was that possible? What was it doing off the Australian coast? Why had the Australians attacked it? And what weapons had they used? And why hadn't there been any retaliation? They were demanding access to politicians for answers, and when none was forthcoming, they formulated and aired their own theories. These ranged from the far-fetched to the downright fanciful. Among them, rumours circulated that a UFO had attacked the fleet. What had to be accepted was that 5520 sailors were missing presumed dead. And not a single body had been recovered.

A riotous mob of radicals had attacked the Australian Embassy. The army arrived just in time to rescue its staff and the severely outnumbered police trying to protect them. More than one hundred and fifty of the combatants were killed in the ensuing mêlée.

The US borders had slammed shut, with only military and diplomatic personnel allowed in or out.

Over the next few days, the heavy-handed approach by the authorities was slowly restoring order.

~

Although not as tumultuous as those occurring in the US, events in Australia took a turn for the worse as well. After being arrested and confined in their homes, all the people the Americans had requested to be detained had disappeared without a trace. And so had the several police officers who were guarding them. And the Minister for Defence was missing as well. Nationwide searches for them were proving fruitless. It was as if they had vanished into thin air.

Adding to the turmoil were the devastating events off the east coast. America was reeling, and Australia was getting the blame. Not that they had anything to do with it, but this was the story being published by the media in the US. The Australian public were demanding to know what a US carrier strike group was doing patrolling off their coast. What had caused the calamity that had befallen it? And most were fearful of the retaliation coming their way. The Australian share market had taken a hit and there had been a run on the banks. There were also widespread demonstrations occurring.

An interim Defence Minister had been appointed. When he entered his new office, he was startled to find the previous minister slumped over his desk. Efforts to revive him had been to no avail, and an autopsy revealed his brain stem was missing.

~

There was a nervousness about the room as Judith entered. The Prime Minister had called all those in the inner circle who had knowledge of the alien presence to an emergency meeting. Politicians and their senior staffers dominated the group, with Judith and the military hierarchy being the few exceptions. She was the last to arrive.

The Prime Minister raised his hand and called them to order. Everyone turned their attention towards him just in time to see him crumple to the floor. A moment later, the Minister for Home Affairs followed him. The others in the room rushed to provide aid and called for medical assistance.

After checking the Prime Minister's vital signs, Major General Henderson began administering CPR with General Mitchell doing likewise to the Minister for Home Affairs. They continued with their efforts until the paramedics arrived. Once the two patients were evacuated to hospital, the rest of the group continued to mill around in a state of shock.

Judith went over to Major General Henderson and murmured, "Valiant efforts, sir, but we both know it was in vain. People cannot survive without brain stems, can they?"

A visibly shaken Minister for Foreign Affairs approached them and said, "I tried to warn them. I knew it would come to no good."

She was still furious with the decision taken by the Prime Minister to accede to the US demands. His most vocal supporters had been the Minister for Defence and the Minister for Home Affairs. Her vehement protests had been brushed aside, and she had fallen out of favour with three of the most influential members in her party. But how quickly things change in politics! None of them were around anymore.

Major General Henderson sat and held his head in his hands. If, as Judith had alluded, the aliens had done this, he too could well be lying on the floor. Dead. He had ordered the operation to apprehend George and Viktoria. He looked at Judith and asked, "Why do you think they spared me?"

"And me, I was directly involved in Heidi's arrest. I can only presume they spared us because we were following orders, not giving them. What a mess we're in now. I, for one, am glad to have you still around to help us get through it. We need all hands on deck. And the aliens have gone tactical."

38

They had been here for three days now, and there had been no contact with the outside world. Anna and Belle were not forthcoming with any news—just telling them they had to remain hidden. They had spent most of their time either exploring the island or in the gym. And in the evenings, of course, they played music.

Belle had taken it upon herself to expand Bernie's culinary skills. She was quite a chef. And Bernie surprised most of them, Heidi in particular, by being a very willing student. And everything was laid on; none of the guests had ever seen a more thoroughly equipped kitchen and pantry.

Anna and Viktoria spent a lot of time sitting on the sofa talking quietly to each other in Ukrainian. Anna seemed to do most of the talking.

~

It was yet another beautiful spring day on the island; a cloudless sky with a crisp breeze blowing gently from the southwest. Its occupants were making the most of the benign conditions. Jessica, who had her strawberry blonde hair somewhat contained by the hat she was wearing to shade her freckled face, was sitting on a small sandy beach watching Heidi as she swam nearby. The others were undertaking the much more arduous scaling of the rugged hilltop.

As they neared the peak, they heard a boat in the distance. They watched it continue to approach the island, arcing in from the south towards the beach. Bernie and George exchanged worried looks.

"Let's get back to the others. This could be trouble," Bernie warned and headed off in that direction at breakneck speed. The rest of them followed, but Viktoria soon lagged behind and Anna slowed to stay with her. Belle continued on sure-footedly, only slightly slower than the two guys.

The boat, which had several fishing rods protruding from a rack at its rear, continued to approach the beach before anchoring just offshore. Two men, one of them carrying a small backpack, jumped into the water and waded to the beach.

As they started walking towards a rocky ledge, they noticed Jessica, who had just risen to her feet, farther up the beach. They were even more surprised to see Heidi emerging from the water to join her. It stopped them in their tracks. The last thing they expected to see was two women on their own.

Heidi shaded her eyes from the bright sunlight as she watched the men continue their approach, then reached down for her towel and wrapped it around herself, covering much of the wetsuit she was wearing. Heidi raised her eyebrows in question and got a pursing of her lips from Jess in return as they turned their attention back to the approaching men.

When he determined they were within earshot, the younger of the men called out, "Well, bugger me. I thought mermaids were just a myth. Good afternoon, ladies." He grinned widely as he said this and nudged his mate with his elbow. They continued their approach, and when they reached the girls, the comedian held out his hand and introduced himself. "I'm Tim. And this is me mate Steve. First time we've ever seen anyone on this island. What are you doing here? Not in any kind of trouble, I hope."

Jessica was closest to him and returned his handshake. "Good afternoon, I'm Jess and this is Heidi. No, we aren't in any trouble, just getting some exercise. It's a beautiful day, isn't it? Are you guys out fishing—having any luck?"

"Yeah, yeah, got a few. Just pulled in to stretch our legs. Where are you anchored? This is the best spot with this wind, nice and sheltered. You should think about shifting to here."

Heidi helped Jessica avoid answering by shaking hands with Tim and enquiring, "So, you guys come here a bit, do you?"

"No, not often. It's kind of out of the way, isn't it? But the forecast for today was so good we couldn't resist. Where are you visiting from? Let me guess—you're mainlanders."

Jess didn't know what he was talking about, but Heidi had met a few Tasmanians and knew the phrase. "Yes, that's right. Stand out, don't we?"

This got a laugh from Tim. "Nah, just a lucky guess." He dropped to sprawl on the sand, gazed out over the ocean, and said, "Looks so peaceful on a day like this. Hard to believe what happened to the yank ships, isn't it? Just terrible—so many missing."

This comment startled both girls. Heidi crouched down beside him and asked, "What do you mean? Has something happened?"

"You certainly have been isolated, haven't you? Two days ago, there was a major catastrophe off the coast over to the east. The US Navy was conducting exercises and lost one of their aircraft carriers and a battleship. Several other ships were damaged. There are thousands of sailors missing, presumed drowned. Chances of survival in those waters are very slim. The Americans are in a right old state, but the authorities are remaining tight-lipped about what happened." He looked towards his mate. "Word on the street is a UFO attacked them. Can you believe that?"

Both Heidi and Jessica gasped and exchanged horrified looks. Heidi was about to say something when she noticed Bernie and George hurrying down the beach towards them.

She got to her feet and Bernie went straight up to her, standing between her and the newcomers. They noticed his aggressive stance and Tim nervously stood up as Steve took a backwards step. George moved over to stand a couple of metres to their side. As he studied them, Bernie relaxed slightly. They were about the right age and fit, but they didn't have the hard look of special forces soldiers.

Steve grinned and held out his hand. "G'day mate. Should've known these lovely ladies would have guys in tow. I'm Steve."

After they shook hands, Tim introduced himself, doing likewise. His eyes widened as he looked over Bernie's shoulder to notice another girl approaching. And not just any girl. The two he had been talking to were attractive, but this one was in another league altogether. She was far and away the most beautiful girl he had ever laid eyes on. A very trim little package.

Bernie noticed George's expression change and turned to see what had caught his attention. He needn't have bothered.

George said, "Here comes Belle."

She continued jogging down the beach until she joined them. She was panting a little, but Bernie noticed she seemed at ease with the intruders' presence. In fact, she was paying more attention to their boat than to them. That kind of relaxed him a little, but the fact she was studying the boat made him think perhaps there were others hiding on board. Maybe the threat would come from there.

"Nice boat, is Bar Crusher, yes?"

Steve said, "Yeah, my pride and joy. Not that I get to use it all that often. Usually too busy." Both he and Tim noticed the girl's accent but had no idea where she was from. Farther away than the mainland, that was for sure.

"You are farmers, yes?" This stumped her friends. They were becoming used to Belle and Anna coming out with random comments, but this was the first time they knew of where either had made a mistake with their words. Confusing farmers with fishermen. It also took the two newcomers by surprise. How did she know that?

Tim asked, "What, is it that obvious? How can you tell?"

Belle smiled, gesturing with her hand as she did so. "When I was little girl I visited my uncle's farm sometimes. These are my happiest memories. Of that time."

"Yeah, they're great places for kids, aren't they? Where was his farm, not on the North Coast, I bet?"

"No, far away. At Mezyn in Ukraine." As she said this, she had a distant look in her eyes, as if reliving past events. A wistful smile played across her face.

The mood was broken by the arrival of Anna and Viktoria. Tim and Steve looked at each other in disbelief. Another two, exactly the same as the last one. Gorgeous.

Belle introduced them. "These are my sisters, Anna and Viktoria. I do not know these men's names, but they are fishermen ... and farmers."

She emphasised the last word as if it was somehow important.

Tim piped up. "I'm Tim and this is me mate Steve. Pleased to meet you."

Heidi anxiously interrupted them. "We've been out of contact with the news lately. Tell the others what happened to the US Navy."

Tim retold the news about the loss of the naval ships and the rumour a UFO had attacked them.

Bloody hell!

Bernie and George gasped in shock, then turned towards Anna. She returned their eye contact but remained silent. Bernie asked, "When did you say this happened?"

"Two days ago. It was all over the news. There was a massive search and rescue operation. Most of those rescued are aboard the other US ships, but several have been airlifted to hospitals in Hobart and Melbourne."

George said, "That's dreadful. Those poor sailors." He turned towards the direction they had come from and said, "Come on everyone, we'd better be getting back. Nice to have met you guys. Have a safe trip home."

They all said their goodbyes and left, leaving the two fishermen gaping after them.

Steve looked at Tim and said, "Bloody hell, did you get an eyeful of those chicks? And one of them seemed to like farmers. Wish I was single like you. I'd be doing a line for her."

With a shake of his head, Tim said, "Out of our league, mate. Chicks who look like that don't live on a farm."

They made their way over to the shade beneath the ledge they had originally been heading for and opened the beers they had in the backpack.

Tim raised his beer. "To mermaids."

Steve agreed. "Mermaids."

They clicked cans together and proceeded to drink.

~

The group walked in silence until they reached the opening to the elevator. There was no talking during the descent to their current accommodation, either.

Waiting until they emerged from the lift, Bernie asked, "What happened, Anna? Did you attack the US ships?"

"Yes."

"Why, in God's name?"

"They were going to attack this island. To kill us all. I warned them not to do this, but they did not listen. My mother is very angry with them."

Bernie put his head in his hands for a moment and asked, "What do you mean, attack this island? Why would they do that?"

"Because they want to destroy us. They thought this is where my mother is."

Heidi started crying, and said, "But, Anna, this has resulted in thousands of deaths. And is going to cause untold more of them, of loyal and trustworthy men and women just doing their duty. Just following orders. People like Bernie and George. They most probably knew nothing about you or why they were targeting here. Please, your mother must stop her attacks. No more killing, please—for my sake."

"She has stopped them. For the moment."

Heidi sobbed, "Those poor people! And their families; they must be devastated at the loss."

Anna went over to her and tried to comfort her.

~

A semblance of calm had returned to the group. Over dinner, Anna and Belle had reassured them things weren't as bad as they'd heard, and they'd find out more when their mother was ready.

After they had washed the dishes, Belle said, "I am going to make peppermint tea. Would anyone else like one?" They all agreed that sounded nice. Bernie and George wished they had Jess's magical fridge here, but they accepted her offer all the same.

Bernie had an idea.

"Anna, it was such a beautiful day today. Why don't we all go back up to the surface and I'll show you my stars? They'll look magnificent in this clear air."

Anna immediately stood and, smiling, said, "Your stars, Bernie?"

"It's a figure of speech, my favourite stars, then."

Anna chuckled, turned to George, and winked at him. "Just teasing, Bernie. I know this." She headed for the elevator door, with Belle trailing her. They all got in the lift, drinks in hand, and went up to the surface.

~

They formed a circle, each finding a comfortable place to sit.

Bernie pointed to a spot in the sky and said, "That's the Southern Cross. See the shape. That particular group of stars means a lot to us Australians. And you can use it to tell where south is."

Anna looked at Belle and Viktoria and said, "These are not stars we are used to seeing."

Belle pointed at another group. "These, yes. We know them. Orion and his belt."

George gave a little laugh. "The people who named them must've had vivid imaginations."

Bernie agreed. "Too right. Or had some strong liquor in them. You can tell where north is from Orion's belt and a few other stars that appear to be close by."

Anna and Belle both wanted to know how and listened intently as he explained it.

When he finished, he said, "I've shown you my stars, Anna. Which one is yours?"

Anna was still looking skywards, but now shifted her gaze to Belle then waved her hand towards her.

"Belle is scientist. You show him, Belle." Belle went over to Bernie, sat right beside him and leaned in close so he could look along her arm as she pointed towards a star. It was hard to make out, it was so dim.

"This one. Humans do not think it is important, have not even given it name. But it is very special to us. It is where people who made our mother live." After a slight pause, she corrected herself. "Of course, they do not actually live on star, but on planets in its system."

This put them all in a reflective mood, and they sat in silence and gazed at the heavens for a while.

Heidi commented, "The stars are so bright tonight. It seems you could almost reach out and touch them."

Anna gave her a quizzical look.

Heidi explained, "It's a manner of speaking. I don't mean you can actually reach them from here."

Anna nodded, but from the look on her face, Heidi presumed she didn't quite get it.

Viktoria reached out and touched George on the arm. "If you see streak of light, it is shooting star. When you see one, you can make wish and it will come true. You have to make wish while it is still glowing though, and you cannot tell anyone what it is."

Belle and Anna exchanged smiles.

They spent the next half hour or so naming all the constellations they knew. This, with Anna and Belle, was a very comprehensive set. And they all got to make a few wishes as well.

They also saw the lights of an aircraft making the trip between Tasmania and the mainland. Gazing skyward, they saw what it had been like here for eons, mixed with a few signs of the heights to which evolution had reached. And Heidi wondered about the dreams and aspirations of the people passing above them. She reflected on the fact that they, like most of humanity, were completely unaware of those below them.

Belle caught them completely off guard by stating, "Tim is nice man, yes?"

Bernie said, "Belle, it's best if you forget all about him. With what has just happened, and us having to lie low and all."

She shrugged, looked at Viktoria, and said, "Remember days on farm, Vika? They were such good fun."

Viktoria agreed, which caused Heidi and Bernie to exchange a glance. These girls certainly were puzzling sometimes.

Belle said, "I think I will ask my mother if, when I am finished my work for her, I can become farmer. In Tasmania. On North Coast." She smiled widely at the thought.

Viktoria asked, "Speaking of—Anna, do you think I will be allowed to stay in Australia, and when can I resume my acting?"

Anna and Belle both looked at each other and smiled. Still smiling, they both turned to face Viktoria, then Belle moved over and gave her a hug.

Anna answered, "Yes, I am sure they will allow you to stay if that is what you want. And you can start acting again whenever you want to. We are sorry we have had such an impact on your life. We did not intend this."

"It was not all bad; I have met you, George," Viktoria whispered, leaning over to snuggle against him.

George added encouragement. "Australia has a vibrant film industry. I'm sure you'll get lots of work. They won't be able to get enough of you." Viktoria snuggled in even closer.

As was sometimes her wont, Anna took the conversation in another unexpected direction.

Reaching over to touch Jessica, she said, "You miss challenge of work and flying in helicopters, yes?"

"Actually, I'm appreciating the downtime, Anna. I just regret the circumstances that have given rise to it."

None of the others could work out where that comment had come from, or what it was about. Bernie had twigged to the fact that Anna liked helicopters. But how was Jessica involved?

He asked, "What's this all about?"

"Occasionally, I go with Emergency Services as a doctor on the QAir Rescue choppers."

Suddenly standing up, Anna interrupted their conversation, saying, "I must go now. I will be back soon."

She disappeared in a blue flash but returned within the minute.

Heidi asked, "Where did you go, Anna?"

"I was busy."

~

Later that night, as they lay in bed, Heidi turned to Bernie and whispered, "I've been thinking a lot about the girls. What they say. Trying to figure out what it all means. I think we've been missing a lot of clues in their conversations. Anna has said a lot of things I brushed aside at the time. But now I think I'm starting to understand some of it. We've got to take what they say literally. Given they sometimes use slightly the wrong wording."

"That's good news, Heidi. I get lost trying to keep up with them. What do you mean?"

"Well, I'm pretty sure there is only one alien here. Most probably not even an alien, but some form of AI they sent—an Intelligent Probe. One with enormous powers. The girls call it their mother. Anna said her mother came alone and made her and Belle after she got here. And she made them like Viktoria. Bernie; it can copy people. It copied Viktoria to make Anna and Belle. Don't you see? It all makes sense now. Why they look identical. And Belle asking Viktoria if she remembered their childhood. Bernie, they had the same childhood. They are the same person. But Anna also said she and Belle were different to Viktoria in that they can talk to their mother whenever they want to. It must've enhanced them with some kind of communication ability, and God knows what else."

"Really. When did she tell you all this?"

"Oh, dribs and drabs here and there. You know what they're like, coming out with seemingly random comments." She gestured with her hand, trying to make her reply sound offhand. As if this had all just occurred to her.

"OK, wild, but kind of makes sense. But they seem to know everything that's going on. Must have a kick arse intelligence system. Has she said anything about that?"

"Not that I can recall … actually, now that you mention it, Anna said her mother could watch things. She was probably meaning it could spy on whatever it wanted to."

Bernie's expression became a little serious as he asked, "Has Anna ever said anything about me and my work?"

"What do you mean?"

"You know, what I do at work—things like that."

Heidi thought for a while, then answered, "No, Bernie, I don't think she's ever mentioned anything like that? Why do you ask?"

"Just trying to see the big picture here, that's all," he replied noncommittally.

"Babe, I think the picture's so big we may never see it all. And even if we do, I'm not sure we'll be able to comprehend it."

Bernie pulled her in close. "Too big for simple old me, anyway."

Heidi rubbed his arm in support.

"What was everyone thinking? Surely by then they knew what would happen. What Anna and her mother are like."

"They're scared, Heidi. Shit scared. And I don't think they know anything about Anna's mother. Have you said anything?"

"No, I've kept that to myself. And I'm glad I did. I don't trust Judith, not anymore anyway."

Bernie nodded and tried to sneak out the fart he had been suppressing. He was unsuccessful. Heidi slapped him on the arm with a look of disgust.

She pulled the blanket over her head briefly before coming up for air, then said, "That stinks, Bernie. You're disgusting!"

"Sorry babe, you can blame it on Belle's lentils."

"Don't try that, Bernie. Belle had nothing to do with it." She paused for a moment, and while regarding him, a worried expression crossed her face.

"Speaking of Belle, you two seem to be spending a lot of time together. All lovey-dovey in the kitchen."

"Heidi, stop it."

"She is gorgeous, after all, far prettier than me. And I can tell you like her. You seem so at ease with each other, as if you belong together."

"I do like her. And Anna, even more so. When I first saw her at the Opera House, all dolled up to the nines, she took my breath away. They're very attractive girls. Only a fool would deny that. But I can't really explain my feelings. I've got to admit, I was confused for the longest time. After all, we try to understand and analyse things by relating them to what we've already experienced. And we both know we've never run into anything remotely like them before. Given that line of thought, I guess my feelings are most like my love for my sister. They feel like family. And the way I was brought up, that's a bond that can't be broken, come what may. And with all her antics, Anna sometimes feels like a brother-in-arms; she's even got a name. I know they're aliens, but to me they're human. Much more human than most of the people I've met. Why they took such a liking to us is anybody's guess, but I, for one, am bloody glad they did."

He raised himself on one elbow so he could see her better in the gloom of the bedside lamp, then reached over to caress her arm. "What I am sure of is how I feel about you. I'm smitten with you. Have been ever since you got me that drink at the barbie."

He closed his eyes briefly, reminiscing about their first encounter.

"Besides, Belle seems to have her sights set on a certain fisherman she just met. And although we can't see them, this island will be bristling with defences. The fact he made it ashore in the first place is a sign Mummy approves." Bernie pulled her close and kissed her on the side of the neck. "Now, I don't want you thinking any more of this nonsense. It's you I'm in love with, Heidi. Always will be."

<h1 style="text-align:center">39</h1>

The air traffic controllers at Naval Support Facility Diego Garcia had just cleared the incoming USAF C-17 Globemaster to land when there was a huge blue flash across the base. Looking out the windows, they were amazed to see the runway covered with people. Thousands of them. They immediately instructed the Globemaster to go around, cancelling its landing clearance. As they studied the masses on the runway through their binoculars, they noticed most were dressed in naval fatigues. Some were standing looking at each other in confusion, while others were drenched to the bone and lying on the ground. A few were retching. There were also a few in camouflage fatigues, and a small group of airmen were removing their flight helmets. Everyone looked stunned.

The controllers sounded the alarm for emergency services to rush for the runways and urgently reported the event to their superiors, who ordered all available medical officers, defence guards, and any other non-essential personnel to head for the airstrip.

After being marshalled into vacant hangers, the newcomers were given water and questioned as to who they were and where they had come from. The bewildered base commander then called his superiors stateside.

"Sir, I have no way of explaining this, but assembled in some hangars on the base here, I have the entire crews of the *Kansas*, *South Carolina*, *Concord* and all but one from the *Henry Teak*. I also have 4,813 crew from the *Carlton Jackson*. They just appeared out of nowhere. Sir, we haven't had the time or resources for an assessment of their state of health, but they all report to be feeling well, even though some have ingested seawater and several are showing signs of mild hypothermia. They've no more idea how they got here than I do. Except for the four pilots who said they were diving to intercept a UFO approaching the fleet, they all say the last thing they remember is being at their station, or in the water after abandoning ship. Sir, all but the submariners report they were under attack by the UFO."

"Could you please repeat? You're not making any sense."

The base commander repeated his report.

After a brief period of silence came the reply, "Understood. Stand by."

~

There had been a spate of promotions to fill the vacancies at the top of the US command structure. The most unexpected of these involved Admiral Blake.

He had been replaced as Commander of the Pacific Fleet when he voiced his opposition to the planned attack on Australia. He was astounded to leapfrog several others and be appointed as the Chief of Naval Operations. As such, he was now a member of the Joint Chiefs of Staff.

He was still transitioning to this role when he received a summons to an emergency meeting in the Situation Room.

~

When he arrived, Admiral Blake found the room packed.

Maria said, "Good morning, Admiral Blake, please be seated. Now that we're all here, could you turn your attention to the monitor? We have a link with the Commander at Diego Garcia. He has some astonishing news." The monitor came to life and the face of the Commander appeared.

Maria looked into the camera being used for the conference call. "Thank you for staying up to take this call, Captain. I have the Joint Chiefs in the room with me. Could you please bring us up to speed on the situation over there?"

"Good morning, Madam President. Gentlemen. Approximately four hours ago, all the sailors missing presumed lost in the incident off

Australia suddenly appeared on our airstrip." As he said this, the display changed to show the scene recorded from the control tower. It changed again to show one of the crowded hangers.

He continued with his report. "Also among the group were the crews of the *Kansas* and *South Carolina*. No one could understand what they were doing here or how they got here. They reported the last thing they remembered was being at their stations, or in the water after being ordered to abandon ship. I have the commanders of these vessels in the room with me now."

The view widened to show a group of uniformed officers standing close together. The Joint Chiefs exchanged bewildered glances. And relieved ones. The missing sailors were safe. But how had they got to Diego Garcia of all places?

Admiral Blake found his voice first, and asked, "Captain, this is Admiral Blake. You said the crew of the *Henry Teak* are among the returnees?"

"Yes sir, they are. All except one are accounted for."

"Is Petty Officer Marks among them?"

Captain Curtis spoke. "No sir, she is the one member of my crew unaccounted for."

"And the submarines; any idea of what happened to them?"

The captain of the *Kansas* answered, "No sir. We were on station with everything running smoothly, then suddenly we were all standing on the strip at Diego Garcia."

"Captain, we lost contact with you more than a week ago. What was the last date you remember?"

"The 4th sir. September."

"And it seems like the next moment you were on the strip. Nothing happened in between?"

"Correct, sir."

Captain Curtis said, "Sir, they cut the bow off the *Concord* right before our eyes. Clean as a whistle. She went down within a minute. And by all reports, the cause of the loss of the *Carlton Jackson* was the removal of a section of its hull. They have devastating weaponry."

President Gardiner said, "Well, gentlemen, we're all relieved you and your crews have turned up seemingly unscathed. We've dispatched medical teams to help with your rehabilitation. They should begin arriving this afternoon. For the moment, we want you to remain at the base with a complete blackout of any communication with the outside world until we determine how to proceed. You understand our dilemma, of course?"

"Aye ma'am." The response echoed around the group.

~

A blue flash pulsed across the room.

Bethany looked around in amazement. "Where am I?"

Admiral Blake was the first to recover. "Welcome back, Petty Officer Marks. You're in the Situation Room. At the White House. May I introduce you to President Gardiner? She has replaced President Sanger who unfortunately passed suddenly three days ago. Ma'am, Petty Officer Bethany Marks of the *USS Henry Teak*."

Maria gaped at Beth, speechless with shock.

The Admiral turned toward the other woman who had appeared and said, "Hello, Anna."

He got a short and somewhat tersely stated reply. "Admiral Blake."

"Madam President, gentlemen, may I introduce Anna? She is the alien I met on the *Henry Teak*." You could hear a pin drop in the room, such was the silence that comment commanded.

Finally, Maria came to her senses. She stood up and said, "Anna. Thank you for returning our crews unharmed. We are extremely grateful."

Anna bowed her head in silent acknowledgement but when she raised her eyes again, her glare spoke volumes.

Admiral Blake shifted uncomfortably and, stalling for time, asked, "Do you feel all right, Petty Officer? Would you like a glass of water?"

"Yes, please."

Anna waited for Beth to take a sip before speaking. "You have been warned twice now. You should take heed. Third time will be catastrophic for you." There was ice dripping from her voice.

Maria tried to pacify her. "We consider what you did catastrophic enough. We certainly don't want a repeat of that."

Anna swivelled her gaze towards the President, an incandescent rage transforming her face. Maria took a step backwards under the assault of her venom. She thought she might be looking into the face of

Death itself.

"It was in response to actions by you. You exhibit much aggression. If it is war you want, we will accommodate you. And I must warn you, this will not go well for you." Spoken with cold foreboding.

Maria valiantly tried to hold her ground. "The actions you refer to were taken by my predecessor. I deplore them and can assure you I would not have authorised anything of the kind. Please, this is a new government you're dealing with now. We desire nothing more than to come to peaceful cooperation with you."

Anna's eyes still blazed; it was hard to tell if progress was being made. She turned her attention back to Admiral Blake, appearing to be debating whether to say anything further. After a slight hesitation, she snapped her intense gaze back to Maria. "Listen to me very carefully. Heidi and others are to be left alone. If you want to discover what 'fire and brimstone' looks like, continue to test us."

There was a blue flash and Anna disappeared.

Bethany looked around the room and said, "What's going on? Sir, the alien craft returned and attacked us. It disabled the *Carlton Jackson* and sank the *Concord*. Then it came at us and suddenly I was here."

"Yes, Petty Officer, but you are safe now. And the sailors all survived. They've just been returned as well."

"But how? And Anna was here. Why was she threatening you about Heidi? What have you done?"

"All in good time, Petty Officer. Please sit down and take a few deep breaths."

Admiral Blake asked no one in particular, "I wonder why she was brought here?"

President Gardiner replied, "I think because the aliens want her here. And if that's the case, so do I. Admiral, I request you reassign her to duties at the White House. Petty Officer Marks, Bethany, welcome to my team."

She walked towards Beth and extended her hand.

40

Heidi walked into the Signals Directorate building and approached reception. As she neared the desk, a security guard rushed towards her. "Ms Almendinger! We've been searching everywhere for you."

"Congratulations on finding me. I'd like to talk to the Director-General as soon as possible, please. It's a matter of the utmost importance."

"If you'd please come through security and wait while we contact her. I'm sure she'll be delighted to know of your return."

The security checks revealed there was an electronic device in her handbag. When asked what it was, she answered, "Something I need to discuss with the DG."

When informed Heidi had just walked into reception, Judith rushed down to greet her. "My God, Heidi, it's wonderful to see you. Where've you been? We've been searching everywhere for you."

"I've been with Anna. We need to talk privately. At once."

Heidi reached for her handbag, but security pulled it out of her reach.

She looked at Judith, who said, "Her bag please." Once Heidi had it, Judith turned on her heel and they headed towards the lifts.

~

As soon as they entered her office, Judith touched Heidi on the shoulder and said, "I'm so relieved to have you back safe and sound, Heidi. I'm sorry about the police, but I had no say in the matter."

Heidi cringed at her touch and looked back without answering.

As Judith looked at her, she almost didn't recognise Heidi. Her body language was dead. Detached. It was almost as if she was an automaton.

"That's fine. I'm here now and we've got to act quickly before things get any worse."

"Heidi, what's wrong? What's happened to you?"

"Why didn't you protect us? Why did you let all this happen?" She was almost yelling.

Judith didn't quite know how to answer her. She cast her eyes down at the floor and then back up to look directly at Heidi. "I'm so sorry Heidi. I couldn't stop them. They had an arrest warrant."

"But you knew what Anna is like. You knew what would happen."

Such was the force of Heidi's admonishment, Judith took a step back. "I'm sorry Heidi. I'm so sorry. Would you like some time off? Can I arrange some counselling for you?"

"That's not going to help. Let's just get on with it."

"No, Heidi. We need to talk this through."

"I don't want to talk about it. The world has gone to hell."

Judith reached for her phone. "Could I have two coffees brought up, please? Flat whites."

Heidi was just staring past Judith as if she wasn't there. If Heidi wasn't blanking her out, she would have noticed Judith's look of genuine concern.

"I'm sorry Heidi. What did the aliens do to you?"

"Nothing. You still don't get it, do you? They're the good guys here. The ones protecting us."

Judith saw she wasn't getting anywhere, so she left things as they were until their coffees arrived.

But, pretty much as she suspected, that didn't seem to help. Heidi still looked detached. Maybe talking about it would help. She pursed her lips in a sigh of sympathy and said, "You said you were with Anna. Were the others with you as well?"

"Yes, they're all safe. Thanks to her."

Heidi took her coffee over to the window and drank in silence. Judith followed her and gazed outside as well. But neither of them was enjoying the view. Their minds blanked out the visual input as irrelevant, both focusing on internal processing.

When she finished her coffee, Heidi walked back to the desk and placed her empty cup down. She sighed and closed her eyes as she fought to regain control of her emotions.

"Judith, the Americans have gone rogue. They were going to attack the island Anna took us to. With nuclear weapons. Of course, the aliens stopped them, and this time attacked their fleet. I'm sure you know the aftermath of that."

Judith had reached her desk and was in the process of sitting, but she sprang bolt upright in alarm.

"A nuclear strike! Are you sure Heidi? And she had you on an island?"

"She didn't tell us anything about it, but it must be off the northern Tasmanian coast somewhere and yes, Anna told us they were going to nuke it. And, up till now at least, her information has been spot on. From what I've heard, it was a one-sided battle."

Talking about it seemed to help. Heidi was now looking a little more like her old self.

Judith said, "Yes, it was terrible. They're reeling from the loss. We've been trying to decipher their signals, attempting to ascertain why they had a carrier strike group cruising off our coast, but as yet have made no headway. They claim it was just an exercise, but we're sceptical of that, you know, with no involvement with our forces, just them."

"Well, that's all about to change." As she said this, Heidi reached into her bag and took out a small black box on the side of which were several sockets. "This is a decryption device. With it, we can read all their signals."

She paused while Judith studied the device. "But be careful what you wish for. We'll be opening a Pandora's Box."

Judith continued to stare at the device for several moments, replaying the guilt Heidi's comments had triggered, before snapping back to the present. "Did Anna tell you what else the aliens have done?"

"No," she replied with a look of dread spreading across her face.

"They've assassinated Prime Minister Fitzgerald and Ministers

Brown and Curtis. And President Sanger along with several members of the senior US military."

Heidi's hands flew to her mouth.

"Oh my God. I can't believe what she's done. It's just one big, horrible mess. No more Anna—please."

"And the police officers involved in your arrest are still missing. She's probably disposed of them as well. Did she say anything about them?"

Heidi looked about to cry. "No, but she probably has. You've got no idea how angry they are."

"Heidi, you must see a doctor. Do you know any psychologists?"

"No. I'm fine. There's no time for that. I should start the deciphering if I'm not still under arrest."

"I'm not sure of that status, Heidi. But while you're in this building, I'll make sure security keeps you safe this time."

"I strongly recommend you dissuade any further action from the police. You know where that will lead."

"I'll definitely pursue that line."

"Well, why don't I get started then?"

"OK, but only if you're sure you don't need some time to recover."

Heidi shook her head, picked up the device, and left for her desk.

As soon as she was out the door, Judith called Prime Minister Turner.

~

As soon as she hung up, the PM rushed to Judith's office. The two of them were sitting at her desk, discussing Heidi's return and what she had to say.

Amanda was trying to come to grips with the horror of what she had just been told, and to subdue her excitement at being able to access the US messages.

Judith interrupted her thoughts with an unexpected statement. "We've got to be very careful about how we handle Heidi from here on."

"What do you mean?"

"She's very upset at her arrest and what's occurred since then. Given the aliens' unrelenting protection of her, and the extreme measures they're prepared to utilise when doing so, there's a possibility she's one of them."

Amanda recoiled at this statement. "Really? Surely not."

"Amanda, my most vivid memory is seeing Anna for the first time and observing the way she greeted Heidi. It's seared into my mind. It was as if they were old friends. I should've realised all this ages ago."

Amanda frowned and shook her head. "But she has worked here for years. And we have her records; she's grown up here."

"Maybe you're right. Anyway, keep it at the back of your mind. If not one of them, she's part of their bigger picture, that's for sure. An integral part."

Amanda was still frowning at her when she added, "And I'm worried about her. She needs to see a doctor, but it doesn't look as if she intends to."

A blue flash and the appearance of several quite startled police officers interrupted their conversation.

Shit!

Both women jumped to their feet in fright. As she recovered, Judith switched her gaze back and forth between the speechless Amanda and the group of police. They were just staring vacantly back, obviously disorientated and confused.

Finally, Judith asked, "Who are you, and how did you get here?"

The quickest of them to come to his senses said, "I've got no idea where I am or how I got here. The last thing I remember is sitting beside Sergeant Ambrose. We had him detained in Ms Almendinger's house."

Judith walked towards them. "You're in the Signals Directorate Building in Canberra. I think I recognise the two policewomen as those who were here previously and escorted Ms Almendinger away. Am I correct?"

"Yes, madam. If you remember, The Defence Minister came with us and was demanding she give him some kind of communication device that he accused her of having. He was becoming aggressive with her. That's the last thing I can remember."

"I see, and the rest of you?"

After she heard their replies, Judith said, "Ladies and gentlemen, you've all been missing for several days now. As have your detainees. There is a nationwide search underway for you all. I have no idea where you've been or how you got here, but we'll get you to hospital and try to find out what has happened to you."

Amanda asked, "Do any of you know what happened to the detainees? Or where you were being held."

They all shook their heads in reply.

The MP who had replied previously said, "I haven't been anywhere. That I can remember that is. The last thing I do remember is sitting beside Sergeant Ambrose." He looked around at the others as he gave his answer and received nods of agreement.

Judith said, "You're all mixed up in a top-secret operation. After your medical assessments have been completed, you'll be taken to a secure facility while we sort this out. But no mention of this to anyone at the hospital. Is that clear?" As she finished saying this, she reached for the phone to call security.

As they were being escorted out of the office, Judith made another call.

~

Heidi saved the documents she had been working on to her secure folder and went straight to the DG's office. Judith was standing at the door to greet her, and Heidi was surprised to see the Foreign Minister in the room with her.

Judith updated her. "Heidi, Amanda has replaced Prime Minister Fitzgerald. She is now our Prime Minister."

Amanda held out her hand and said, "Welcome back, Heidi. I'm so very sorry about your arrest. One of my first actions as PM was to have your warrant overturned. I was aware of the order, and as part of our government must accept some responsibility, but let me assure you, I was not in favour of it at all. Again, please accept my apology. And we will supply any help you need to get you over your ordeal."

"Thank you, Ms Turner, and the others?"

"The same, Heidi, all cancelled. And it's Amanda. No need for formalities between us."

Heidi turned to Judith and said, "I have several of the US signals between their command and the carrier strike group decoded already. They confirm what Anna told us. Not that I doubted it for a minute, but you can read it for yourself, in black and white."

She waited while Judith and Amanda exchanged glances. "There's something else. They've been repeatedly calling one of their submarines, apparently with no success."

Amanda asked, "Could I see the transcripts?"

Heidi looked at Judith, who pointed towards her computer. Heidi sat at the desk, opened her secure directory, then vacated the chair, allowing Amanda to sit. Judith and Heidi stood behind her as, one after another, she opened the files and read them. No one spoke until the last of the files had been viewed and closed.

As the white-faced Amanda turned towards her, Judith asked, "Where can we possibly go from here?"

Amanda didn't offer an immediate reply. She just closed her eyes and rubbed her temples for a moment before breathing out slowly, then placed her hands on the desktop and pushed herself up. To Heidi, she looked a little fatigued.

"Heidi, could you please carry on with this? In the utmost secrecy. Not a word of this to anyone. And I mean *anyone*. I don't want word getting back to the Americans that we can decode their signals. Not yet anyway. Not until I can get a handle on where their new administration is going with this."

She again closed her eyes, appearing to be coming to some conclusion. "Heidi, do you think you could arrange a meeting with Anna? I'd like to clear up several things with her."

"The last time I saw her, she didn't seem to be in the mood to talk to politicians."

"Thank you, Heidi. Please try to persuade her. I'll be available at any time. And as you decode the rest of the signals, could you please pass them on to Judith immediately? This is crucial information."

After a little more consideration, Amanda said, "Do you think you'd be able to decode their embassy traffic?"

"Yes. I'm sure the device can do that."

Judith interjected. "Heidi, I'd like you to move into my office. I'll get another desk brought in for you to work at. It'll be more secure here. And easier for you to keep me up to date."

Amanda sighed, then went over to Heidi and shook her hand. "Thank you, Heidi. I don't know where we'd be without you. Judith, could you keep me up to date if anything significant comes to hand?"

41

Later that night, Amanda was discussing options with Judith. She had spent the past few hours reading the jaw-dropping naval signals and US embassy traffic.

She pushed her chair back slowly, stood, and paced back and forth several times, then stopped to stare out the window. She stayed there for nearly five minutes.

While still gazing out the window, she said, "I'm going to order the SAS to seize control of Pine Gap. Round up all the US staff and confine them." She looked back at Judith, who was staring at her with wide eyes and her mouth agape.

"Amanda, the Americans are going to scream blue murder if we do that."

"This is us screaming blue murder."

Judith went over to Amanda and touched her on the arm while shaking her head, her eyes pleading not to follow through with this.

Amanda remained resolute. "I want you to send your best people there to collate all their recent communications. But not Heidi. I want her to do the deciphering here. Please make up a list of names. I'll order the operation for tomorrow night."

"I'll make up the list. When do you think you'll require my staff to relocate?"

"As soon as we have control of the site. But of course, not a breath to anyone until then."

~

The next evening at 22:30 hrs Central Australian Time, the power supply to Joint Defence Facility Pine Gap tripped. Inexplicably, the reserve generators failed to start.

Concurrently, four black SUVs raced towards the entrance checkpoint, their lights extinguished; they appeared as fleeting shadows in the starlight. The darkness was no problem for their occupants though, in fact, it was their friend—they were peering through the windscreens with night vision goggles flipped down over their eyes.

The federal police manning the checkpoint raised the boom as they approached, allowing them to speed through unhindered. With pre-planned precision, they dashed to various buildings throughout the site. They had barely screeched to a halt when swarms of black clad operators rapidly deployed and dashed into the buildings. The doors provided no obstacles; they had all the access codes.

~

Caught off guard, the bewildered staff found themselves suspended in time. Their routine shattered, replaced by a stark reality that demanded immediate compliance.

"Australian Army. On the floor. Now!" The command reverberated through the room like a gunshot.

The words hung there, heavy and unyielding. The accompanying threat was visceral, as evil looking weapons pointed straight at them.

Adrenaline surged, hearts raced, and instinct took over. Most dropped to the floor immediately. But not everyone moved swiftly enough. Strong hands seized them, yanked them off balance, and threw them roughly to the floor. Their arms were twisted behind their backs as flexicuffs cut unmercifully into their wrists.

In the emergency lighting's gloom, figures flitted around—phantoms clad in black, their forms merging seamlessly with shadows as if they were born of darkness itself. Night vision goggles flipped out of the way, revealed eyes that held no compassion. Soldiers focused solely on the now, executing their orders with ruthless precision.

~

Although very traumatic for the staff members being restrained, to the SAS operators, the operation went smoothly. That was until they reached the cipher room.

They came around the corner in single file, crouched low in almost a half squat, with their weapons aimed straight ahead.

"Australian Army. Stand down!"

One of the marines standing beside the door instinctively lurched sideways and reached for his sidearm. As it cleared its holster, the rapid spitting of a suppressed weapon mixed with the echo of the barked command. Then came the tinkering of spent cartridges bouncing around on the hard floor. As the marine was thrown backwards under the impact of the rounds tearing into his body, the operator's focus shifted to his companion. But a precious instant had elapsed. The marine had his weapon drawn. A loud boom, boom, booming of a SIG Sauer P320-M18 firing on full auto assaulted their ears. Rounds smashing against his vest halted the operator's forward momentum, then he stumbled sideways as he took one in his thigh. The second and third operators unleashed sustained busts at the marine, driving him first backwards, then to the floor. The acrid smell of gunfire hung in the air, but a deathly quiet descended on the scene. The only sound, the ringing in their ears.

As the fourth operator grabbed his downed mate by his assaulter back panel and dragged him around the corner of the hallway, one of the operators who had just unleashed the hail of fire cautiously approached the two fallen marines and checked for a carotid pulse. He looked back and shook his head.

~

The operation was over within half an hour. Once satisfied the entire site was under their control, the operators contacted the federal police and requested they restore the power supply.

The officer in charge of the seizure then radioed in his report.

~

At 23:15 hrs Eastern Standard Time, the US Ambassador received a call summoning him to Parliament House for urgent talks. As he alighted from his limousine, he received a call from the CIA informing him of the attack on Pine Gap. He terminated the call as security ushered him into the building.

Waiting for him inside were General Mitchell, Major General Henderson, and the new Minister for Foreign Affairs. After hurried and terse greetings were completed, he was invited to sit. When he enquired what this was all about, they informed him he would have to wait for the Prime Minister, who was on her way. Several minutes later, a very tense Prime Minister Turner entered the room.

Amanda opened their discussion. "Good evening, Mr Ambassador, thank you for responding to our request at this late hour. I must inform you I have ordered the seizure of Pine Gap and the detention of all US staff located there. The operation has just been concluded—the base is now under our control. Regrettably, two of your staff were killed while offering resistance."

Her voice wavered a little as she said this. Amanda held the ambassador's gaze as a look of sincere regret washed over her face. She closed her eyes, taking a moment to compose herself, then resumed from where she had left off.

"All other staff who were on duty are unharmed and are being detained on site. Staff rostered off duty have been arrested and are currently being escorted to the site. They will be detained while we review our diplomatic and military alliances with the US. These actions were precipitated by information we have recently received."

She took a quick breath and before anyone could speak, continued, "Furthermore, we request you to inform your government we require all marines based in the Northern Territory be confined to their barracks until they are repatriated to the US. I have instructed our armed forces not to interfere with them as long as they comply."

Her dissertation had a dramatic effect on the Ambassador. He responded in a loud voice. "Madam Prime Minister, I must protest in the strongest terms. Your actions are unprecedented. And the loss of American lives at your hands. Unforgivable."

"It is what it is, Mr Ambassador. When we receive confirmation that your marines have left, we will reopen dialogue with your government. Until then, no calls will be returned."

"With respect, Madam Prime Minister, it is not up to you to decide with whom we have discussions."

"It is when it involves us. Good night, Mr Ambassador."

42

President Gardiner sat in the Oval Office, gazing at the nameplate on her desk. President Maria Gardiner. How had she possibly ended up here? And with such monumental decisions to make. She reflected on life's events for a moment, then blinked and refocused.

She had spent hours rereading the reports on their interactions with the aliens. She had also had long discussions with Bethany, gleaning anything she could from her.

And she had read the extensive files on Heidi Almendinger—the woman Bethany told her the alien was referring to in her ominous warning before she disappeared.

On the domestic front, she had continued with the strong-handed approach of her predecessor and had wrestled control over the rioters and insurgents, with law and order largely being established throughout the country. At least that was a positive.

One of the annoying distractions she was dealing with was the constant hassling she was receiving from the big pharmas. They were pressuring for the documents President Sanger had promised. Secret documents, apparently. At first, she had presumed they were concerning the Swedes' research, but it was now becoming apparent the documents concerned were obtained from the Australians. Covertly obtained. They were stored on a memory stick and designated Top Secret. The stick's current location was in a safe in the George Bush Center for Intelligence.

As well as trying to come to grips with the alien menace, she was instigating changes to the White House senior staff and advisers. That, in itself, was a major undertaking. She had not had any lead time to decide who would be asked to fill the positions. But she knew for sure who would be leaving.

~

Her deliberations were interrupted by a call informing her Pine Gap was under attack. She rushed to the Situation Room. Several aides were already there, but the Chiefs of Staff were still en route.

A call came through from the Ambassador to Australia. Her face paled as she listened to what he had to say, then she almost whispered, "Thank you, Clayton. Our response will take some time to think through." She sat in stunned silence until the door opened and the CIA Director burst into the room.

"Pine Gap has been attacked. Comms are down. Has there been any word from the Australians? Who is attacking?"

"Sit down, Chase."

He sat as instructed, but he continued with his flustered exclamations. "Excuse me, Madam President. But Pine Gap has gone dark. We've got to find out what happened."

"Yes, Chase. The Australians have taken over control of the site. I presume the fact that it has gone dark, as you call it, is because they've shut down our links."

He looked at her as if she'd gone mad. "The Australians? What are you talking about? What the fuck are they thinking?"

"I presume it's in response to our recent activities. They're no doubt wondering what the fuck we were thinking, trying to nuke one of their islands."

"They don't know that. As far as they're concerned, we were just conducting exercises there."

"It appears not. Something has gotten them hot under the collar."

One by one the breathless Chiefs of Staff entered the room. They were brought up to speed with events as they arrived. Once all those close enough to get there in a reasonable time had arrived, the President again gave a precis of the situation.

The last to get there had been the Chairman of the Joint Chiefs. He was livid with rage. *Son of a bitch.*

After giving them a moment to come to terms with the news, Maria said, "It appears the Australians have accomplished, with a group of Special Forces, what the Chinese failed to achieve with a missile."

The Chairman of the Joint Chiefs went ballistic. "They've gone completely off the reservation. We need that site back operational immediately. Without it, we're blind to one third of the goddamn globe. I can have a ranger battalion parachuting in within ten hours. All I need is your authorisation." He was practically ranting.

Maria said, "Sit down, General. We're going to do no such thing. Any other ideas how we react?"

He fired back. "Ma'am, we must take the site back. There's no alternative. And as for bringing the marines home; no way! As soon as the rangers land we should mobilise them to travel there as backup."

"General, you've had your say. Anyone else have anything?"

The Chairman would not be silenced. "Madam President, you are completely out of your depth here. You must authorise the mission. You obviously have no idea how vital that site is."

He was glaring around the room in an attempt to intimidate support from his fellow officers. The president walked to the door, opened it and addressed the secret service agents standing outside. "General Fletcher has just been relieved of his duties. Please escort him from the room and have him detained, incommunicado, until further instruction."

Once he had been removed, huffing and puffing as he left, she turned to Admiral Blake and said, "Admiral, could you please take over as Chairman. Now, were there any other suggestions as to our response to this?" She waited only a moment; it wasn't intended to be an invitation to speak. "Admiral, I want the marines brought home. It is imperative we reopen dialogue with the Australians. All available resources are to be used to get them out of their country."

Admiral Blake looked at her for a moment, still trying to come to grips with the previous exchange. "Yes, Madam President." He looked towards the Chief of the Marine Corps and gave the order. The marines were coming home.

The CIA Director said, "But, Madam President, if the Australians have control of that site, we're not only blind to intelligence gathered in that quadrant of the world, but they'll have access to a lot of our classified equipment. Furthermore, we must consider the welfare of our staff. Have we received any indications as to their status?"

"All they told our Ambassador is that all staff are safe, apart from two marines killed during the seizure. They have also forwarded their identities, along with their regret, but added it was unavoidable given the circumstances."

The Director put his hands over his face. "This is the biggest cluster fuck imaginable."

~

As soon as she returned to her office, Maria called Bethany and requested she join her.

Bethany was still in a whirl coming to grips with her new reality. She was working in the White House! And as a member of the President's personal staff. She felt as if her feet had not even touched the ground, such was the change of pace compared to her previous deployment on the *Henry Teak*. The White House, and America as a whole, were in a complete state of upheaval following the events of the past few days.

Raising her hand slightly, she acknowledged the secret service agents standing outside the room as one of them knocked on the door. She was surprised when Maria herself opened it and welcomed her inside. They were the only two in the room. Bethany felt like pinching herself to ensure she was not dreaming it all.

Maria said, "Bethany, I have a very important role for you in mind. Please hear me out."

"Yes ma'am."

"I'm going to post you to the embassy in Australia. Not as Ambassador, of course, you're far too inexperienced for that. You'll be an aide to the Ambassador. If he pushes back, I'll replace him, but I'd rather he remain in the role, at least until we have the situation with the Australians back on an even keel. Continuity; better the devil you know, you understand."

"Yes ma'am. But what possible use would I be to him? I don't know anything about diplomatic relations."

"I've read your file, Bethany. It's full of terms such as confident, intelligent, resourceful, dependable—I'm sure you'll be able to adapt quickly to the role."

She paused, then explained, "Besides, I'm not sending you there to be of use to the ambassador. I'm sending you there to be of use to me. I need a back door to the Australians. And, more importantly, to the aliens. Official liaisons with the Australians are on hold and with the aliens, they're non-existent. It's vital they be restored or established in the case with the aliens. I believe the key to this is Ms Almendinger."

She tapped the file in front of her. Under the TOP SECRET stamp was Heidi's name in bold print.

"Obviously, she is very close to the aliens. Requesting her apprehension triggered the devastation of our Pacific Fleet. And you heard the warning given to us when you were brought here. The Australians are communicating with the aliens through her, and I want a piece of that action. And she appears to be very much in the loop with the Australian hierarchy."

She pursed her lips as the two women looked at each other in silence. Beth didn't think it necessary to speak yet. In fact, she was still busy processing what Maria was telling her.

"You've had contact with her. I'd like you to develop that to the point of establishing a way we can give and receive messages. If not officially with the Australians, at least timely. Under the radar, so to speak. And any comms channel with the aliens will be a quantum shift in our ability to get through this somewhat intact. Our woefully ill-conceived actions towards them have taken us to the very brink of the abyss. We need to let them know we've changed direction."

Maria studied Bethany. The length of her previous statements exacerbated the silence now pressing in around them.

Finally, Beth blinked and found her voice. "Yes ma'am, I'll certainly try. But I hardly know Heidi. I've only met her once, at the meeting in Australia after the ICBM incident."

"Exactly. That meeting was in Australia. And you were on a very short list. The aliens' list. Bethany, you are the key to getting us out of this mess."

Bethany nodded solemnly and replied, "Yes ma'am. I'll do my best."

43

President Gardiner walked towards the rostrum.

She had spent considerable time deliberating on how to proceed and had consulted with her key advisers. Her mind was now made up. She was going to break with tradition, more than a century of it. A new age was dawning. A new epoch, in fact. She was going to level with the American people. She was going to tell them about the aliens. Of course, she wasn't going to tell them everything about her nation's or the aliens' activities. There are several rungs to levelling after all. But it was going to be bombshell content none the less.

She looked directly at the central camera and started. "My fellow Americans ..."

~

Several hours later, as the public tried to come to terms with what the President had just told them, the Commandant of the Marine Corps was standing on the tarmac at Naval Air Station Pensacola. He was watching the first of the Globemasters containing the marines, previously deployed at Robertson Barracks in Darwin, touch down.

~

The marines were not the only ones back on US soil. The staff from Pine Gap were also home. They were all now housed at Camp Peary, the secretive CIA training facility in York County, Virginia.

The status of Pine Gap was inevitably going to be leaked. The US knew this, but they wanted it to remain unknown to any potential adversaries until they could sort things out with the Australians.

And the Australians would have a lot of questions to answer and actions to explain. The other countries in the Five Eyes Alliance would inundate them with questions that demanded answering. And their answers could spell the end of this critical alliance.

44

The power brokers from the Australian government convened at Parliament House. They were discussing the address to the nation by President Gardiner. All major news channels were in a frenzy, giving their expert opinion, or that of anyone they could find who purported to be an expert. And there was no end to that list. Everyone's tastes were being catered for.

Amanda held up her hand and called for the noisy conversation to come to order.

"Now we have another world of hurt unleashed. How to deal with our media. And deciding how much we divulge."

She looked at her watch and said, "Let's break for lunch and mull things over. We'll reconvene at two."

As soon as she was alone, Amanda reached for her phone.

"Judith, why don't we have lunch together? There are several things I want to talk through with you. How about we get some takeaway and go down by the lake?"

"I'd like that."

"Good, I'll meet you at the Promenade Cafe."

~

They sat on a bench with their gaze fixed across Lake Burley Griffin. The air hummed with the promise of spring, but neither seemed to appreciate their surroundings. Amanda, in particular, was deep in thought.

While still looking over the lake, she said, "I'm heartbroken about the deaths of those marines at Pine Gap. I'm finding it hard to cope, knowing that I'm responsible."

Judith turned to her and reached out and soothingly rubbed her arm.

"Amanda, you're not responsible for that. If anyone, the American government is. It's not your fault. Don't blame yourself."

"It mightn't be all my fault, but I do blame myself. I'm finding it hard to live with."

"We all have to live with ourselves, Amanda. It's the price we must pay for the decisions we make. You are in the position of having to make big ones. Using military force is a horrific thing, and it carries a terrible price. But you made a good one here. Let's move on."

She rubbed her arm again, then removed her hand and returned her gaze to the lake.

Amanda wrung her hands as she did likewise. She pushed her regret to the back of her mind and focused on the events of the morning.

"What do you make of the President's speech?"

"Forthright about the aliens. Unbelievable that they'd be prepared to divulge that. Just shows how desperate they've become. And of course, no mention of targeting one of our islands. Naturally. That'll never come out of their mouths—your thoughts?"

Amanda turned towards Judith. "I'm flabbergasted. As you pointed out, they must be desperate. And it puts us in quite a position with what we say. Officially, that is. Our media will be all over us."

Judith frowned and turned back to gaze over the lake.

"So, you intend to issue a media statement?"

"I don't see any other choice."

Judith swivelled her head to look directly at Amanda.

"Well, I've got an idea on how to manage it. You release the video of the UFO taken from our aircraft. And you trot out Pilot Officer Lawson with you at the news conference when you do it. A thoroughly briefed Pilot Officer Lawson, that is. As to exactly what he can and cannot say. And dressed in full uniform, including his campaign medals. The video will completely floor everyone. The optics of you standing beside him will be perfect. All the questions will be directed at him, not you. Then we sit back and analyse what their reports look like. We can respond with clarifications to steer the conversations in the direction we want."

This suggestion hit a chord with Amanda. She straightened her back and enthusiastically replied, "Fantastic idea. What's this pilot like? Can we rely on him to play along?"

"He's a military officer, Amanda. He's been on ice since the incident, so to speak. His squadron deployed to the Middle East almost immediately after it occurred. They are part of our force that you recalled as a reaction to the thwarted US attack. Once you meet him, it'll be up to you to make that call."

"Right, I'll get him sent here straight away."

They sat in silence for a few moments as they returned to taking in the view over the lake.

After further consideration, Amanda said, "I think I'll have to say something to warn the other countries about what the aliens threatened to do if any nuclear weapons are used. In all good conscience. I couldn't live with myself with the consequences of what that will entail."

This caused Judith to frown. She disagreed but needed to choose her words carefully here.

"I'd advise against that at this stage. We don't want anyone knowing the aliens have been communicating with us. Anyone who doesn't already know, that is. This all needs to be managed carefully."

"But what about the Chinese? They could be preparing for another attack. They've already shown they're prepared to use nuclear weapons and might see this as their chance for a first strike at the US."

"That's a risk requiring detailed appraisal. Unfortunately, Heidi's device cannot decrypt the Chinese signals. That, in itself, is telling. The aliens mustn't want us finding out what the Chinese are up to, and we're still guessing as to their intentions. But we're making very educated guesses. Their assertion that the whole ICBM incident was a fabrication by the US is ludicrous. And their silence since then has been deafening. They haven't been mobilising, and the intelligence the US was sharing with us indicates they are not about to do anything as rash as any further attacks. In fact, their military has apparently completely shut up shop. Something has them rattled. No prizes for guessing what that might be. And yes, the fact the Chinese deployed a nuclear weapon is a moot point. It wouldn't surprise me if they're shy a general or two as a result. Wondering how they lost their brain stems. And I hazard a guess Anna and Belle both speak fluent Mandarin."

Amanda took this all on board. She was still worried, though.

"What about some other rogue nation that has an axe to grind with the US? Seeing this as their big opportunity?"

"We haven't been picking up any signs of that. And we've been looking, believe me."

Judith paused and gazed back out over the lake to give Amanda time to mull over her advice.

"Knowledge is power. When you know what your adversary knows, you are at a distinct advantage. The trick is to keep it so they don't know you know what they know. Don't mention anything about any communication with the aliens. And don't mention anything that will alert the Americans that we can decipher their signals."

Amanda nodded, showing she'd take this advice. As she did so, she stood up.

Judith rose to join her and said, "There is one other matter you should be aware of. The Americans are sending Bethany Marks to their embassy here. Petty Officer Bethany Marks, who was at the original meeting. I think that's highly significant."

Amanda immediately turned toward her and said, "Highly significant indeed. Do you think they're offering an olive branch? Or do you think she is being sent to spy on us?"

"Amanda, I think it's them attempting to open a back channel. I think President Gardiner is a very astute woman, and I can see a glimmer of light at the end of a very long and dark tunnel."

~

Like everyone else, Pilot Officer Lawson had followed the news about the US fleet and he had watched the American President's speech with intense interest. But he had a much better idea of what had transpired than any of his fellow officers. He couldn't understand why the UFO had attacked their fleet. It seemed things had escalated somewhat since that fateful evening of his encounter with it. Maybe that was why his squadron was recalled at such short notice. He kept it all to himself, of course, which wasn't as hard as it would have been for some. He kept a lot of things to himself.

He was surprised, and intrigued, when he received the summons to Canberra. It must be something to do with the UFO. But he had told them everything that had happened; he wouldn't be able to offer any further enlightenment. And if they were looking for a way to defeat it, he wouldn't be much help, either. As far as he was concerned, they were in a complete mismatch.

He stood at attention as the Prime Minister greeted him.

"Pleased to meet you, Pilot Officer Lawson. Thank you for coming. Please—sit."

She pointed to a chair beside the round coffee table in her room and took the other one.

"I presume you've seen the news coming out of the US. The President's speech about the aliens?"

"Yes ma'am." He shifted about nervously.

"It has forced our hand into doing the same. The media are going to be all over us demanding to find out what we know, especially considering the frosty relationship that has developed between the US and ourselves. If they don't get answers, they'll invent their own. We need to take control of the narrative."

Pilot Officer Lawson sat and listened in silence, wondering what this had to do with him.

"I'm going to release the footage of the UFO you took from your cockpit. And I'd like you to accompany me to the press conference when I do so. You can imagine the bedlam that's going to ensue. I'd like you there to answer questions relating to it. Will you agree to do this for me?"

"Yes ma'am. Of course, ma'am."

"Thank you. Now, you can answer any questions regarding the events in the video. But don't mention anything else. Absolutely nothing about the meeting with the aliens or anyone who was in attendance. Or of the Chinese missile. Not a word about any of that. Not even a syllable. Is that clear, Pilot Officer Lawson?"

"Yes ma'am, clear as crystal."

~

The gathered press stood in hushed astonishment, even their breathing stifled, as the video played on the giant monitor fixed to the front wall of the gallery. When it finished, the screen reverted to a still image of the black diamond shaped object.

The Prime Minister held up both hands with her palms facing towards the audience to quell the barrage of questions.

"This is recently de-classified footage of an incident that took place between one of our military aircraft and an unidentified object over the Northern Territory. I'm sure you are all familiar with President Gardiner's speech in which she informed the world there is an alien presence here. And that it was they who devastated the US fleet off our coast. We must assume, if that is the case, this object is associated with that presence. Let me introduce Pilot Officer Lawson. He is the pilot of our aircraft from which this footage was taken. He will describe to you the events of the day. Pilot Officer Lawson ..."

After he had explained the sequence of events, the barrage of questions resumed in earnest. All of them were directed to him and were about the UFO and his impressions of it. The PM didn't have to field a single response. They had a new star. The media briefing went exactly as Judith had predicted. Perfectly really. There's a first time for everything.

45

The Swedish Ambassador requested that a meeting between himself and Prime Minister Turner be arranged, informing them he had important, time critical, information to pass on.

Amanda was annoyed he would call at such a time. She presumed it was a follow up regarding their request for a trade delegation and she had enough on her plate as it was; much more pressing issues to deal with.

But, upon further consideration, the request intrigued her. What did the information entail? And he had described it as time critical. He and his government would have seen both the US's and her press conferences. She was uncertain what they knew of the aliens leading up to this, but now they were at least aware of their presence. And, of course, she remembered that Heidi had asked that they cooperate with the Swedes. At Anna's request. That spelled out that they might be a little more aware of the situation than expected.

She instructed her staff to arrange the meeting.

~

Amanda welcomed the Ambassador. "Good afternoon, Mr Ambassador, what is it you'd like to discuss?"

"Thank you for receiving me, Madam Prime Minister. My government has asked me to pass on information about recent interactions they have had with a mysterious benefactor. A young woman. They were puzzled as to who this woman was and where she obtained the information and materials she passed on. They are now convinced that she is actually a messenger from the aliens who have been interacting with the US and your militaries."

In light of her recent discussions with Judith, Amanda was uncertain how much information about the aliens she wanted to share, but she decided to pursue the conversation.

"That's an astonishing revelation, Mr Ambassador. What did they say this young woman was like? And what was her attitude? As you can tell from our press conferences, they do not appear to be here as benefactors, but quite the opposite. They attacked us."

"That is the urgency of this request. My government has assured me the information given has proven to be authentic. But it is so advanced they could not understand where it has come from. They say, now that we know about the aliens, it's obvious that is where this all originated."

The Ambassador paused to catch his breath. He was obviously very excited. And he wanted to stress his next point.

"Madam Prime Minister, we think the aliens' intentions have been misinterpreted. We think, if approached in the correct way, they will be prepared to help us all. Unfortunately, she has not been answering our calls, but we will keep trying. We desire nothing more than to help you establish contact with them. And ease any tensions that may have developed. When we make contact, if you agree, we can inform her of your wish to do so."

Amanda sat in silence and deliberated further on what she was going to share with the Swedes.

After some thought, she said, "What you're saying is incredible. You've met one of their messengers?"

"So I have been informed. And she said they have a presence in Australia. They are in contact with someone here as well."

Amanda continued with her deception. "Someone here. In Australia?"

"Apparently. That is what their messenger told my government."

"And she talked directly with your government?"

"All I've been told is that she met with several of our ministers. I don't know which ones exactly."

Amanda paused again while she decided how to proceed.

She put her head in her hands for several seconds, then, with her decision made, raised it and said, "Perhaps it will be best if I can talk to the members of your government who were at the meeting. It's probably best if we do so via a conference call from your embassy. Do you think you could arrange that?"

"I'm sure it will be possible, Madam Prime Minister. What would be a suitable time for you, remembering the time difference between our countries?"

"I'll make myself available at any time suitable to them. As you stated, this could be time critical."

"I can make the arrangements now if you like."

"Perhaps it will be best to make any calls from your embassy. On secure lines. Once it's arranged, please let me know and I'll meet you there."

"Thank you, Madam Prime Minister."

The Ambassador hurried back to his embassy.

~

Amanda was not overly surprised when her aide informed her the meeting had been arranged. Only an hour had passed since the Ambassador had left. The Swedes were indeed taking this seriously. It was the early hours of the morning in Sweden at the moment.

The Ambassador was waiting for her at the embassy entrance and led her straight to his office. He initiated the video conference call with the group of Swedish ministers gathered half a world away.

"Good morning, Nils, I have Prime Minister Turner with me now. She informed me the two of you have not met. Nils Gustafsson, Amanda Turner."

Nils said, "Thank you for agreeing to talk with us, Prime Minister Turner. First, let me again offer our country's condolences on the passing of Prime Minister Fitzgerald."

He paused to show his sincerity, then continued, "I have several members of my government here with me. We were all present at the meeting with the young woman that Walter has told you about."

Each of the ministers introduced themselves. Amanda had come prepared with a list of all the Swedish Ministers along with their photographs, so she could keep up.

After the introductions were completed, Amanda said, "Prime

Minister Gustafsson, Walter has told me you consider this woman to be involved with the aliens."

"Yes, Prime Minister Turner. That is the case. And please, it's Nils. With everything that's occurring at the moment, it would be nice for us to be on first-name terms. I have to say, the young lady was extremely polite and very generous. She showed no signs of hostility whatsoever. It's hard for us to understand why they are showing such hostile intent towards you and the US. It is our greatest desire to help tone down the relationship that has developed between you. We'll offer any assistance we can to help achieve this."

"Thank you, Nils. We're very grateful. Our dealings with the aliens are not as strained as you believe them to be. I am sad to say, it appears to be a different story with the Americans. And Walter has just told me one of our citizens has been to visit you."

Nils said, "Perhaps it's best if Sara answers that."

Sara related the details of Heidi's visit.

Amanda said, "I see. Does this citizen of ours have a name?"

Nils butted in. "Unfortunately, we are not prepared to divulge that information at present. In the interests of protecting the individual concerned. I hope you understand."

"Indeed. And thank you for your concern for their welfare."

Amanda reopened her tablet and held a photo in front of the camera.

"Would this be the person we are talking about?"

She carefully studied the faces at the other end of the call as she did so. Their expressions gave her the answer she expected, even though nothing verbal was offered.

She opened a second photograph and held it in front of the camera.

"And would this be your mysterious young benefactor?"

After a moment's pause, Amanda said, "I see you recognise them both. These two young women are well known to us. And rest assured, you need not fear for their safety. From us, or anyone else for that matter."

Amanda wanted something else cleared up as well. She asked, "Nils, have you talked to the US about any of this? After all, they are the ones faring the worst with the actions of the aliens."

"No, Amanda, not at this stage. We wanted to talk it through with yourselves first, given the knowledge that at least someone in your country was in contact with them."

"Thank you for that. I agree—at this stage—the less they know, the better. The aliens appear to not be on good terms with the Americans at present."

"It certainly appears so."

"You seem to have had quite a few ministers at your meeting. Did your benefactor show any preference as to who she talked with?"

Nils indicated Sara should answer. "Actually, she talked at length with our scientific experts. And I have to say, from my experience, scientific experts appear to be a staid group of individuals. But when discussing the document, they were anything but that. I have never seen anyone more animated in my life. She did, however, request a further meeting with both me and our Minister of Climate and the Environment. She was very keen to discuss addressing climate change, specifically within the EU. And she has requested that we arrange for her to address their assembly. That was taking a little time to arrange, but, with these latest revelations, we suddenly have the green light. We have it scheduled for two weeks' time."

"Enlightening. Is this also where your request for a trade delegation to discuss regenerative agriculture with us originated?"

"Yes, it is. We thought a collaborative approach might be more productive."

"I'm sorry for our initial response to your request. We had a lot to deal with at the time and our resources were stretched thin, to put it mildly. But, it's an area we are interested in. Considering recent events, I think it's now time for us to pursue this. We would be very welcoming to your delegation. In fact, we'd like it arranged as soon as possible. And, Nils, I'd be delighted if you were to visit us with the delegation. I'd very much like to develop a closer relationship between our two nations. Perhaps even a first-names one."

Amanda gave a cheeky smile as she added this last statement. Nils mirrored her expression, a smile playing across his face.

Amanda closed the call after saying, "Thank you for sharing this information, and for all of you getting up so early in the morning, or staying up so late, as the case may be. I'm very much looking forward to meeting you in person."

46

Beth was greeted by US diplomatic staff at the airport and taken straight to the embassy. Waiting for her arrival were the Ambassador and the CIA Chief of Station. Neither of them was particularly pleased at her presence, but they hid the fact during their greetings. The Ambassador didn't want some rookie here getting in the way. He had a minefield to tread with the Australians. And the CIA didn't want Naval Intelligence, which they suspected her to be, stomping around on their turf. The Pine Gap affair was going to require kid gloves to resolve, and the CIA wanted to be the ones doing the handling.

She was informed of the location of her office and of the accommodation arranged for her. They spent the next several hours grilling her about the mood in the White House, and about any information she had of their intentions going forward.

Bethany was somewhat jet-lagged from her trip, but she was so hyped up with adrenaline that she stayed focused during the entire time. *Tell them what they want to hear. Keep your cards close to your chest.* That kind of thing. They then excused her and told her to go and rest to get over her trip.

~

Beth was trying to think of ways to 'accidentally' run into Heidi.

Her intel briefing had informed her Heidi had a group of friends who sometimes went to music gigs. Jazz clubs; that kind of thing. Beth was going to try that avenue.

She spent the evening of her arrival walking beside the lake, just in case of a chance meeting. Unfortunately, she had no luck on that front, but these things take time. Anyway, it was a relaxing walk after being cooped up during her long flight.

~

As her first weekend in Australia approached, Beth decided she'd spend Friday night at the Jazz Bar. It offered an outside chance of running into Heidi, but also a good way to unwind and maybe meet a few interesting people. She liked jazz—could even sing a little. Apparently, the club sometimes invited impromptu performances from the crowd. It promised to be an enjoyable night out—if nothing else. The Ambassador considered her too low in the pecking order to warrant a protection detail. That suited Beth just fine.

~

Beth was enjoying herself. The jazz was fantastic. Live music! It was not something she could enjoy while at sea. She missed that side of civilian life.

And she had put her name down to perform. She had chosen *What a Wonderful World*. It was her all-time favourite, and although not originally written as a jazz song, it had become a cherished classic in their community.

As yet, she had not been called to the stage.

~

Heidi sat on her verandah watching the moon rise while she sipped a glass of wine. She was exhausted; things were frantic at work. There were so many messages to decode. And their content was either frightening or encouraging, depending on the particular message, or on your point of view.

She was startled to see Anna walking up to her house.

"Anna! What brings you here?"

"I visit my friend. Spend some time with you."

Heidi suspected there was a little more to the reason for her visit than that, but let it pass.

"Come on in. I'll get you a glass of wine." After Heidi handed Anna's glass to her, she said, "To friends spending time together."

Anna smiled and clinked glasses. They both drank the toast.

"Where is Bernie?"

"He's working late, meetings—that kind of thing. Everything's pretty hectic at the moment, as I'm sure you're aware."

"Heidi, we should go to jazz bar. Relax and have good time. Take your mind off work, yes?" As she said this, Anna stood up and reached out to take Heidi by the hand.

Heidi had been planning to retire early and didn't particularly feel like going out tonight, but she wasn't going to say no to Anna.

"What a good idea. I'll just freshen up and get changed. I see you're dressed for a night out already."

Anna smiled and continued to sip her wine while Heidi went into her bedroom to get changed.

~

Upon hearing her name announced, Beth walked purposefully towards the stage. She was a confident young woman, so it wasn't all bravado. Yet amidst all her excitement, she felt a touch of nervousness; she hadn't sung in public since high school.

Heidi and Anna had just walked in the door when Beth turned towards the audience. Heidi recognised her immediately. She cast an accusing glance at Anna, who smiled cheekily back before cutting short any further admonishments from Heidi by moving closer to the stage. Heidi trailed behind.

As she was being introduced to the audience, Beth noticed them. She caught her breath.

Oh my God, they're here.

Not one; both of them!

Their presence distracted her, and suddenly her heart was racing and her skin goosebumped. Focusing, she closed her eyes and took a deep breath to clear her mind.

She gripped the microphone lightly, almost in a caress, and relaxed into the moment, soothed by the expectant hum of the crowd and the embrace of the stage lights. Her voice lost its usual military timbre and, using much softer and emotional tones, she said, "Ladies and gentlemen, this song is dedicated to a dear friend, one who has stood beside me through events none of you could even comprehend." Smiling and making eye contact, she continued, "This is for you, Anna."

She signalled to the band, and they started the intro music. She swayed to its beat until it was time for her to begin. The audience fell silent; their entire world focused by the stage lights. She sang from her heart, glancing around at the audience during her performance, but returning to look at Anna whenever she sang the line 'What a wonderful world'.

There was a standing ovation and yells of approval, not only from the audience, but from the band members as well. She gracefully bowed her acceptance of their acclamation, turned and gestured towards the band, clapped them, then left the stage. She walked straight over to Anna and Heidi.

Anna greeted her in her usual way, and said, "That was beautiful, Bethany. Who knew you could sing like that?" She patted Heidi on the arm. "This is my friend Heidi, you met her at meeting. You remember her, yes?"

Beth reached out to grasp Heidi's hand. "Yes, of course I do. Hello, Heidi, nice to see you again."

As they shook hands, Heidi replied, "Yes, Bethany, it is. Although I wish things had not progressed the way they have since that meeting."

"So do I, believe me. And my country has precipitated most of it. For which I am truly sorry."

Their discussion was interrupted by a waiter approaching and handing Beth a glass of bourbon. "From the gentleman over there." She turned her head towards a group of middle-aged men sitting around a table. One of them raised his glass and Beth returned the salute.

Turning her attention from him, she looked back at Anna, and said, "Well, it appears I'm right for a drink. What can I get for you ladies?"

They sat together at a vacant table while Beth ordered their drinks. Anna engaged in small talk about where Beth had learned to sing until the waiter returned.

Beth was elated she had made contact, not only with Heidi, but with Anna herself. And the fact they were together, apparently socialising, reinforced President Gardiner's assumptions about Heidi's central role in interactions with the aliens.

She was wondering how to proceed when Anna said, "Your new President is much different from those who preceded her."

This was her in. Anna had directly mentioned the President. The next few exchanges were going to be crucial to her mission.

"Yes, she is. Very much so. Anna, she's desperate to have a way of talking things through with both yourselves and with the Australians. To try to resolve our issues. Behind the scenes. She thinks this can be achieved via Heidi and me. That's why she sent me here."

Anna held eye contact with her for a moment, then looked at Heidi, inviting her to speak.

"Bethany, I'm not even a part of our government, let alone senior enough to act in that capacity."

"Exactly, Heidi. Neither am I. Until a couple of weeks ago, I was a Petty Officer aboard one of our ships. Under the radar, that's us. Out of the official loop. We're not damaged goods. And we have the contacts. Official channels of communication between our countries are so damaged it might take years to re-establish them completely. And we have no way of liaising with the aliens as you do through Anna. We desperately need that to avert the nightmare facing us."

Heidi looked at Anna for guidance on how to proceed.

"You should speak with Bethany. Pass information. If American President wants to get message to us, she can do this through you. If she wants to get message to your government, you can tell it to Judith."

"Yes, if that's what you want, Anna, of course I'll agree to it. But Judith isn't part of our government either."

"Message will get through. She has ear of Prime Minister."

When Heidi nodded, Bethany couldn't hide her elation. She had not even been here a week and things were in motion. She looked at each of the others and said, "Thank you both so much. Heidi, how do you think we should meet to pass messages? Without either of our authorities becoming aware of it, that is?"

Again, Heidi looked to Anna for guidance.

"You should join fitness classes. Same ones. You can meet there."

They both agreed that was a good idea.

Later in the evening, as she left the club, Bethany sent a single text message. She used the phone given to her personally by the President. It was a brief message.

"Yes! On both counts."

47

President Gardiner sat in the Oval Office staring at the message on her phone. Bethany had pulled it off. And almost as soon as she'd arrived. Although elated, the coming events daunted her; she wasn't sure if she could follow through to a satisfactory conclusion. But she had to succeed—in this instance, failure was definitely not an option.

She reached for the phone and called the Australian Ambassador.

"The last of our marines from Robertson Barracks are now back stateside. I hope their absence will be a short one. In our haste to comply with your wishes, most of their hardware was left behind. Of course, you also have possession of all our hardware at Pine Gap. The upside is it will be there upon our return."

She paused, but Ambassador Walsh remained silent.

"As this was your country's demand when you severed diplomatic ties with us, I assume we can now get them re-established. Please inform you government of our great desire to do so."

"Yes, Madam President, I will. Although I must warn you that, if at all, it will be a very cold relationship going forward. We are furious at your unprecedented actions."

"Thank you, Mr Ambassador. Consider that noted. Furthermore, I respectfully request arrangements be made for me to visit Australia. I wish to talk to Prime Minister Turner face to face. I don't want any possibility of what I have to say being misrepresented or misinterpreted." There was a very terse edge to her voice.

The ambassador swallowed nervously and replied, "Yes, Madam President. I will pass on your requests."

~

The President's request for an official visit placed Amanda in a quandary. It would be a major step in re-establishing the previous and longstanding relationship between their two countries. However, she was not prepared to exacerbate the current anti-American sentiment simmering within her country. Rumours were rife that the US had been preparing to attack Australia. And the seizure of Pine Gap had been leaked. By the United Kingdom, of all places. A visit by the President could cause major rioting and civil unrest. It was too early for her to agree to the request.

~

Once informed of this, Maria recalled Bethany to the US. She wanted to give her specific instructions, but not via any electronic means. Not that she was worried about the Australians intercepting her communications; she was concerned her own embassy staff would decode them and realise Bethany's true role. That had to remain a secret between the two of them.

When she arrived in Washington, Bethany was escorted directly to the White House.

Maria said, "I'm delighted with your progress in establishing contact with Ms Almendinger. Your message seemed to indicate you made contact with Anna as well. Is that the case?"

"Yes ma'am. They approached me, in fact. Anna seemed OK with the idea of us passing messages between our governments. In fact, when I suggested it, she told Heidi to agree."

"That's the best news I've heard since first finding out about the aliens. Let's get straight down to business. I see it as imperative that I meet with the Australian Prime Minister. As soon as possible. We must get back to normal relations with them. I'd like you to plead our case to them via your contact with Ms Almendinger. If they won't agree to me visiting Australia, then suggest a visit here by Prime Minister Turner. I need to know if she'd agree prior to me extending an official invitation. A refusal by her at that stage would just throw fuel on the fire with both our media. Once we're back talking to the Australians, we can tackle the far more difficult, but crucial, task of getting the aliens to establish an official liaison with us."

"Yes ma'am. I'll do my best."

"I'm sure you will, Bethany. And, of course, it's imperative your true role there remains a secret from all our embassy staff, including the ambassador."

"Is that why you brought me back here instead of just phoning me?"

"Exactly. But I can't have you flying back and forth each time we need to talk. We need a few simple code words."

"Yes ma'am."

"OK. 'Yes' stands as the code for her changing her mind and agreeing to my visit there. 'Maybe' serves as the code for her agreeing to visit here. 'No' for neither option being agreed upon—no progress with any of it as yet. You can text the messages on the phone I gave you."

"OK, ma'am, yes, maybe, no. Got it."

"There is one other thing you need to do for me, Bethany." As she said this, Maria opened a drawer of her desk and retrieved a USB memory stick. She placed it on the desktop and pushed it towards Beth.

"This is something that belongs to Anna. Could you please return it to her for me?"

Beth picked it up and said, "Is this what I think it is? And what do I say to her?"

"Actions speak louder than words, Bethany. Sometimes, the action speaks for itself."

~

Heidi was pulling on her tracksuit top as she prepared to leave the gym when Beth approached her.

"Hi, Beth. You've missed some classes. Have you been ill?"

"Hello, Heidi. No, I've been away. Quick trip back to the States. Business trip, actually."

"Oh, nothing of my concern, then."

"Actually, it was directly concerned with you. Can we talk?"

"Let's go over to my car. Out of the weather. We can talk there."

"Are you sure it isn't bugged?"

"No need to worry on that account, Beth—Anna, you know."

Beth gave a wry smile. "Great."

Heidi started the engine to get the heater going.

"So, what have you been up to, Beth?"

"I've been talking with the President, of all people. She is desperate to patch up relations with Australia. She's very disappointed Prime Minister Turner refused her request to visit here, and she has asked if you could help to persuade her to change her mind. And if not, would she agree to visit the US?"

"I didn't know about the President wanting to visit. It seems strange Prime Minister Turner refused. At any of the meetings I was at, she always seemed to plug the 'communication is key' message."

"Well, anyway, could you do this for us? Pass on the message?"

"Of course. But all I can do is pass it on. I don't have any way of arguing your case for you."

"I understand that."

Beth opened her purse and took out the memory stick. She showed it to Heidi and said, "President Gardiner asked that I return this to Anna. She wants me to give it to her personally, if possible. Do you think you could arrange for us to meet?"

"I'll ask her if she'll come to the gym for our next class. It'll kill two birds with the one stone; she loves to exercise."

48

The Swedish delegation gathered at their embassy for a formal reception. It was a black-tie event, with small groups clustering in quiet conversation. A string quartet provided a subdued background, adding to the elegance of the evening. The Australian officials who were going to take part in the forthcoming meetings were also in attendance. It was an event designed to get everyone to at least meet each other, if not to become familiar. The subtle hum of their conversation announced the promise of connections forming, relationships developing. The language for the evening was English — necessary as none of the Australians present spoke a word of Swedish —and possible, as all the Swedish delegation, like most EU residents, spoke at least passable English.

Amanda was having a one-on-one chat with Nils.

"Nils, these aliens ..."

"I know. The technology they have shared with us is mindboggling. I know you are holding things back. Can you tell me more—?"

The Ambassador's approach interrupted them. He had the aide accompanying him repeat his message.

"Excuse me, sir, a young lady has just approached security and told them she wishes to attend the ceremony. She says we should ask Prime Minister Turner if that would be agreeable. She identified herself as Anna. No last name, I'm afraid. There is no one with that name on the invitee list."

The three men looked to Amanda for a response, but she just closed her eyes.

Anna has come here! This is going to get interesting.

Opening her eyes, she said, "Yes, I know Anna, and I would be delighted if she were to join us."

Both Walter and Nils still had puzzled expressions. This was highly unusual and not at all accepted protocol. They were looking for a further explanation. Amanda grinned and touched Nils on the arm.

"The evening is about to get very exciting, Nils. I believe you will recognise the young woman, or think you do."

Nils' mind raced. A young woman? Recognition? Amanda's playfulness was contagious.

"Of course, Amanda." Turning to the aide, he continued, "Could you please have the young lady brought up?"

As the aide left, Walter continued to look at Nils with a puzzled expression, wondering what was going on.

As if she already knew their exact location within the gathered crowd, Anna singled out their group as she entered the room. She wore a dazzling smile as she walked towards them.

Anna held out her hand in greeting. "Good evening, Amanda."

"Good evening, Anna. What a pleasant surprise. Please, let me arrange a drink for you."

Both the men were still processing Anna's arrival. Walter still wore his nonplussed expression and Nils' eyes appeared about to pop out. Amanda motioned to an aide to arrange the offered drink.

Removing her hand from Amanda's grasp, Anna turned slightly and offered it to Nils.

"Pleased to meet you, Nils. I am Belle's sister, Anna." She gave a subdued bow in his direction. Then, inclining her head briefly towards the ambassador, she followed on with her greetings. "Walter."

Nils grasped her offered hand, feeling the warmth of her skin. Her grasp was gentle, giving no indication of the power rippling within. He found his voice. "It is my greatest pleasure to meet you, Anna. I must say, you and Belle look remarkably alike."

"Yes."

A waiter approached and offered Anna a tray containing a flute of champagne.

Nils raised his glass and said, "To new friends."

Anna modified the toast. "And to countries cooperating."

They all drank to that.

Anna held eye contact with Nils as she lowered her glass, then glanced around the room briefly. "Your first time in Australia, Nils, yes?"

"Indeed, Anna, and what a remarkable country it is."

Anna leaned in, her voice conspiratorial. "My friends live here."

"They are truly fortunate people to have a friend like you," whispered in reply.

Anna smiled, a mixture of grace and devilment. She turned to Amanda and said, "You should speak with President Gardiner. Perhaps it is better you do this in neutral country. So neither of your nations sees you as backing down." Anna held eye contact with Amanda and had a look telegraphing it would be wise to accept this advice.

While Amanda was still considering how she would answer, Nils butted in. "If that is what you decide to do, please let me offer to host the talks in Sweden. It will be our great honour."

Anna was still looking intently at Amanda.

Amanda paused, then breaking eye contact, looked at Nils and said, "Thank you for your kind offer, Nils." She looked back at Anna. "If President Gardiner is willing, I would make myself available to meet her in Sweden."

She lent in closer to Anna and continued the conspiratorial tone Anna had adopted with Nils.

"Would you like to join us, Anna? I understand President Gardiner is desperate to talk with you as well."

"Yes, I will come."

Anna's smile was enigmatic, a Mona Lisa curve.

49

They were standing at the top of the run. The day's skiing instructions were over and they were relaxing. Bernie held up his phone while Heidi and Anna posed, smiling and hugging one another, and took a photo.

Anna said, "Take one of Bernie and me, Heidi."

Bernie passed over the phone and pulled Anna in close. She twisted and put both her arms around his neck, smiling towards him. Heidi captured the moment. Then, with her arms still around his neck, Anna pulled herself higher, leant in and pressed her forehead against Bernie's, saying softly, "Thank you, Toast."

"You're welcome, Arc. And it's me who should thank you. For everything."

Their embrace continued; an icy mist marked each exhale as their breathing subconsciously synchronised, enhancing their connection — a silent testament to their shared warmth.

Anna suddenly pulled away.

"Race you to bottom."

She grabbed her ski poles and took off down the slope. Bernie immediately did the same and skied in pursuit, leaving Heidi fumbling to put the phone in her parka pocket before following.

Anna was waiting when they arrived, almost simultaneously, at the bottom of the run.

"Ha-ha, I am good at this. It is much fun. You have to try harder,

Bernie."

"Yes, Anna, you take to skiing like a duck to water. You're too good for me. I was trying my hardest. Believe me."

Heidi, still a little out of breath, panted, "That's enough exercise for one day. Let's head back to the chalet."

~

Bernie was having a shower while Heidi sat beside Anna on the lounge. She thought that, although Anna had seemed in high spirits recently, she appeared a little pensive at the moment. Despite, or perhaps because of, all the events that had occurred during the last year, Heidi felt contented. They had become such good friends.

And Heidi wasn't the only one with a new friend. Mother Nature now had one as well. Heidi just knew things were going to get better from here on. She was positive of it.

She said, "Anna, I'm so glad to have met you. I can't imagine my life would feel full without you."

As a wistful look played across her face, Anna replied, "Yes—our lives. We are humans and it is our fate to get old and die. But my mother has promised me she will always remember us. She will be lonely without us, but she will remember us as we are now. With her, we will be forever young."

Anna pulled Heidi in close and pressed her forehead to Heidi's. Smiling, she repeated softly, "Forever young."

She pulled away slightly so she could look Heidi in the eye. "Heidi, I will not be able to visit so often anymore. I have much work to do for my mother. But I will think of you often."

Heidi blinked back tears. "I understand, Anna. You and Belle have done so much already. How is she, by the way?"

"She is well. This is why I will be so busy. Our mother wants me to do Belle's work for her. Belle wants to go farming. And have many babies. We are happy for her."

"And you, Anna. Are you interested in anyone romantically?"

"No, too busy for this, and my mother's work is too important. But I am still young; perhaps someday. If I meet someone who I do not frighten."

"Once people get to know you, Anna, you aren't frightening at all. Quite the opposite, in fact. You give us all hope."

Anna smiled at the compliment and appeared to be preparing to stand, but stopped when Heidi asked, "Why me, Anna? Of all the people in the world, why pick me?"

Anna relaxed back into the lounge and cuddled in closer to Heidi. Her expression changed yet again, this time to one Heidi could not quite categorise. She reached up and caressed one of Heidi's earrings, her touch lingering as if she wanted to maintain the embrace. Caught up in the moment, Heidi suddenly understood. She realised why she hadn't recognised the fleeting expression that had played across Anna's face. It was so enigmatic. Anna, once fierce and unyielding, now revealed a softer side. It was an unspoken plea for closeness, a wistfulness that made her vulnerable; human.

Anna whispered, "Would you like to watch movie with me? It is my mother's favourite. She loves it and watches it over and over."

"Of course, Anna. I'd love to."

Suddenly the wall opposite them dissolved into a startling clear 3D image. All of Heidi's attention was transfixed on the scene, reliving past events as if she was there once again.

~

The mournful echo of the church bells announced the passing of midday. Nuremberg's town square was awash with people, some hustling with preoccupied purpose, some milling around seemingly aimlessly, while others appearing to be doing nothing more than idling the day away.

In stark contrast to the crowd, one man stood motionless and isolated near its centre, no emotion showing on his face. It was his clothes that set him apart. And what he was holding. Combined, they screamed to all but the blind that he didn't belong here. Perhaps it was his impeccable black formal dress suit, or maybe the double bass instrument he was supporting in front of him. Even more incongruous with his attire was the dark tint in the adaptive lenses of the glasses he was wearing.

A small girl, perhaps eight years old, somewhat tentatively, somewhat boldly, approached the man to stand directly in front of him. She stopped with just enough distance between them to maintain her personal space. In contrast to his grandiose attire, she was clad casually in faded jeans, a simple blouse, and a red cardigan. Her blonde hair added further contrast between them. She bravely stared the man directly in the eyes and raised the cheap wooden recorder she was clutching in her right hand to her mouth.

She soloed the opening bars of Beethoven's *Ode to Joy*.

He matched her gaze, then repeated the melody. The deep, visceral sounds of the double bass reverberated several octaves lower than those of her simple instrument. He was not quite smiling now but had a look of benevolent encouragement. Emboldened, she resumed her lines. He waited until she had finished before continuing with the tune. The little girl smiled shyly and lowered her instrument, not knowing the rest of the music.

While he was playing, and seemingly from nowhere, another musician appeared. A violinist. Similar to the little girl, she was casually dressed. Although no longer playing, the little girl stood her ground, occasionally moving subtly to the beat but mostly standing stock still, feeling and rejoicing in the music she was hearing. Gradually, more and more musicians appeared, the flash mob expanding to a full orchestra. Their rich sounds resonated throughout the square.

This performance, of course, captured the attention of the milling crowd. They stopped to listen, watch, and feel the music. It seemed to entrance them, obviously elevating their mood as evidenced by their faces and demeanour.

Suddenly, an entire choir burst into accompaniment, their powerful voices adding another dimension to the performance. They were singing in German, their native language. This was the language in which the song was meant to be sung, so nothing was lost in the translation. Many of the audience also joined in, lost in the moment, and non-self-consciously singing with whatever quality of voice nature had bestowed upon them.

The performance ended in a crescendo of sound, and, true to its title, the entire assembly was beaming with rapturous delight, none more so than the performers who bowed their thanks to the generously applauding crowd.

~

Heidi had seen this all before; not in such breathtaking clarity, but on her TV screen. The YouTube clip was one of her own mother's favourites, and they had watched it together on numerous occasions during her youth.

Using the same sweeping hand gesture she had used when first introducing herself and Belle, seemingly a lifetime ago, Anna said, "All of this, Heidi, because of you—and your music."

"Anna, it was just a performance. I didn't teach the music; the orchestra already knew it and had practised it many times. My role was just to play the first part to get the performance started."

Anna's gaze pierced through the mundane. "We know this now, Heidi." Her voice held the weight of revelation. "But it has taught us so much about humans and what they are capable of. Potential they have. What they strive for. How they want to behave. And it has shown us power of fantasy."

"Yes, Anna, it's very uplifting music. But as you've come to discover, we humans very rarely behave this way."

Anna became serious. "Heidi, this planet is very special to people who made my mother. It supports life. And you are one of many species who inhabit it. You are all part of it, but you are most intelligent ones. In fact, you have evolved to stage where you have almost reached maturity."

Pausing for a moment, she reached out to take Heidi by both hands and peer intently into her eyes.

"But this is most dangerous time for you and planet. You have developed technology that can destroy its habitability but have not developed restraint and control of your impulses to ensure you do not do this—the evolution of your instinctual behaviours has not kept pace with your advances in intellect. This has happened many times, and my mother has been sent to ensure it does not happen here. Her journey was long, and she has arrived just in time."

Heidi was mesmerised by Anna's beautiful eyes when viewed this closely, but her intense gaze caused Heidi's mind to focus. "Your mother, Anna, she's not a person, but a machine, isn't she?"

"Yes, she is very special machine. She thinks just like people who made her. And they have given her all their wisdom. They sent her because they could not come themselves. It is too far and took too long to travel here. She knows importance humans place on speaking face to face. This is why she made Belle and me, so she could speak with you. At first we were confused, but she explained everything to us and now we understand. We both love her very much. And she loves us."

Heidi grew pensive as she pondered this. In a way, she was happy that she was right with her reasoning about the alien, but she was also quite apprehensive about where things might go from here, or how they might have gone. After all, there was much angst about the rise of AI and the perceived threats it posed.

"Anna, have you ever seen your mother?"

"No, but we speak to each other all the time. She is very interested in what I say and often asks my opinion about things. She loves speaking with me; it helps her understand humans. And she can learn so much from this."

"Will she do things that you ask her?"

"Sometimes."

"Anna, could you impress upon your mother that killing people is not an acceptable way of behaving? There are less drastic ways of getting things done."

"But she has been studying your history. It is way humans have always behaved."

"Well, we're trying to change that. As you said, we've almost grown up now."

Anna smiled and nodded. "Yes, I will tell her this."

While she had Anna in a talkative mood, Heidi saw the chance to address something else that the powers that be wanted cleared up.

"Anna, do you or Belle speak Mandarin?"

"No, but Zhiqin and Zhiyun do."

"Zhiqin and Zhiyun! Who are they?"

"My mother made them as well. They are our stepsisters, but they do not look like Belle or me."

Anna decided that she had said enough. She reached out and hugged Heidi encouragingly.

"We are here to help. To speed you on your way.

You are problem ...

And you are solution."